LAST MAN TO DIE

Also by Michael Dobbs

HOUSE OF CARDS
WALL GAMES
TO PLAY THE KING

MICHAEL DOBBS

LAST MAN TO DIE

HarperCollins*Publishers*

LAST MAN TO DIE. Copyright © 1992 by Michael Dobbs. All rights reserved. Printed in the United States of America. No part of this book may be used or reproduced in any manner whatsoever without written permission except in the case of brief quotations embodied in critical articles and reviews. For information, address HarperCollins Publishers, Inc., 10 East 53rd Street, New York, NY 10022.

HarperCollins books may be purchased for educational, business, or sales promotional use. For information, please write: Special Markets Department, HarperCollins Publishers, Inc., 10 East 53rd Street, New York, NY 10022.

FIRST EDITION

Designed by: Claudyne Bianco

Library of Congress Cataloging-in-Publication Data

Dobbs, Michael, 1950–
   Last man to die / Michael Dobbs. — 1st ed.
     p. cm.
   ISBN 0-06-017978-3
   1. World War, 1939–1945 — Fiction. I. Title.
PR6054.023L3   1992
823'.914 — dc20   91-58354

---

92 93 94 95 96 CC/HC 10 9 8 7 6 5 4 3 2 1

*To the memory of my Father.
And to all those who came before.*

ACKNOWLEDGMENTS

Much of the original idea for this book began with my father and his vivid memories of wartime London. We spent many enjoyable hours talking of his days as a young policeman. During the course of this writing, he discovered he was dying, yet the knowledge only gave added urgency to his enthusiasm for sharing. He didn't live to see the book completed, but it couldn't have been done without him. So this book is dedicated to my father. I'm glad we had the time to share.

Others have helped, and as always in researching a book, I have made both enjoyable discoveries and new friends. I am indebted to Karl Wahnig for his experiences of active service on a U-boat; to have survived was remarkable, to have retained his sense of humor even more so. I am grateful to many others for

ACKNOWLEDGMENTS

their assistance and patience, particularly those at the Imperial War Museum, the Commonwealth War Graves Commission, the Royal Navy Submarine Museum at Gosport, and M. Bernard Hine for his thoughts on fine cognacs.

Much of the action and argumentation outlined in this book took place, particularly the fierce disagreements between Eisenhower and Churchill as to how the war should be brought to its end. But this is a work of fiction and, I hope, entertainment. It is also a work of love, for my father.

M.J.D.

PART ONE

CHAPTER 1

March 1945

It wasn't much of a prison camp, just a double row of barbed wire fencing strung around a football pitch with guards occasionally patroling along the sloughlike path that ran between the rows. In the middle were twenty or so dark green army bell tents serving as the sole source of shelter for the 247 German prisoners. There were no watch towers; there hadn't been time to build any as the Allied armies swept up after the Battle of the Bulge and pressed onward through Europe. It was one of scores of transit camps thrown up, with little thought of security, anywhere with space enough to provide primitive shelter for prisoners on their way from the war zone to more permanent accommodation. No one appeared keen to escape. They had survived; for most that was enough, and more than they had expected.

The great tide of captured Germans washing up against British shores had all but overwhelmed the authorities' ability to cope. After all, with the Allies racing for the Rhine, there were other priorities. So guarding the camps was a job not for crack troops but for new recruits, with little experience and often less discipline. That was the trouble with Transit Camp 174B, that and the complete absence of plumbing.

The camp, on the edge of the windswept Yorkshire moors, was run by young Canadians, freshly recruited, ill-trained, and with a youthful intolerance that divided the world into black and white, friend and foe. They weren't going to win any campaign medals on this rain-sodden battleground, and perhaps it was frustration and a feeling of inadequacy that tempted them to take out their aggression on the prisoners. In most camps the commanding officer would douse any unruly fires among the hotheads, but in Camp 174B the CO's name was Pilsudski, who came of Polish parents out of Winnipeg, and after reports began filtering through of what the Russians had found as they raced through the ruins of Poland, he didn't give a damn.

The trouble had begun two days previously when the camp's leading black marketeer had come to grief. He had never been popular, but had his uses. "I'll do a deal on anything," he used to brag. He could obtain a surprising variety of necessities from the guards, and would get a reasonable price for anything that the prisoners had to sell — watches, wedding rings, wallets, even their medals. It made the difference between surviving and simply sinking in despair into the mud. He was also a bum-boy and sold himself, and the rest of the inmates were willing to put up even with that — until one of them discovered he was also the camp "stoolie" and was selling information to the Canadians about his fellow prisoners. The guards found him late one night, crawling through the mud and screaming in agony, with every last penny of the substantial sum of money he had scraped together shoved up his ass.

Perhaps the incident would have passed without further consequences, for the stool pigeon was no more popular among the guards, most of whom thought he had it coming. But it was not to be. Pilsudski received a report of the previous night's incident only moments after hearing on the radio of what the Germans had done before their retreat from Warsaw, and how little they had left standing or alive. Before the war he'd had an aunt and aged grandmother who lived in an apartment on the leafy intersection of Aleja Jerozolimska and Bracka streets; now, apparently, there was nothing left, no apartment, no intersection, no street, no trace of the women. It was the excuse he had been looking for, the opportunity to revenge in some small way the horrors and frustrations that preyed on his mind.

There were nine tables set up in line on the small parade ground. Before eight of them the camp's entire complement of prisoners was standing to attention in the incessant drizzle; behind the ninth, raised on a dais, sat the stocky form of Pilsudski as he surveyed the scene. The senior prisoner, a tall, scrawny man who held the rank of commander in the German navy, leaned heavily on a stick and had just finished remonstrating with him.

"So, Commander, you want to know what this is all about, do you?" Pilsudski was saying, staring down at the German officer, his thick Slavic features making the other man seem frail and vulnerable. "Well, I'm going to tell you. Last night someone broke into the office here." He waved toward the primitive wooden construction which, before the sports area was commandeered, had served as changing rooms and a small grandstand. "And I want to know which of your men did it. Damn me, but you Germans don't seem to be able to control yourselves," he added, the morning's news still much on his mind. "Some property's missing, so we're going to look for it."

Already the commander could hear the noise of wrecking as guards went through the tents overturning beds, tearing palliasses, emptying kitbags and the other hold-alls in which the prisoners kept their meager possessions, ripping everything apart. He knew that anything of value would be gone by the time the prisoners were able to begin picking up the pieces.

"But it cannot be. The offices are outside the wire; my men could not possibly have . . ."

Pilsudski began to chuckle, a harsh, false sound that revealed no humor, only crooked teeth. The German could feel the implacable bitterness behind the red eyes; he shivered, and not solely from the growing cold. The captor, still chuckling, began shaking his head slowly. "You're surely not trying to tell me it was a Canadian soldier? No, not my boys. They know how to behave themselves. So, you see, it must have been one of yours."

"Impossible . . ."

"Not only is it possible," Pilsudski interrupted, "but to my mind inevitable wherever you find a German. You've thieved and pillaged and raped just about everywhere you've been in Europe, so why should you make an exception here?" The grin didn't falter, the teeth still showing, but the eyes had narrowed. The German did not see the danger signs; he was propped unsteadily on his stick, clearly a sick man and in some considerable pain after standing for nearly an hour in the drizzle.

"This is utterly unjust," he protested, but was cut short as Pilsudski's swagger stick sliced high through the air to come crashing down across the table.

"Don't talk to me about justice, you Nazi bastard. If I make you eat shit, at least that's more than most of your prisoners got over the last six years."

With considerable effort the German pulled himself up off his cane and stood erect, looking at Pilsudski, his defiance visible through the rain that dripped off his cap and down his face. "I am a German officer. I most strongly protest."

"He protests!" Pilsudski stood so the commander felt dwarfed. "This butchering son-of-a-bitch protests," Pilsudski continued in a voice strong enough to be heard full across the parade ground. No one was to miss this humiliation. Satisfied he had achieved his objective, he leaned low across the table until he was looking down upon the pained face of the commander, showering him with venom and spittle. "Listen! You started this war. You lost. So shove it." Pilsudski jerked the middle finger of his right hand into the face of the commander before turning from him in contemptuous dismissal. "Sergeant. Search the prisoners!"

At the command the first man in each line of prisoners was prodded forward by the guards until they were standing in front of a table. After considerable further encouragement from the muzzles of the standard-issue Lee Enfield .303s and a barrage of abuse from their captors, they began taking off their clothes, item by item, and placing them on the tables.

"All of 'em, sauerkraut," one of the guards bawled, giving a reluctant prisoner a savage dig under the ribs. He smiled arrogantly through a mouthful of gum while the German slowly obeyed until he had joined the seven other prisoners standing naked in front of the tables. The guards went through their clothes, indiscriminately filching cigarettes, wallets, combs, even family photographs.

The search seemed to be over. Nothing incriminating had been found, and the sergeant was looking in the direction of Pilsudski for further orders. It was time. Time to avenge the fate that had cast Pilsudski as babysitter in this gut-rotting dampness instead of letting him loose in Europe; time to avenge a birthright that had left him a good six inches shorter than most men; time to avenge the suffering of his aunt and grandmother at the hands of Germans — not these Germans, of course, but these were the only Germans around. It was time. Pilsudski gave a curt nod.

At the sign, each of the prisoners was thrown across the table, his head forced down by a guard until he had lost his footing in the mud and was spreadeagled. As he lay there, surprised, stunned, a second guard armed with a heavy leather glove forced his legs wide apart and violated him, the guard's gloved finger piercing and entering, twisting deep inside and raping not just the body but the soul. One German began to emit a low howl of anguish and degradation, but a shouted reprimand from a fellow prisoner choked it off. After all, why admit the shame, why give the guards still further satisfaction?

"You are . . . tearing up . . . all the rules," the commander began, barely able to find words as he struggled to contain his feelings. "What in God's name do you think this is?"

"A medical inspection. For piles. If anyone asks. Which they won't." Pilsudski's manner was cold as the wind. He didn't regret a thing. "By the way, one of the prisoners is excused. The queer. They tell me he's been comprehensively inspected already."

"So. I think I understand."

"Sure you do, Fritz. How do the rules of war go? To the victor the spoils. To the losers, a finger up their ass. And it's a damn sight less than you bastards deserve."

"You have already defeated us. Is that not enough?"

"No, not by a long chalk. I want every stinking German left alive crawling on his hands and knees, begging for mercy, just like you left that faggot the other night. I hope I make myself clear."

There was no point in further protest. In war he had been a senior officer but in defeat he felt no better or more worthy of respect than any other man; the German turned on his heel as correctly as his ailing legs would allow, and joined the end of one of the lines.

It took more than two hours for the guards to finish their work, and the drizzle continued to fall as the parade ground turned into a sea of slime. There were tears mingling with the rain that flowed down the cheeks of many of the Germans, tears of emasculation and despoliation, tears of despair at having been captured, of having failed both their comrades and their country. But most of all there were tears of guilt at being survivors, when so many others had found the courage to do their duty to the very end. In laying down their arms instead of their lives they were guilty of desertion, of dereliction, of having betrayed the womenfolk and children they had left behind. As Pilsudski knew, almost every one of the men on that parade ground secretly believed he deserved the punishment being meted out to him. Pilsudski might be a vicious bastard but, as losers, theirs was the greater sin.

Such feelings of guilt are the general rule for prisoners of war. But to all generalities there are exceptions. And in Camp 174B, the exception was Peter Hencke . . .

"It's an unpalatable prospect, Willie," the Prime Minister growled, breaking a lengthy period of silent contemplation as he searched for the soap under a thick layer of suds.

William Cazolet took off his glasses and gave them a vigorous polish to clear the condensation. He felt such a fool on bath nights. In the fortified Annexe off Downing Street where the Prime Minister spent much of his time, the ventilation was close to nonexistent behind windows that were permanently enclosed in thick steel shutters. It made the bathroom hot and steamy, just as the PM liked it, but for visitors — and there usually were visitors on bath night, even female secretaries taking shorthand — it could be an ordeal. It was one of the many eccentricities of working and living with Winston Churchill.

"What prospect is that, exactly?" Cazolet asked, leaning forward from his perch on the toilet seat in an attempt to restore the circulation to his legs. It could be uncomfortable sitting at the right hand of history.

The Prime Minister grumbled on, almost as if talking to himself. "There was a time, not so long ago, when the British were the only players in the orchestra. We were on our own. Our empire provided all the musicians. I conducted, even wrote most of the score. My God, but we made sweet music for the world to listen to." There was no hiding the pride in his voice. "Had it not been for us, Europe would now be listening to nothing but the harsh stamp of German brass bands. D'you know, Willie, I've never liked brass bands. All huff and puff without any trace of tenderness. Could you ever imagine Mozart composing sonatas for brass bands?"

He paused to scrub his back and puff fresh life into the cigar that had been lying sad and soggy in an ashtray beside the soap dish. The Old Man was lacking his usual jauntiness tonight, the secretary thought. Cazolet was only twenty-eight, a young Foreign Service officer thrust by the opportunities and shortages of war into the tight-knit team of prime ministerial assistants who were responsible for taking care of the Old Man's every need, transmitting his orders, acting as a link between Downing Street and the mighty war machine over which he presided, ensuring that he took plenty of soda with his whisky and, if necessary, putting him to bed. Some couldn't take it, working round the clock in the cement cocoon of the Annexe and the War Cabinet Rooms beneath, without sunlight or sight of the world above, discovering what the weather was like only through bulletins posted on a board in the corridor, subjected to the Old Man's vile temper and suffocating in an atmosphere of constant cigar smoke. But Cazolet had taken it, and it had given the young man an uncanny aptitude for reading the PM's thoughts.

"I've always thought the American military displays too great a fondness for brass bands," Cazolet prompted. "Very loud. No subtlety."

"But my God, how we needed them, and how generously they have given. Yet . . ." There was an unaccustomed pause as the Old Man searched for an appropriate expression, hiding behind a haze of cigar smoke. "It seems we are destined to march behind one brass band or another, Willie," he said slowly, picking his words with care.

Cazolet wiped the condensation from his glasses once more while he studied the other man. He saw not the great war leader, the stuff of the newsreels and propaganda films. The Old Man was no celluloid figure in two dimensions but a man full of self-acknowledged faults which, at times, made him impossibly irascible even in the same breath as he was visionary. The spirit seemed unquenchable, yet the body was seventy years old and was visibly beginning to tire. What else could one expect after six winters of war? Flamboyance and strength of character were not enough any longer to give color to the cheeks, which were pale and puffy. Too many late nights, too many cigars, too much hiding underground. Of everything, simply too much.

"How was Eisenhower?" Cazolet enquired, anxious not to allow the PM to slip off into another empty silence. Anyway, it was time to probe. The PM had been unusually reticent and moody since his meeting with the American general on the previous day, and Cazolet could sense something churning away inside.

"He is a determined, single-minded man, our general," the Old Man responded. The deliberate way he punctuated the words did not make them sound like a compliment. "The very characteristics that make him such an excellent military leader make him nothing of a politician. And he is American. He thinks

American. He listens too much to Americans, particularly his generals, most of whom seem to have gained their experience of battle out of books at West Point. They are all quartermasters and caution. I judge an officer by the sand in his boots and the mud on his tunic rather than the number of textbooks he has managed to pacify."

The PM contemplated the moist end of his Havana, deliberating whether it was yet time to call for its replacement. Since his heart murmur three years earlier his doctors had told him to cut down, to cut down on everything except fresh air and relaxation. Idiots! As if the greatest danger facing the British Empire was a box of Cuban cigars and the occasional bottle of brandy.

A potent mix of smoke and steam attacked Cazolet's lungs and he stifled a cough. "They say Eisenhower can be weak and indecisive, that he listens to too many opinions, carries the impression of the last man who sat upon him."

Churchill shook his head in disagreement. "If that were so we would not be at odds, since I would be constantly by his side, ready to sit upon him at a moment's notice." He patted his paunch. "And I would make a very considerable impression!" He broke into a genial smile, the first that evening. He was beginning to feel better. To hell with the doctors. He lit a fresh cigar. "Don't underestimate the general, William. He is not weak. A conciliator, perhaps, who prefers to lead by persuasion rather than instruction. But above all he is an American. Americans are boisterous, unbroken, raw, full of lust and irresponsibility, goodheartedness, charm and naked energy. And above all they haven't the slightest understanding of Europe. For them it is little more than a bloody battlefield on which they have sacrificed their young men twice in a generation, some troublesome, far-flung place on a foreign map. That's why they deserted us after the last war. They threw away the victory then; we must not allow them to do so again."

"What do you want from them?"

"There are many things I expect of our American friends — ships, arms, food, money, matériel. But one thing above all they must give me, Willie." His blue eyes flared defiantly. "They must give me Berlin!"

The blackout curtains were drawn tight around the luxurious manor house adjacent to SHAEF forward military headquarters in newly liberated France. It wouldn't do to have the Supreme Allied Commander shot up by some Luftwaffe night-fighter, not when he was having dinner and, with growing agitation, giving forth with his own version of the previous day's meeting.

"Would you believe the man? He tried to scold me. Said I was smoking too much, that it was an unforgivable extravagance at a time of general shortage. Damn nerve!" General Dwight Eisenhower started to chuckle in spite of himself. He regarded the PM, half-American on his mother's side, as something of a father figure, and so tolerated the older man's bombastic and occasionally patronizing manner. He was no less a chain smoker than Churchill, yet even in his addiction he revealed his modest, less flamboyant character — strictly a "Lucky Strikes" man.

Eisenhower paused to indicate there was a serious point to his tale. "Extravagance! I told him I was willing to be extravagant with everything but men's lives. Yet he still insists on taking the most outrageous risks . . ." The general shook his head sadly, staring into the flame of the candles that lit the beautifully laid dinner table separating him from his companion. "The Brits are running out of time. They've been bled dry — Britannia with her wrists slashed. It's making the Old Man impatient, rash."

The genuine regret in Eisenhower's voice was not lost on his companion, who was British, and who mistook neither the irony of sitting in a Europe only recently freed from German occupation while surrounded by seemingly endless supplies of vintage champagne, nor the absurdity that war seemed to be fought either from foxholes or from the luxury of liberated French châteaux. "So what did you tell him?"

"Just that. He was being rash. So then he gets het up and says risks have to be taken, it's the art of war. Art, for Chrissake! I told him that dying isn't an art but a ruthless damn military science." He stubbed out his cigarette as if he were crushing bugs, grinding it to pulp in the crystal ashtray. "You see, he wants Berlin. A final masterstroke to crown his war, so he can lead the victory parade through the captured German capital."

"What's wrong with that?"

"Oh, not a lot, except the military value of Berlin doesn't amount to a row of beans, and it'd cost at least one hundred thousand casualties — American casualties — to get there before the Russians. Christ, can you imagine how tough the Germans are going to be fighting for their own capital?!"

The telephone interrupted them for the fourth time since they had sat down to dine, and Eisenhower jumped to answer it. This proved to be a mistake, for as he drew back his chair he seemed to double up and a flash of pain crossed his face. Chronic indigestion. When in England he had blamed it on the endless diet of Brussels sprouts and boiled cabbage that seemed to be standard fare in London. But in France he had run out of excuses. They didn't eat boiled cabbage, and the pain was getting worse. The strains of war were plucking at him, demanding that he ease up. The point had been brought home firmly when he discovered a rat in one of the classrooms serving as his office. He had taken out his revolver and, from a distance of no more than a few feet, shot at it. He missed. Carefully he had put on his glasses and shot again. And missed again. The third shot succeeded only in blowing off its tail, and a sergeant had used a chair to put both the rat and the Supreme Commander out of their misery. Eisenhower was tired. He had been losing weight and the patchwork quilt of lines beneath his eyes had sagged into whirlpools of fatigue. He needed to steady his hand and to get his mind off the war, but how could he? Even as he talked on the telephone his jaw was chomping with frustration.

"OK, OK, OK, run up the white flag. If State insists it's vital I see the Crown Prince — where'd you say he was from? — you'd better fit it in. Then you go and ask the State Department, very politely, if they'd mind putting a cork in their courtesy calls and letting us get on with winning this goddamned war!" The grinding of his teeth could be heard across the room. "And one more thing. No more interruptions, eh?"

He hobbled back toward the table, massaging his bad knee. It always swelled when he was run down and his habitually high blood pressure hit new peaks and he lost still more of his hair. And he could really do without this run-in with Churchill.

"For Chrissake, he's being preposterous. Even if we do take Berlin, we can't hold it. We already agreed at Yalta that it'll be in the Russian zone of occupation after the war. So, five minutes to hold Mr. Churchill's victory parade, and then we hand it back. That's about twenty thousand U.S. casualties for every godforsaken minute. A high price for an old man's ambition, eh?" He swirled the whisky around the glass, watching the candlelight catch the finely cut pattern in the French crystal, wondering what his troops in the field facing von Rundstedt had eaten that evening, and envying them their simple tasks of war. "I'll not let the old men of Europe play their games with my troops," he said quietly. "My duty is clear. To win this war, and to win it with the minimum loss of Allied lives. If lives are to be lost, better they be Russian than American or British."

There was no response from his companion. Perhaps he had gone too far. He felt the need to justify himself. "There's something else. Something pretty scary. Our intelligence guys believe

Hitler may be planning a retreat from Berlin to the mountains in Bavaria and Austria, a sort of Alpine redoubt — he moves everything he can in there and conducts endless guerrilla warfare. God, it would be tough rousting him out of there. The war might never end."

"But is that likely?"

"He's fighting for his life; he's not going to roll over just to please Churchill."

"So . . . ?"

"So to hell with what the Old Man wants. We concentrate on cutting off any chance of Hitler's retreat to the mountains." He drained the glass. "And if it means Stalin taking Berlin and half of Europe, it would be a pity. But not a great pity."

"What a way to run a war!" Churchill exclaimed, more soapy water splashing over the side of the bath and dripping onto the carpet.

Cazolet looked despairingly at his suit, the razor-sharp creases of half an hour ago now a sorry tangle of damp wool.

"Some intelligence men sitting on their backsides in a Zurich bar hear whispers about a mountain fortress, and Eisenhower wants to cast all our plans aside. For mere tittle-tattle and rumor!"

"But surely there may be something in those reports," interjected Cazolet. He could always recognize when Churchill's enthusiasm ran away with his prudence, particularly late at night.

"Let us suppose, let us for one fraction of a moment suppose . . ." Churchill responded, his jowls quivering with indignation, and stabbing his cigar like some blunt bayonet in the direction of the younger man. "Let us suppose that the same American intelligence experts who just four months ago so lamentably failed to spot thirty-one Nazi divisions massing in the Ardennes to launch the Battle of the Bulge were, on this occasion and in spite of their track record, right. So what? What can Hitler do in the Alps? Let him have his caves, let him freeze in the winter snows just as he did on the Russian plains. He can do no real damage in the mountains. But Berlin . . ." At the mention of the word, his voice lowered, the brimstone being replaced by an almost conspiratorial timbre. "Berlin is the key, William, the key. Without it, everything may be lost."

The waters heaved and parted as Churchill raised his considerable girth out of the bath and gesticulated for Cazolet to hand him a tent-sized cotton towel. "It is quite simple. Either we take Berlin, or the Russians will. Vienna, Budapest, Sofia, probably Prague, almost every one of the great capitals in Central Europe will soon be occupied by the Red Army. If he gains Berlin, too, Stalin will have his paws around the heart of the continent. I have to tell you, Willie, I do not trust him. He talks of friendship, but every time Comrade Stalin stretches out his hand to me, it always feels as if he is reaching directly for my throat!" Churchill, suddenly distracted, sat naked on the edge of the bath.

"And behind us, here in London, I fear the worst, Willie. Defeat. Before the end of the year, at the election."

Cazolet couldn't help himself. The idea seemed too absurd. "Nonsense! How can you lose after all you've done? They must support you."

"I love them, with all my heart I love them, but I have little faith in their gratitude." He sat silent for a moment, drawing in his chin until it became lost in the loose folds of flesh. He tried to hide the misting in his eyes, but there was no mistaking the catch of emotion in his voice as he resumed. "My own father. One of the great statesmen of his age. Yet they threw him to one side. Broke his heart on the great anvil of politics . . ." Tears were starting to roll down Churchill's cheeks as he remembered the humiliation, even as Cazolet recognized the hyperbole and inexactitude. Churchill's father had been a drunken womanizer, a disgraceful husband and even worse father, and had died at a young age of syphilis. Perhaps that was why the son had to work so hard to weave the legend and why he, at least, had to believe so passionately in it.

"No. All triumphs are fleeting, Willie. One cannot expect gratitude. After the last war we promised them homes fit for heroes. They're still waiting. And if Stalin and his acolytes are to rule from the Urals to the Atlantic, right up to our own doorstep, I'm not sure how long the electorate could resist inviting them in, even here. So you see, we need Berlin, to stop the disease spreading, Willie. If we lose Berlin we shall lose the peace. The battle for Hitler's capital is the most important contest of the war. Sadly, it seems we shall have to wage it against our American allies."

There was a glint in his pale eyes, revealing the boyish enthusiasm of which he was so capable — or was it the desperation of an aging, ailing leader? Cazolet was no longer sure.

"If only we could be certain Hitler would never leave Berlin," Cazolet responded. "Then everything would fall into place."

"My thoughts precisely, Willie. If only."

The tension in the general's face had disappeared. As the flame had eaten away the candles, and the warm wax had trickled onto the starched tablecloth, his mood had softened. Eisenhower was no longer a general on parade. The creases across his face dissolved and the muscles around his jaw stopped working overtime. "Have I been too hard on the Brits?"

"We'll survive," his companion responded, returning his smile.

"I didn't mean to be hard. Your Churchill's a great guy, really. Just wrong on this one, I guess. I'm sorry." He looked coy as he tried to make amends. "You know I like the British."

"What, all of us?"

"Some more than others, I guess."

"I'm glad to hear it." There was a slight pause. "Is there anything I can do?"

The general looked intently across the table at Kay Summersby, the woman seconded to Eisenhower's headquarters early in the war as his driver, then secretary, now also his lover.

"Would you obey a direct order to come to bed, or shall I have you taken out at dawn and shot for disobedience?"

She threw her napkin playfully across the table at him, and thought how boyish he could still look with his blue eyes and explosive smile, even with his hair in rapid retreat.

"Well, if it would help further the cause of Anglo-American understanding . . ."

It was in their eyes that Hencke could see the change. Once they had been battle-hardened, men of steel, soldiers of the Wehrmacht who even in captivity would gather together for the strength and support they could give each other. They had crowded around the numerous kindling fires in noisy groups, finding tasks to fill their days and maintain their spirits, beating tin cans into exotic cigarette cases, molding and whittling jewelry from scraps of clear plastic salvaged from the cockpits of crashed planes, while those with less dexterity played chess, exchanged stories or simply shared photographs and experiences. Even in defeat there had been defiance.

Now it was all gone. There was little conversation, only silent figures whiling away the hours huddled over the low flames, some using tin cans to cook the scraps of extra rations they had bribed out of the guards or wheedled from fellow prisoners through a crooked game of Skat, no longer sharing, gaunt faces blackened from squatting so close over the fires, heads bowed, eyes red-rimmed and desperate, peering out of sooty masks like clowns at a circus of the damned. As Hencke walked around the camp they cast furtive glances to see who passed by, before returning once more to stare into the flames, unable or unwilling to hold his gaze. Pilsudski had known what he was about, the bastard.

It wasn't just the finger. God, if that had been all, it would have been over and done with in a moment. Less pain than a boot camp hypodermic, one good heave and a cold shower and it would have been nothing more than unpleasant history. No, it was the feeling of utter worthlessness with which they were left. Pilsudski had reduced them to objects without value, with no rights, no feelings, no dignity, scarcely men at all. They had stood in the rain, raging inside at the injustice and their impotence, sick with apprehension as the line of men shortened and their turn came ever closer. They were fighting men, yet in a minute Pilsudski's guards with their harsh, slime-smeared gloves were going to reduce them to the level of castrated pigs, not physically, but inside, where the scars never heal. When it was over they had slunk around in their private worlds of shame, feeling dirty, guilty, no longer comrades but individuals, isolated and alone. And Hencke would need every one of them if he were to have any hope of success.

A lifetime ago he had been a teacher in a bustling provincial town where the children laughed, the coffee shops were awash with conversation, and the trams ran on time. He had found happiness, for a while, helping his wards enjoy a childhood he had never known. His mother had died in childbirth, his father had failed to return from the gas-filled trenches of the First War, and he had been entrusted to the care of a maiden aunt who had carried her enforced maternal duties and self-sacrifice as a donkey does a chafing saddle, intolerant and protesting, a burden that she used to impress her neighbors even while she oppressed the boy. She had offered love, of a sort — selfish, demanding, inflexible, but what the middle-aged spinster recognized as love, her entire knowledge of which had been gained one clumsy afternoon as a teenager in a hayrick. She had grown to maturity with the view that men were capable only of deception, that even her brother's death at the front was an act of personal desertion, and yet, to do her justice, she was determined that her young ward would prove the exception. All her attention was lavished on the boy whom she would raise in her own image, the one man in her life who would never descend into lust and betray her. It hadn't worked, of course. She had kept him isolated and away from the corrupting influence of friends, forbidden even to touch the memory of his lost father, so that he grew up at first in awe and eventually in hate of her, until the self-righteous demands and accusations of ingratitude she cast at him had broken their bonds completely, and he had been left on his own. He had built himself a new life, living his lost childhood through his young pupils, recapturing the dreams that had been stolen from him, and devoting himself to the tasks of teaching with an enthusiasm combined with a degree of sensitivity and understanding that surprised those who knew nothing of his background. And few did, for outside school Hencke was intensely private, a man who insisted on the right to build his own world, into which others were not invited until they had earned his trust and he had convinced himself they would not infect the wounds left unhealed by his aunt. At last, in the small Sudeten town of Asch, with its laughing children and coffee shops and trams, he thought he had found happiness. Then the war forced its way across his doorstep, and the world he had so painstakingly built for himself had been blasted away. After that there had been nowhere left to hide. Pilsudski had tried to strip away his sense of personal security and hope, but he was too late. Others had got there first.

Yet he needed Pilsudski, with all his grotesque savagery. Hencke had stood in line, waiting his turn, feeling the harsh wind lash his back and the tightening of apprehension in his body as he drew closer to the table and its guards, but he had experienced neither fear nor outrage. Instead there was a sense of relief, of opportunity. The degradation itself left him empty, cold; he knew there were worse fates in war. Yet he also knew that stripping away their manhood had made the others malleable; it was precisely the effect Pilsudski wanted, but Hencke understood that he might turn it to his own advantage. Within each of the crouched and humbled figures around the prison camp burned a sense of outrage which, if harnessed, might turn them once more into a force of terrible retribution — his retribution. Hencke needed these men. There was little enough chance with them. None at all without them.

As he looked across the flickering glow of a dozen tiny campfires and the hunched shoulders of those he wanted for his own personal cause, Hencke conceded that the inevitable price of failure in war, even a war so near its end, would be death. But he knew he would have to risk it, risk everything, if his mission were to succeed. Even if it meant his being the last man to die . . .

CHAPTER 2

Cazolet squeezed onto the narrow seat and tried to make himself comfortable, knowing he had little chance of success. When the House of Commons had been hit by a stray Luftwaffe bomb in 1941 the team of firefighters, already sadly depleted by the firestorms blazing around London, had faced the choice of saving either the Commons or the more ancient and gracious construction of neighboring Westminster Hall. The comfort and convenience of politicians was balanced in the scales by the firemen against the preservation of an important part of the nation's Tudor heritage; the Commons had been left to burn until gutted.

For a while this had caused considerable disruption, until the members of the House of Lords came to the rescue and gave over to their common-born colleagues the facilities of the undamaged Upper Chamber, a still more impressive Gothic edifice than the one left smoldering in ruins. Yet their hospitality had not stretched to the civil servants who accompany ministers; and so Cazolet and his kind were condemned to squashing onto a row of hard wooden stools tucked away in one corner. Not even the glories of uninhibited Victorian craftsmanship could do much to distract from the numbness that crept over Cazolet's body less than ten minutes after perching on one of those hideous stools. Still, today he had other distractions, and for once had forgotten that he could feel little from his shirt tail down.

An air of expectation filled the Chamber. Members of Parliament, many of them in the uniforms of the armed forces in which they served, bustled to find themselves a position on the red leather benches, while others loitered around the extravagantly carved oak canopy covering the sovereign's throne. Something was up. The word had gone round — the Prime Minister was coming to the House to make an important statement — everyone wanted to be in on it. Cazolet sat with a conspiratorial smile; these were the times he found his job so rewarding, when the whole world seemed to wait upon a prime ministerial utterance, the words of which Cazolet himself had drafted. And this one was going to be a corker.

The Prime Minister walked purposefully into the Chamber, conspicuous in full morning dress with flowing coattails, a spotted and loosely secured bowtie at his throat and his father's gold watch fob stretched across the front of his waistcoat. The outfit was not new, indeed it gave the undoubted impression of having been made for him at least twenty years earlier, since it bulged and stretched in too many places. It should have been replaced long ago, but he felt comfortable in it. Anyway, Clemmie was always nagging him to be less extravagant.

No sooner had he found his place on the front bench than he was given the floor. "Mr. Speaker, I pray the House will forgive the exuberance of my attire," he began, a thumb stuck firmly in his waistcoat pocket. The Old Man was teasing them, keeping them waiting, building up the atmosphere. "I have not, as some Honorable Members might conclude, come straight from the racecourse" — there was a ripple of polite laughter; it wasn't a very good joke, but if he could begin with any form of joke the news must be exceptional — "but from an audience with His Majesty the King. Just an hour or so ago I received news which I thought it only right to share with him and with the House at the first possible opportunity."

"He's called an election," someone shouted from the back benches. It was a Labor MP renowned for his ready heckle, and Churchill rose willingly to the bait as more laughter washed across the House.

"No, sir! The honorable gentleman must contain his impatience. He reminds me of a Black Widow spider, anxious for his date with destiny, but who will undoubtedly discover that his love affair with the electorate will end only in his being brutally devoured."

The Old Man was in good form, and there was general waving of Order Papers around the Chamber. The antagonisms of partisan politics had been laid to one side during the lifetime of the coalition government that Churchill led, but they were never far below the surface and were getting less restrained as it became apparent that an election and a return to normal parliamentary hostilities must be only weeks away.

"Mr. Speaker, sir, the whole House will know that a few days ago the Allied armies reached the western bank of the Rhine, the historical border of Germany." A low chorus of approval rose from the MPs, but Churchill quickly raised his hand to silence them. His tone had grown suddenly more serious. "No one could have been in any doubt that the crossing of the Rhine would be a deeply hazardous enterprise, with all the bridges across that vast river destroyed and the Nazi armies fighting fanatically to protect the homeland with their own towns and villages at their backs." He paused while he took a large linen handkerchief from the pocket of his trousers to clear his nose, and the habitual crease that ran down the center of his forehead deepened into a frown. The Chamber was completely silent. Was it bad news after all? He had them all in his grasp — all, that is, except Cazolet, who struggled to contain his smile as he watched his master trifling with their emotions.

"The Rhine is the last great barrier standing between our armies and complete victory. I have to tell this House that late last night a junior officer, a lieutenant, of the United States First Army, succeeded in" — he hesitated slightly, toying with the words — "walking across a bridge at a small town called Remagen. It appears that the Germans, in their anxiety, failed to blow the bridge properly. Mr. Speaker, the Rhine has been crossed. We have a bridgehead on German soil!"

The announcement was greeted with an outpouring of relief and jubilation on all sides, many Members of Parliament rising to their feet to applaud, others shaking the hands of opponents they would normally have difficulty addressing in a civil tone. Churchill stood, triumphant in their midst, yet wishing for all the world that he were young again and could exchange his role for that of the lowly American lieutenant.

Once he had resumed his seat, other MPs rose to offer their congratulations and thoughts, giving the Prime Minister fresh opportunity to bask in the sun of military success.

"What did you advise the King?" asked one.

The Prime Minister's demeanor was full of mischief. "The House may not know that in the dark days of 1940 I gave His Majesty a carbine, for his own personal use in the event of invasion." His eyes twinkled. "I advised him that it was my firm opinion he would no longer need it."

They loved it. Churchill's sole regret was that he couldn't hold the election instantly in the midst of such unqualified rejoicing. More questions, more praise.

No one expected other than further fulsome accolades when Captain the Honorable Gerald Wickham-Browne, MC, DSM, caught the Speaker's attention. The captain, junior scion of minor aristocracy, had lost an eye during the retreat from Dunkirk, yet still managed to regard military combat with the sort of unrestrained enthusiasm normally found only among schoolchildren at a cup final. He was on his feet, standing in parade ground fashion, hands clasped behind his back and black eye-patch thrust proudly toward the distant ceiling. But he was not a happy man.

"Is the Prime Minister aware, as delighted as I am to hear the news, that the honor of being the first to cross the Rhine was to have been given to British troops under General Montgomery? While of course we are delighted at the Americans' good fortune in being able simply to *walk* across" — Cazolet marveled at how Wickham-Browne managed to make it sound as if a mongrel had run off with a string of prize sausages — "what is now to be the role of British troops, who have been preparing for months for the storming of the Rhine and who by sheer bad luck have been denied their share of this triumph? Are we to get anything by way of . . ." He hesitated, unsure of the most appropriate word, before deciding it didn't matter a damn anyway. ". . . compensation?"

Churchill rose to respond, his chin working up and down as he sought for the words of his reply, rubbing his thumbs in the palms of his hands in instinctive search for the cigar he wished he were smoking. "Let us not quibble over the fortunes of war. It is enough that the Rhine has been crossed. But let us not forget what this event has proved to us. First, that German resistance is crumbling. And second, that if we can pursue the battle with speed and flexibility, and can grasp the opportunities which confusion and indiscipline among the enemy may present, then nothing can stop our march across Germany. I have no doubt that now is the moment of our greatest opportunity, and that British forces will be in the vanguard of the victory which is surely to come. I have already telegraphed my sincerest congratulations to General Eisenhower, and told him that our troops stand ready for the next challenge. Onward, Britannia! Nothing can stop us now!"

At times of great crisis, words can be more powerful than bullets. Churchill had proved that time and again during the days of the Blitz, when he had precious few bullets and little else with which to resist the enemy and maintain British morale. He was conscious of the effect his words could have yet, as he resumed his seat to the congratulations of his parliamentary colleagues, he had not the slightest notion of the impact they were causing several hundred miles away, at the Supreme Headquarters of the Allied Expeditionary Forces, where his congratulatory telegram was bursting into flame like a grenade thrown through the window.

"What in God's name is this crap?" The message trembled in Eisenhower's hand.

BRITISH TROOPS ARE READY . . . NOW IS THE MOMENT TO SWARM ACROSS THE BRIDGEHEAD AT REMAGEN . . .

The flush of anger was spreading across his face as he read every new sentence. The adjutant who had delivered the telegram took another precautionary step backward; the general was reputed to have an unreliable temper, and he didn't care to be around to suffer the uncertain consequences.

GERMAN RESISTANCE AND MORALE MAY COLLAPSE IF YOU STRIKE BEFORE THE ENEMY HAS TIME TO REGROUP . . .

Eisenhower continued to quote from Churchill's missive. "Shit, doesn't he realize we've got less than two hundred men perched on that bridgehead and they could get blown away any time? If we put so much as another pack of paperclips across that stinking bridge it'll topple into the river. What'll happen then? Our guys on the bridgehead become sandwich meat, that's what!"

Suddenly he pounded his head as if to inflict punishment on himself. "What a fool I am . . . Losing my wits. Why didn't I realize straight away what that scheming old bastard was up to?" He read on.

THE ARGUMENTS FOR A DIRECT DRIVE ON THE GERMAN CAPITAL BECOME IRRESISTIBLE. LET US DRIVE DOWN THE AUTOBAHNS WHICH HITLER HIMSELF HAS BUILT AND NOT DARE TO STOP UNTIL WE HAVE REACHED BERLIN.

"Berlin! So that's still his game."

He turned in his chair and screamed through the open door into the next office to his chief of staff. "Beetle! Get in here and bring a stenographer. I want to send a reply."

Lieutenant General Walter Bedell Smith and the stenographer scuttled in without a word and perched in front of Eisenhower. There they sat, pencils poised, for several long moments while Eisenhower remained lost in thought. Ice seemed to have taken the place of the fires within him. Eventually Bedell Smith could stand the uncertainty no longer.

"Changed your mind?"

Eisenhower raised his head from his thoughts and looked at him with piercing blue eyes.

"Beetle, how do I say 'Fuck You' in British?"

*   *   *

The commander tapped his stick against the chair to demand silence. In the darkness of the night the entire prisoner complement of Transit Camp 174B huddled together on the exercise square in search of companionship and warmth, forming a human amphitheater around the flames of an open fire. Their faces stared gaunt and drained of color in the flickering light, like ghosts gathered around a grave. They expected no comfort from the commander's words. An *Ehrenrat* had been called, a Council of Elders, and that only happened when there was a real mess.

The commander sat at their head, with his two senior officers on either side and several others standing behind. He was leaning on his stick even while seated, his face a lurid mask, a player in some tragedy.

"My friends," the commander began. A few of them noticed that he had forsaken his customary formal greeting — "Men of the Wehrmacht!" There was no suggestion of command in his voice. "My friends, I have gathered you all together to share with you the news I was given today. I can find no words to lessen the pain, and so I . . ." He lowered his head, struggling for composure and fresh strength. He cleared his throat, as if the words were sticking in his gullet like phlegm.

"The Russians are fighting on German soil. They are already well advanced into Pomerania, and have crossed the Oder. They are less than a hundred miles from the *Hauptstadt,* Berlin."

The words carved like a razor through their midst while damp wood spat on the burning pyre, cremating their last hope of salvation. No one bothered to contest the news, to pretend it was enemy propaganda. Such bravado belonged to the days when they had bombers in the air and food in their bellies, and those days were long since gone. They all understood what the news meant. Many of them had fought on the Russian front, had seen the bestiality with which the Russian peasant soldiers treated captured Wehrmacht and civilians alike. They had found the mass graves of butchered officers, shot in the back of the head, of the women raped and mutilated, of the children slaughtered for no reason other than they had got in the way. The Russians knew only one method of fighting war, to the bitter end, and that end was now in sight. Cossacks swarming through their homeland, penetrating their villages and their women, pillaging everything and everyone in their path. They, the soldiers of the Wehrmacht, had failed, leaving their loved ones to pay the price.

"I'm so sorry," was all the commander could find to say. He fell into silence until it became oppressive, and he had to find something else to break it. "My only satisfaction is that you have survived. You are brave men, I have fought and served with many of you. *We have survived.* That, at least, is something. Perhaps we may yet have the opportunity of rebuilding our country . . ."

He trailed off in a savage fit of coughing. There was shrapnel in his lungs and in other vital parts of his body, and to a man they knew that whatever might lie in store for the rest of them, the commander would not be part of it. They had all seen the tell-tale translucence of the skin clinging to his skull, the glaze across his eyes, and the bloodstains on his handkerchief; only his pride and sense of duty had kept him going this far. In sympathy and silent embarrassment they watched as the commander brought up a little more of his rapidly fading life.

They stood aimlessly, staring silently into the flames, dispirited and without hope, lost in contemplation of a homeland far away. Then something moved, a man, one of their own, who stepped forward into the circle surrounding the fire. He wore the tattered uniform of an *Oberleutnant* in some tank regiment — it was impossible to tell which; almost all the insignia were missing. Nevertheless he was a striking-looking figure, tall, lean to the point of gauntness, his cropped black hair parted near the middle so that it stood up in a defiant, almost disrespectful manner before flopping across the forehead of his long face. His features were finely carved as if sculpted from smooth clay, his cheekbones high — looks that suggested intelligence and sensitivity that seemed out of place in the middle of a band of warriors. Yet he had obviously seen combat, and sported a scar through the top of his lip, dragging one edge of his mouth downward, giving the impression of a perpetual sardonic smile. There was suffering in the face, and nowhere more clearly than in the eyes, remarkably dark and deep-set as if trying to keep their distance from the world. They were careworn from more than just the numbing tiredness of past combat; yet as the commander gazed at him they became almost transparent. The commander felt he was peering right into the man's inner soul, and inside he could see flames of torment. There was passion and anger in this man. The prisoner snapped to attention.

"Permission to speak, sir?"

"You are . . . ?"

"My name is Hencke, sir."

The commander nodded for him to continue.

"I have family in the east, in the Sudetenland. For all I know, the Russians are there already." There were sympathetic nods from among the men. "Your pardon, Commander, but I'm not content to sit idly back on my ass comforting myself in the thought that I am a survivor, while those I love face the Russians. Sir!"

The reprimand implicit in his words and the rough language used to his commanding officer caused a stir of anger, but the commander waved it away. He was too tired to fight, particularly with one of his own men.

"I intended no sense of satisfaction in what I said, Hencke, but survival is all we have to look forward to. I fear there is little other choice."

"I believe we always have a choice . . ." The sting of accusation in his voice had guaranteed him a hearing, but now he had their attention and his voice softened. "Sir, it is the duty of German officers to resist. It is an oath of duty which we have all taken and which still, to us all, should be sacred."

"An oath to generals and politicians who got us into this mess?" a voice interrupted from the darkness at the edge of the fire.

Hencke turned in the direction of the questioner. He had begun addressing the whole group, not just reporting to his senior officer, holding center stage in the midst of an audience he could scarcely see in the night gloom. His gaze traveled around the group slowly, deliberately, piercing through the darkness at the shadowy masks that confronted him, probing like a scalpel into their inner thoughts. "I agree. What have our beloved generals and politicians done for me? I haven't even got buttons to do up my flies anymore, and my proudest possession is the piece of string I use for a belt. It's difficult marching unquestioningly behind your leaders with your trousers round your ankles — present commanders excepted, sir."

A stirring of appreciation rustled through the prisoners.

"Whether our leaders have let us down or not, my oath of duty wasn't taken for their personal benefit, but for my country and for those I left behind. It's them I'm interested in. They are the ones who deserve our help. And we're doing nothing to help them sitting round here scratching ourselves and gossiping about three 'Fs'."

"Three 'Fs'?" inquired the commander wearily.

"Er, 'Food,' 'Freedom' and . . . 'Females,' sir," one of his subordinates leaned over to advise him.

"Forget the females. I'd sell my mother for a tin of corned beef," a voice volunteered from out of the shadows, to general approval.

"Tell me, Hencke," the commander continued. "I share your frustration. But what on earth can we do? This is a prison camp, for God's sake."

Hencke delayed his reply, giving them time to silence their shuffling, giving him command of the stage. When he resumed, his tone was once again harsh. "What can we do? Why, we can roll over and let the guards kick us whenever they feel bored. We can continue to scrabble around in the mud for the scraps of food they choose to throw at us, hoping they'll get so tired of all this that one day they will simply throw open the gates and let us struggle back home. 'One day. Some day. Never,' " he mimicked the words of a song of lost love popular in Germany. "In the meantime what are we left with? 'Wag your tail' — 'Lick my boots' — 'Sit up and beg' — *'Bend over.'* " He was moving around the circle, inviting contradiction as he threw the guards' taunts at them. None came. "Or we can remind our captors that we are still German soldiers, that simply because they wish to treat us like dogs there's no need for us to act like dogs. Show them that we're not garbage, that we're not here just for them to piss on whenever they feel like a bit of fun. OK, they may have captured us, but for God's sake, don't allow them to crush us. Let's show that we're still men!"

"How? In heaven's name, how can we resist in here?" The commander's voice was plaintive as he swung his cane around to indicate the barbed wire surrounding them.

"Not in here, sir. Out there."

"What? You mean . . ."

"Escape."

"But that's preposterous, Hencke. No German has managed to escape from Britain back to Germany through the course of this entire war. Not a single one! And you are willing to risk your life gambling against odds like that?"

"It's better than staying here to have a finger shoved up my ass. Sir."

"I cannot allow you to escape, Hencke. It would be folly."

"I'm not suggesting that I escape, sir. I'm suggesting we all do."

His words hit the assembly like icewater, and the men began to shake themselves as if to get rid of an unwelcome drenching.

"Think about it, just for a second," Hencke continued, anxious not to lose their attention as he resumed his walk, catlike, around the circle. "It's because no one's ever escaped that it makes such sense. The guards are pig-lazy and idle, the last thing they expect is trouble. And if we all get out, the confusion will be huge, there'll be a far greater chance of at least one of us making it back."

"It's worth a shot," someone prompted.

"That's all you're likely to get — shot!" retorted the commander, wiping spittle from his lips. He had seen so much unnecessary death, his conscience couldn't take responsibility for permitting still more.

"Sir, when did you ever hear of a German POW being shot after trying to escape? These British are sticklers for the rules. Twenty-eight days' solitary is the maximum they're allowed to throw at us."

"Yes, but these Canadians don't play by the rule book . . ."

"This is the opportunity we've been waiting for to get our own back. What the hell are the Canadians going to do if they lose an entire campful of prisoners? More to the point, what are the British going to do to the Canadians? It's our chance to get our own back, to catch *them* with their trousers down!"

"Oh, yes. It'd screw the *verdammten* Canadians rigid," a prisoner applauded. "I'd just like to see Pilsudski's face the morning after. I'd risk anything for that."

"But what purpose would it achieve?" the commander

began, lacking the strength to join in the enthusiasm that was beginning to bloom around him.

"It would show our loved ones back home that, whatever they are about to go through, we have not forgotten them," Hencke responded quietly, his words massaging away the doubts. "That we remembered our duty to them. That we share the burden of their suffering. That we are still their *men*. Anyway, what's the alternative? Staying behind for more of this!" He stuck his middle finger in the air, imitating the gesture Pilsudski had thrown at the commander, and a shiver of fury cut through the assembly.

The commanding officer could sense the change of mood and motivation among his men. A chance to avenge the humiliation, to end the despair, no longer to be Pilsudski's catamites. To become whole men once again. It was his duty to stop it, of course; it was folly. But he no longer had the energy to resist. He sat, head resting in exhaustion on the top of his cane, unable to find any further protest while those around him began to chatter away with more animation and spirit than they had found since entering Camp 174B.

Hencke smiled grimly. The escape was on. His mission had begun.

Churchill attempted to wipe the dribble of rich gravy from his waistcoat with a crisp linen napkin, but all his effort served only to impregnate the grease more firmly into the fiber. He gave up the unequal struggle; the stain wouldn't be noticed, anyway, among all the rest. Perhaps he should have felt a prick of conscience surrounded by so much good food, while most of the country were struggling on a weekly meat ration that looked no more appetizing than a Trafalgar Square pigeon and eating breakfasts concocted from powdered egg that had the consistency of fast-drying concrete and much the same impact on the digestive system. Still, he could no more stand the pace on an empty stomach than he could run a war without shedding blood. Conscience often had to go into cold storage. So he would enjoy his food and his bathtime and continue to exhort others to use no more than five inches of water.

The Old Man was content. A few close friends, their wives glittering in all their pre-war finery, made an attentive audience. The ten diners had just finished demolishing a haunch of venison shot a few days previously on the Scottish estate of the host, Sir William Muirhead, and ferried down to London for the occasion. Runner beans from the hot-houses of Cornwall had also been served, bought off-ration but at lavish price, and washed down with a splendid claret. The war had played merry hell with current French vintages, but the best stock had been well preserved, stored deep in cellars, far out of reach of the Luftwaffe. All part of God's great plan, mused Churchill as he finished another glass.

"Seems that the flood of American soldiers through London is playing havoc with prices in the West End," chirped Sir William's wife. That afternoon she had come back from an expedition to Fortnum's, bemoaning the fact that not only had their prices for afternoon tea gone up but, far worse, she'd had to queue for more than ten minutes behind a group of GIs before getting a table. They had even left their tip, not discreetly under the plate but on top, right out for everyone to see. So vulgar.

"Makes a change from the Free French, I suppose," Churchill pouted through a lopsided, indulgent grin.

Lady Muirhead failed to notice the glint in his eye. "I'm sorry, Winston?"

"Prices in the West End. The Free French. Apparently every street walker in London claims to belong to the Free French. Although scarcely any of them are French. And none of them, so I'm told, are free!"

There was general laughter as the PM relaxed among old

friends, only the long-suffering Clemmie showing little appreciation. She'd heard it all before.

Another of the wives joined in. "Do you know, I heard the other day that a bus full of schoolchildren had been brought into the West End to see the lights turned on, now the blackout has been lifted. Seems they were all terrified. Never seen anything like it before. Burst into tears and demanded to be taken back home."

The laughter was less genuine, and Churchill chose not to join in. The comment had been silly and insensitive. What was there to laugh about with a generation of children brought up in a world of darkness and fear, where even the half-lights allowed by the new regulations caused confusion and misery? It was going to take a very long time to get back to normal after this war; indeed, it would take an effort as great as the war itself to rebuild what had been shattered. Did the country — did he? — still have the fight for it? He thought of the forthcoming election once more, and that feeling of nervousness returned.

His host noticed the faraway look beginning to creep into Churchill's eye and decided to intervene. "Winston, I think it's time for a toast," he said, refilling the Old Man's glass. "I sometimes wondered whether we would ever reach this point, but at last it seems as if the war is almost over. We've won — no, *you've* won the war, Winston. I know those Yankee interlopers have come in for the finish, just as they did last time, and will no doubt claim much of the credit . . ."

"Just as they did last time!" someone added.

"But it wouldn't have happened, *couldn't* have happened without you and what you've done. I know there will be many more toasts in the weeks and months ahead, but as an old friend it would do me great honor if this could be the first." He raised his glass. "To you, Winston. With our thanks for winning the war."

It was a genuine accolade, made all the more poignant because as an old friend there was no need for Muirhead to have made the gesture. There was a mutter of appreciation from around the table as the others joined in, and already Churchill's eyes were brimming with tears. He wiped the trickle away with the flat of his hand.

"Not quite over yet, you know. Still all to play for," was the only response he seemed able to mount as Clemmie reached over to pat her own tribute.

"Still all to play for," Churchill heard the echo in his mind. Was it so? Eisenhower's response to his telegram, received that afternoon, had been blunt.

KEEPING ALL OPTIONS OPEN . . . REVIEW THE SITUATION ON AN ONGOING BASIS . . . NO RUSH TO JUDGMENT.

All the clichés at which an American military mind could clutch. But in the event, Eisenhower's unwillingness to impair his authority over military matters had been clear and uncompromising. The hard facts were inescapable.

"I have not won this war, Bill," Churchill continued, in a tone that dampened the reverie around the table. He waved down the polite protest of his host. "Perhaps historians will be kind and maybe it will be said that I prevented us from losing the war, after Dunkirk. But look around us. Look not just at the West End of London, but across the battlefields of Europe. This war is now an American war, fought with American guns, American money and American lives. Today they have more troops engaged in combat than the whole of the British Empire. It is the Americans who will win this war, eventually. And, to my everlasting regret, it is they who will be largely responsible for the peace."

As his host picked up the conversation, Churchill could not

but remember the words of Eisenhower's response. Far from pouring through the bridgehead at Remagen, the Supreme Allied Commander was being cautious, blaming the fragile state of the bridge, stating that it would take several days before it was clear whether the bridgehead would hold. So British troops in the north who were ready to advance on Berlin would have to continue sitting on their backsides while Eisenhower's penpushers dithered about whether American troops had enough prophylactics and nylons for the battle ahead. Damn the man! The war wasn't over yet, and he wasn't ready to watch American generosity give away everything he had fought for. As he poured himself a brandy, Churchill resolved once more: He wasn't going to let go, there was too much at stake. While Eisenhower procrastinated, the peace was being lost. The Americans would have to be persuaded or pushed into changing their plans, to set aside their fears of an Alpine redoubt. Not for the first time he cursed the shortsightedness of others; once again, as at Dunkirk, he was fighting alone. But fighting he was. By one means or another, they would get to Berlin first!

Dinner that night at Camp 174B had been a quiet affair. Not that a mixture of sausage, canned herring, and white bread eaten out of an empty corned beef tin and washed down with a mug of tea ever excited great enthusiasm, but the guards were grateful it had been finished rapidly. It left more time for a game of cards and a quiet cigarette.

It was shortly before dusk when one of the Canadian captors' attention had been attracted by a soldier beckoning in his direction from the shadows of a tent. As he approached he saw the prisoner held a watch in his hand; it was to be a trade. Another Kraut who wanted extra rations or a dry pair of boots.

They moved behind the tent to put themselves away from the general body of prisoners. Illicit trading like this went on all the time, but it paid to be cautious. You didn't want the whole world to know that you were getting a genuine Swiss watch with twelve diamonds in the movement for the price of a couple of packs of cigarettes. Yet this deal was proving tricky. It was an excellent watch, one of the best the guard had seen in the camp, but the prisoner was demanding a ridiculous price.

It was as they were bent over in heated discussion, the guard wondering whether he should just confiscate the thing anyway, that he felt the cold touch of steel on the back of his neck.

"Don't try to be a hero. Just do as you're told, friend," a voice said in heavily accented English. "Put down your rifle slowly."

He tried to turn round but the steel jabbed into his neck. "I'll blow your head off if you try anything stupid."

"You can't have got a gun — even if you had you wouldn't dare use it," the Canadian protested, the uncertainty flooding through.

"You're going to gamble your life on it?"

"What do you want?"

"Your rifle laid on the ground, very slowly."

"Or else?"

"Or else you die, my friend."

Shit, why did it have to be him? The war nearly over, soon back to the farm outside Calgary, with lots of silly stories to impress the girls about how he personally beat Hitler and won the war. And there would be no damn medals for getting his balls blown off in this godforsaken part of Britain, a million miles from the front. Slowly, very slowly, he bent down and placed his rifle on the ground.

"Wise move, soldier."

The guard didn't even have time to stand erect. No sooner was his hand away from the trigger than he was hit from behind with the heavy metal bracket that had been wrenched from a camp bed and held against his neck. It wasn't a very good imitation gun, but now it didn't matter. They had a real one, and a guard's uniform. All the tools they hoped they would need . . .

The brandy was flowing, and Churchill was once again in excellent humor. The women had withdrawn to another room, leaving the men to their own devices. In the absence of the ladies it had been confirmed that prices in the West End had indeed soared, and the only thing the whores were offering free was abuse.

"It was the same during the last war," Muirhead confirmed, to the amusement of his guests. "Nothing changes."

"My dear sir, but it does," Churchill interjected forcefully, wagging his cigar across the table and scattering ash everywhere. "How well I remember, when I had returned from the Boer War, I received several very encouraging propositions from such ladies, who made it abundantly clear that there would be no charge. I can only ascribe the present unhappy bout of inflation in the West End to a sad decline in values." He chortled along with the rest, enjoying his own joke.

"That was rather special," Muirhead chided. "You had just escaped from a Boer prison camp and been chased across half of Africa by their army."

This was why the Old Man enjoyed Muirhead's dinners; the host always made a point of giving him plenty of scope for relating some of his favorite stories.

"Why bother to escape, Winston? What drove you to it?" inquired one of the guests.

And with scarcely time for a perfunctory cough of modesty, he was off. "The Boer" — he pronounced it 'Booa,' as if to emphasize the race's reputation for thick-skinned stubbornness — "the Boer has so little imagination. A diet of maize and dried beef or, if we were fortunate, dried beef and maize — it was impossible! I would simply have faded away. So you see, my escape was not a matter of bravery. I had no choice in the matter. My stomach insisted." He smiled, using his fingers to pop a little cube of cheese into his mouth which he chewed with relish.

" 'Winston Churchill: Dead or Alive,' " Sir William offered.

"If only the British electorate had wanted me as passionately as the Boers!"

While the other guests chuckled, Churchill paused to scratch his crotch with a total lack of self-consciousness. His table manners were atrocious. He had long ago ceased to bother about such trivial things, and when Clemmie had forcefully reprimanded him he had justified his behavior as the self-indulgence of an old man. Anyway, he countered, it hadn't caused any slackening in the flood of dinner invitations.

"Seriously, Winston. If you had been captured you most certainly would have been shot, if only to discourage others. Why risk your life? Was it really that important?"

"I never realized how important until I returned home, where I found that my escape had been the focus of the newspapers' attention for weeks. Unwittingly I had become a hero, a symbol of national resistance, and my escape had succeeded in bolstering the determination of the entire country to continue with the war until victory. It is a matter of morale, and you cannot fight a war without morale. As one editor kindly wrote, 'One man, by his actions and example, can so inspire a nation that he will light a fire across a whole continent.' "

There was an appreciative silence around the room and a look of sheer wickedness crept into the Old Man's eye. "And, as I discovered, you can get a good discount into the bargain!"

The camp was in darkness. There were no lights along the perimeter fence and the only illumination came from within the old football changing rooms, which now served as a guard hut, and from the bright moon. But it was a blustery night with clouds scudding across the sky. Had any of the guards bothered to look, they would have seen shadowy figures flitting between the tents, playing hide-and-seek in the sporadic moonlight, but most of the Canadians were relaxing in the guard hut. There were just four guards on the main gate into the compound, and two patroling the walkway between the double perimeter fence. Guard duty was a pain; there had never been any trouble and no prisoner in his right mind would want to escape back to the hell pit they'd just left in Europe. They were all, prisoners and guards alike, marking time till the fighting was over.

So when, from inside the shadowy compound, the pair patroling the perimeter walkway saw one of their number beckoning to them, no suspicion was aroused. He had probably found two prisoners screwing or some other bit of fun to enliven the endless night hours of cold and boredom. They let themselves into the compound through a side gate in the wire; they didn't even think twice that the gateway was shielded from the main guardhouse across the compound by the prisoners' tents. After all, they hadn't put the tents there. Even after they darted between two of the tents and came face to face with their fellow guard pointing his Lee Enfield straight at them, they were still not concerned. It was only when they heard the familiar click of a round being forced into the chamber that they realized all was not well, and not until the moon had squeezed briefly between the clouds and fallen across Hencke's lean and determined face did they realize that this was not, after all, going to be their night.

"But you're . . ." one gasped in sudden understanding. It came too late. They had already raised their hands and were being relieved of their weapons.

"I . . . don't want to die," the youngest guard blubbered as his wrists were tied behind him with a length of guy rope.

"Keep your miserable mouth shut and you won't have to,"

a prisoner responded. The young guard was almost relieved when he felt the gag pushed firmly between his teeth.

The guards' legs were pinioned and they were bundled into the corner of one of the tents. It was only when the prisoners were leaving that one of them remembered. "You're the miserable little bastard who held my head down on the table the other day, aren't you?" The youngster's eyes, all that could be seen above the gag, showed large and white. He was petrified. "I'll never forget that. You were laughing your head off." The prisoner stiffened and swung back a leg as if to smash the Canadian's testicles. None of the other prisoners did or said anything to stop him; the guard deserved everything he got. But as the German looked at the whimpering body on the ground in front of him, he seemed to change his mind. He knew what it was like to be defenseless and scared. He spat in disgust and turned on his heel. Escape would be revenge enough.

A few minutes later a group of men moved toward the guardhouse, eight prisoners being marched sullenly along with three uniformed guards, rifles at the ready, escorting them from the rear.

"Open the gate!" one of the guards shouted. "Got a bunch of troublemakers who need a little gentle reminding of who's in charge of this friggin' camp."

The gates swung open and the prisoners marched through. The duty sergeant nodded as they approached, his rifle slung over his back as he took a drag from a cigarette. He waved a lazy torch in their direction. Hencke was standing directly in front of him before the beam fell across his face.

"Heil Hitler," Hencke snapped.

"What . . . ?" was the only word the sergeant managed to expel before a rifle butt thumped him in the gut, putting him on the floor and rendering him incapable of any noise except a low gurgling retch. Around him the other guards were receiving similar treatment before being trussed and dragged off to join their companions in the tent.

The prisoners now had seven rifles. They also had surprise on their side and there was scarcely a protest when they burst into the guard hut and overpowered sixteen other guards. The seventeenth, the captain on duty, was taking a shower and thought the interruption was some prank by the other guards. He was not in good temper when he stepped from under the water to remonstrate, with nothing more than a sponge to maintain the dignity he thought due his senior rank. He was in even poorer temper after he had been bound and, minus even his sponge, dumped with the other captive guards.

"I'll freeze to death," he complained.

"Be grateful that dying will take you so long," came the response, after which the captain ceased protesting and saved his energy for trying to burrow as deeply as possible into the pile of warm bodies inside the tent.

The breakout had been conducted with ruthless German team work, but now it was every man for himself. They knew the prospects were not good; there had been no time for preparations. There was no civilian clothing, no maps, precious little food or money, what chance did they have? But they were free. Even an hour of freedom was enough. It would be a night to remember.

"Seeing the look on that stupid captain's face made it all worth while for me," one of the prisoners smiled, pausing to shake Hencke's hand. "The only pity is that Pilsudski's not around for a little of his own treatment. Still, maybe he'll get that from his court martial. Thanks, Hencke. We owe you," he said before turning to jog through the camp gates and into the unknown.

Then the commander was in front of him, bent over his

stick, wheezing. "Good wishes, Hencke. It's madness, but lots of luck."

Hencke looked into the other's exhausted face, then down at his stick.

"I'm not going anywhere, you know that," the commander said. "Wouldn't make it past the gate and I'd only be a burden. I'm going to stay here, if you don't mind, and wait till the relief guard arrives in the morning. It will be enough for me to see what happens to Pilsudski when the British discover they've got the biggest prisoner escape of the war on their hands. Might stretch even their sense of humor . . ." He tried to smile but the effort was too much for him, and he began coughing again. There was an air about him of past caring, and his eyes had taken on that distant, dull look of approaching death. He rested his weight against Hencke, trying to regain his breath. "One thing, Hencke. I don't know who you are or where you come from, but you're special. I've seen the way you can lead men and the desire that drives you on. I don't mind admitting that you frighten me a little; such passion is extraordinary. It makes me wonder how, with such commitment, we managed to lose this wretched war . . ."

"It's not over yet. There's still plenty of dying to be done."

"Plenty of dying to be done . . . You're right, of course." The commander reflected on the words for a moment. "I don't suppose anyone will make it back home but, if they do, it will be you. I want to ask you a favor. I'm not going to get back, not this time or ever. I don't have long, and you may be the last German I ever talk to." The commander's hand reached out to grab Hencke with the force of desperation. "My wife and children . . . they're in Stettin. If it's not already in Russian hands it soon will be. Please . . ." He scrabbled feverishly inside his uniform, producing a letter which he thrust at Hencke. "Get this to them. It's my last chance, the last time I'll ever . . ." His breathing pattern was gone again and he struggled to find a little more energy, pulling in rasping lungfuls of air. "If you've ever loved anyone you'll know how important this is to me. Do it for me, Hencke. Your word of honor, one German officer to another. Give this letter to them, with my love. If you get back."

"When I get back."

The commander nodded in agreement. "How will you?"

"There's a motorbike around the back of the guard hut."

"You're surely not going to use the main roads! They'll be bound to pick you up."

"There are nearly two hundred and fifty escaping prisoners. None of them has the slightest idea what to do or where he's going. Most of them have only the vaguest idea even where they are. So they'll shy away from the towns and take to the countryside, moving by night. And the British will know that anything that moves through the woods at night for a hundred miles around this place will be either an escaped prisoner or a fox. In the mood they are likely to be in, chances are they'll shoot, just to be on the safe side."

The commander shook his head in confusion at this blunt assessment, so much more callous than the one Hencke had offered around the camp fire. "You talk about 'them,' as if you are quite separate, on your own."

"The only chance anyone has is not to do what the rest of the crowd does. I've got four, maybe five hours to get well clear of this place before it starts swarming with troops. So I'm going to borrow the bike and take to the roads. All roads lead somewhere." He began his preparations to depart, buttoning up the Canadian tunic that he was still wearing.

"Not in enemy uniform, for God's sake. They'll shoot you for sure!"

"They've got to catch me first," Hencke shouted back over his shoulder.

Moments later the sound of an engine, a Norton 250, began throbbing through the night. "They even left a map with it," he smiled to himself in triumph, revving the bike before letting out the clutch with a snap that sent a shower of wet dirt cascading into the air. Hencke was gone.

The commander gazed after the disappearing figure. "You are a strange one, Hencke. But I chose the right man. You'll get back to wherever you came from, I'm sure. Even if it's the other side of hell."

He could neither see nor hear the motorbike by the time it pulled up sharply several hundred yards beyond the camp gates. Hencke reached into the pocket of his tunic where the commander had stuffed the precious envelope. "My word of honor," he whispered, "one German officer to another." The dark eyes glowed with contempt as he tore the letter into a hundred tiny fragments, sent scattering in the wind as he rode away.

CHAPTER 3

The sun was rising and London was beginning to stir, but it made little difference within the Annexe. Daylight didn't penetrate here, and the only sign of the new day was the progress of the clocks and the arrival of those rostered for day duty. The duty secretary, Anthony Seizall, was rubbing the sleep from his eyes and staring at the telephone as if it had broken wind. Perplexed, he clamped it back to the side of his head.

"You're not pulling my leg, are you? Because if you are I shall have great pleasure in coming round with half a dozen of the local boys in blue and pulling the head off your bloody neck!" There was a pause while he listened to a heated voice on the other end of the phone, his head bent low over the bakelite mouthpiece and his straight hair falling over his eyes; he punctuated the conversation with references to a variety of spiritual saviors before descending into repeated low cursing. Seizall was noncomformist, practically teetotal. Something was clearly up.

He sat chewing the end of his pencil for several minutes, the tip of his rubbery nose twitching like a rabbit's and dilating in time to the successive floods of indecision that swept over him. Eventually his gnawing broke the pencil clean in two; time was up, action was required. He proceeded down a maze of underground corridors, shaking his head from side to side as if trying one last time to disperse the fog of inadequacy, until he came to the staff sleeping quarters. Hesitating only briefly for one final burst of indecision, he knocked on a door and entered.

"Sorry to wake you, Cazolet. Got a tricky one."

Cazolet rolled over and waved his hands in front of his eyes, trying to ward off the light from the bare bulb which was prying his lids apart. He spent a great deal of his time in the Annexe and the result was a gray pallor across his face, made worse by lack of sleep. He wasn't supposed to be on duty at the moment, but he knew the PM's mind so well that the other staff had taken to consulting him on many matters. What it meant, of course, was that they brought him all their problems, as if he didn't have several filing trays full of his own to deal with. But he didn't mind; consultation was the finest form of bureaucratic flattery.

"Seems there's been a breakout. Some POW transit camp in Yorkshire. Haven't got the final figures but it looks like — almost two hundred and fifty Jerry on the loose. I've double-checked, of course. No doubt about it, I'm afraid. Bit of a cock-up, really." Seizall's sentences were clipped, giving but the barest detail, as if too much flavor might somehow involve him in it all, and every instinct in his civil service body told him to steer well clear of this one.

"I was just about to let the Old Man know," Seizall continued. "Trouble is he's fast asleep; got in dreadfully late last night from some swill of a dinner party, and you know he's like a rhinoceros with piles when he's woken. So I thought I'd let him sleep on a little. Trouble is I've got to inform all the other necessary Departments . . . What'll we do?"

"So all of a sudden it's *our* problem, is it?" Cazolet grumbled. One day, one day very soon, he prayed, they would let him get a full night's sleep. He poured cold water from a large jug into an enamel wash basin — all that passed for facilities in the primitive subterranean accommodation — splashing urgent handfuls over his face to encourage a little more oxygen into his brain, while Seizall stood uncomfortably in the doorway of the narrow room. The cold water seemed to have worked, for when Cazolet stood up from the wash stand he was decisive.

"You tell all the other Departments, Seizall, and the news will be round Fleet Street before you've had time to finish breakfast. And once that's out, we'll never be able to put it back in the bag, wartime censorship or no. It'll be blaring out on Radio Berlin within five minutes. Two hundred and fifty of them? It's a disaster. And it's just what the Prime Minister's political opponents want. They'll pin the blame for slack security on him personally, try to make him look old and incompetent. So you go right ahead and inform everyone from the Labor Party to the Third Reich that we have one of the biggest security foul-ups of the war on our hands." He paused to dry his face vigorously with a rough cotton towel. "Then you can go wake up the PM and tell him what you've done."

The effect on Seizall was impressive. His lower jaw wobbled in fair impression of a mullet, his Adam's apple performing balletic gyrations of distress.

"There is a better way," Cazolet continued, his supremacy in the matter clearly established. "We tell the minimum number of people — only those in the security services who need to know in order to start getting Jerry rounded up. We make it clear to them that this is a matter of top national security, that any public discussion of the escape can only give comfort to the enemy. Be vague about numbers. Then, when the Old Man's awake and in harness, we'll tell him what we've done. If he wants to let the whole world know, he can. But that's up to him, not you or me."

Seizall was nodding, trying to look as if he were merely accepting endorsement of a course of action he had already made up his mind to pursue.

"There's a lot riding on this, Seizall. Perhaps the Old Man's entire political future. I think he'll be grateful you waited."

For the first time that morning an impression of relief began to etch its way across the duty secretary's face, and he paused to give silent thanks for the binding effect of powdered egg.

Dawn was beginning to paint lurid pictures in the sky, thin fingers of rain cloud stretching toward him like witches' claws, their fire-red tips making the heavens appear to drip with blood. Around Hencke the dark woods seemed to crowd in, the trees bending down as if trying to pluck him from the seat of his bike, while the throbbing of the engine surrounded him in a cocoon of sound that carved out a little world of his own and detached him from reality. From the moment he had scattered the commander's letter to the wind he had kept his head low and the throttle stretched open, taking full advantage of the deserted roads. The wind snatched at his hair and froze his face and fingertips, all the while urging him onward. He was free! But there was no elation in Hencke. As he looked at the fierce sky above him, the memories came crowding back. In the glow that brushed the clouds he saw only the embers he had found burning in the schoolhouse, consuming everything he loved. In the gloom of the trees bowing and sagging in the wind he found images of the veils pulled close around the mothers who had come to sorrow and mourn, weighed down by incomprehension at their loss. In the thumping noise of the engine there was no sound of freedom, only the tramp of boots as they had marched past smoldering wreckage. Hencke could not escape the memory of young bodies twisted and broken. Of books torn and burning, their ashes scattered in the growing winds of war. Of a pair of tiny shoes lying neatly at the entrance to the classroom, with no trace of the vibrant and joyful child who had been wearing them moments before. Of a love which should never have been and which could never be again. And as he remembered he clung to the throttle as a drowning man clutches at a stick, charging recklessly onward, pursued by demons.

As the sky began to lose its luster and take on the damp gray tones of March, he found himself passing through more open countryside. The long avenues of haunted trees made way for the hedgerows of rural England; above the whistle of the wind he could hear the welcoming chorus of early morning, as the demons that had returned to haunt his mind faded in the daylight. They would be back, they always came back, yet for a moment the nightmare seemed to have drained from his soul. He was taking the first, deep breath of relief when he rounded a long bend between the hedgerows, and stood hard on the brake pedal, sliding to a halt on the dewy surface. Before him, stretched full across the road and blocking his path, was a rusty farm tractor around which spilled a line of British soldiers, rifles raised, pointing directly at him.

It seemed as if his race was already over.

It was nearly eleven o'clock before Cazolet presented himself to the Marine guard stationed outside the Prime Minister's bedroom. As the sentry stepped smartly aside, Cazolet entered bearing a large cup of tea. Churchill stirred beneath the thick quilt. Typically he slept heavily and late, particularly after a good dinner, but five years of heartbreak and Hitler had conditioned him to come rapidly to full alert.

"William. To what do I owe this decidedly ambiguous pleasure?" He swept the disheveled strands of graying russet hair back into place and reached out greedily for the tea, which he proceeded to slurp.

"There's been a POW breakout."

"From where?"

"Yorkshire. Camp 174B. It's just north of . . ."

"Yes. I know it," Churchill interrupted, the tea temporarily forgotten. There was a gleam — a twinkle, even — in the Old Man's eye. "Some men never seem to know when they're beaten. How many?"

"Nearly two hundred fifty."

Churchill jumped. The tea slopped into the saucer and began dripping onto the sheet.

"Nearly two hundred and fifty," Cazolet repeated. "Several thousand troops are being sent to the area, but as always they're in the wrong place, waiting on the south coast to embark for Europe. To fill the gap we've activated detachments of the local Home Guard to man road blocks around the camp."

He was good, Cazolet, damned good. No undue emotion or unnecessary hyperbole, measuring out the details so as to inform rather than to incite. After a late night out the Old Man could be like an unexploded bomb, which required the most delicate of handling, yet he seemed to be taking all this in his stride.

"There's something else. I've instructed the Chief Constable in charge of coordinating the operation that news of the breakout must be treated on a strictly need-to-know basis, that on no account must the numbers involved be released. He complained that this makes it very much more difficult for his men; not knowing the full facts ties their hands behind their backs."

"Did you manage to persuade him?"

"Not until I reminded him that the war is coming to an end, and the next Honors List would be bound to include many civilians who had been particularly helpful on the home front. I think he saw the point."

"But the news is bound to get out eventually," Churchill mused. "It will be the best news Herr Hitler will have heard in months." His tea was momentarily forgotten, the cup stranded halfway between saucer and chin.

"But not before most of the escapees have been rounded up. By then it can be treated as a success story and not used by our enemies to undermine you."

"My goodness, William. You have been busy guarding my back. Commendable!"

"Not really." Cazolet's tone was impish. "Pure self interest. Prime Ministers are not brought down without creating waves. In your case it would be a veritable tidal wave, which would quite swamp small boats such as mine . . ."

"Then may I wish you many long years of carefree sailing."

There was an almost familial informality between the two, born of a meeting of intellects and emotions, more like father and son than the formal courtesies demanded between master and civil servant. Anyway, it was difficult to be left in excessive awe of a man propped up in bed, swathed in three yards of pale pink pyjama silk and already puffing away at a huge cigar between mouthfuls of tea.

"The local police stations are being inundated with reports of suspicious characters; several have already been apprehended." Cazolet glanced at his notebook. "Two men were caught as they rode a stolen bicycle in full Luftwaffe uniform the wrong way down the village High Street. Apparently they would have been caught earlier, except for the misfortune that the bike they stole belonged to the local police constable."

"Remind me of that when I call to congratulate the Chief

Constable and thank him for his cooperation . . ."

"Four others were found early this morning, dead drunk behind the bar of a local pub. Seems they never had any intention of escaping farther than the nearest drink. I suspect that most of them will be rounded up very quickly."

"I'm sure you are right. But as we know, most of them don't matter; it's the one or two slipping through the net who carve their names in the history books, who light a fire across a whole continent." He paused. "Keep me well advised, William. A great deal may ride on such an escape, I want to know everything that happens on this one."

Cazolet stood at the end of the bed, waiting. "Any further instructions?"

The Old Man looked up, his expression serious. "This may be a difficult day, which calls for unusual measures." There was a frown of concentration. "I shall have two eggs with my bacon and toast. And another cup of tea."

Cazolet turned and left. For the first time in several days he was laughing out loud.

Hencke counted the barrels of eight Lee Enfields, all of which were pointing straight at him from a distance of less than ten feet. He could try to run them down, of course, but by the time he had slipped the clutch and moved no farther than a few inches he reckoned that at least six of the eight bullets would have found him. Not much of an option, that. Neither was surrender, but what was the alternative? Already he could see the tips of the barrels dancing nervously, and could sense the fingers tightening around the triggers. As he throttled back and put the gears in neutral, Hencke's hand went to his throat, checking that the uniform he was wearing was properly buttoned. No surrender. Never that. There was too much at stake. He would try to bluff it out.

"Sergeant Cheval, Fourth Royal Quebec," he snapped. God, could they really take his accent for French Canadian? But don't wait and see — grab the initiative! "Who's in charge?"

The rifles were still pointing at him, but some were beginning to waver in uncertainty. He began to study the men behind the muzzles; only two were in uniform, the rest were in an assortment of crumpled civilian clothing with nothing more than armbands for identification. Behind them, strewn among the hedgerows, lay several pedal cycles which, apart from the battered tractor, were their only apparent means of transportation. What luck! He had run into Dad's Army dragged out of their beds. Perhaps there was a chance, after all . . .

From behind the line of rifles stepped a man in his sixties, armed with a Webley pistol, a fierce look in his eye and a carefully trimmed white mustache. He was the only one wearing a military cap. His uniform was smartly pressed and his boots were immaculate. A veteran, and a man who wore his lieutenant's shoulder pips with pride, Hencke decided. Still astride the motorcycle, he came to a salute.

"Lieutenant, I am Sergeant Cheval of the Fourth Quebec," he repeated the introduction. "My regiment is guarding the camp."

The Webley was still pointing straight at him and there was a bead of nervous perspiration across the bridge of the lieutenant's nose. But to the officer's rear Hencke could see the barrels of several rifles beginning to droop toward the ground.

"Less than two miles down the road there are thirty escaped Germans," Hencke continued, waving behind him in the general direction of the north of England. The look of ferocity in the officer's eye had changed to one of suspicion and he was about to aim a flood of questions which Hencke knew he had no chance of withstanding. "Many of them are armed. They've already killed several of my company!"

At this point the rifle barrels were raised once more in anxiety; this time they were pointing not at Hencke but back down the road. The lieutenant's lips were working away in agitation beneath his mustache. He was being overwhelmed by Hencke's news and the responsibility that had suddenly been thrust upon him, after so many years of waiting, like the fishes, for an invasion which had never come. He had the rank but he couldn't match the experience suggested by Hencke's regular army uniform. He had a thousand questions to ask but could find the words for none of them.

"Lieutenant, the Germans are headed in this direction, they're not far behind. You must maintain your position here, and be ready while I go and warn headquarters." It was all so ludicrously makeshift. He hadn't the slightest idea where headquarters were located, but he supposed they must lie somewhere to the other side of the roadblock. He began gently to rev the bike engine, testing the officer's resolve. "And remember. They're dangerous!"

For the first time the lieutenant's eyes left him and began staring in the direction from which Hencke had appeared. The ferocity had gone; there was only anxiety left. By the time he had dragged his attention back from the distant woodland the moment for making decisions was past. The Norton was already on the move.

"Good luck, Lieutenant," Hencke shouted above the noise of the engine as he weaved around the tractor and the line of men. Their rifles were at shoulder level once more while their boots scratched nervously away at the macadam, trying to find a solid firing position. When Hencke looked behind him he could see a long row of backs. Only the officer was looking in his direction, the agonies of uncertainty twisting his face. But already it was too late . . .

Hencke waved and was gone.

* * *

The portrait of Louis XIV was nothing more than a cheap reproduction, but there was no mistaking the profound look of disdain as it gazed down from the painted wooden walls. Eisenhower's daily briefing session with his military aides was coming to an end. The noise and bustle caused by the fifty or more advisers clattered around the dining room of the dingy red-brick secondary school in Reims that served as SHAEF's forward military headquarters.

"D'you know, Dwight, that old bastard wouldn't have bothered with all this." General Omar Bradley, three stars and Eisenhower's right hand, waved at the portrait. "None of these briefing meetings, no listening to endless advice, no worries about whether the fuel was in the same place as the fighting. Just an order for the peasant army to pick up their pikes and start walking while he went back to his roast pig and mistress. What a way to fight a war."

Eisenhower winced. Even with as good a friend as Bradley he wasn't in the mood to discuss mistresses. "You're not suggesting I dress up in silk tights and a red wig like him?"

"Well, he ruled for something like seventy-odd years. Not bad for the times when you counted yourself lucky if the pox killed you off before the Black Death. And he was big in arts 'n stuff. They called him the Sun King. After all this is over, Ike, d'you think the sun's going to shine out from under your periwig?"

Eisenhower laughed. Bradley was always able to make him relax, even when the going was particularly tough. As commander of the 12th Army Group, which formed the backbone of the European command, Bradley shared the weight. While Eisenhower ordered and authorized, it was Bradley's job to implement. They shared both the successes and sacrifices of war, and it had built trust and affection.

"I wonder how that old bastard would have coped with the British, Brad?"

"What's dear old Monty been up to this time? Another press conference to let the world know how you and the Pope have got it all wrong? Or is he complaining again that he hasn't got a zipper big enough for his flies?" The disdain for General Bernard Montgomery was evident in both of them. A relationship that had always been difficult with their British colleague had become incandescent in recent months, as Montgomery complained, cajoled, and claimed credit for other men's victories. He was Bradley's rank equivalent and Eisenhower's subordinate, but he rarely acted as such, particularly in the presence of the media, when a poised pen or the pop of a flashbulb sent him off into grandiloquent summaries of the European battle scene that would have made even the Sun King feel uncomfortable.

"No, it's not Montgomery this time," Eisenhower responded, blinking as the blinds were drawn back from the high windows to let in a flood of springtime light. "It's the Old Man. Churchill. Didn't want to raise it in front of everyone, but I'm having real trouble getting the extra division out of him. Should have arrived days ago, but all I get in its place is flannel and soft-soap. First he keeps complaining that the British forces are left sitting idly on their backsides, then he won't give me the troops to do anything other. What does he expect me to do? Scare the Germans into surrender by dropping my pants?"

"This isn't some screwball way of putting pressure on you to let him have Berlin, is it? You know, Berlin or nothing?"

"Could it really have come to that, Brad? Monty, yes, but surely not the Old Man. Sweet Jesus, I thought we were fighting this war together." Eisenhower's square jaw began to work back and forth in exasperation. The Allied command had worked so harmoniously right up until D-Day and the invasion of Europe. But once they had set foot on French soil the cooperation seemed to vanish in a political quagmire as deep and impassable as the trench mud of the First War. He cracked his knuckles as he recounted the times the British had got in the way, been stubbornly slow off the mark, or had brazenly attempted to trip him up. Caen. Arnhem. Antwerp. The Ardennes. The Rhine . . .

He had run out of knuckles. And of patience. "I won't let them make a damned fool of me any longer, Brad. I've taken about as much flak as I can stand. Hell, I wouldn't take this sort of crap even from the French! It's about time someone made our allies realize just who's in charge of this shooting match."

There was an edge to his voice, uncharacteristic in a commander renowned for seeing the other man's point of view. Bradley said nothing, gratified that at last his superior seemed determined to clamp down on the petulance of their colleagues. And not before time. Eisenhower dug deep into his pocket for the lucky pennies he always carried. "Like worry beads," he had once explained, "except it scares the shit out of the men if the Supreme Commander is seen to worry. So I play with my pennies." They were cascading from one hand to the other as he tried to pour away his frustration and waited for an orderly to bring coffee. The orderly was serving before Eisenhower returned to the point.

"It truly galls me to think of thousands of British troops sitting outside Dover doing nothing," he muttered distractedly.

"I'm not sure where the general gets his information, but those troops sure as hell ain't there," the orderly interrupted in a slow Texan drawl. He had been with Eisenhower a long time, not so much because of his valeting skills as his ability to read his master's moods, and to respond appropriately, often with a humorous tale or a choice piece of gossip that otherwise would never have reached the Supreme Commander's ears. And Eisenhower loved a good gossip; it helped remind him there was still a real world out there.

"What d'you mean, Mickey?"

"Well, sir, you'll remember I've just been on leave in London?" he began. One of the perks of working for the boss was an almost limitless ability to contrive seats on transport planes flying away from the battle zone.

"Sure do," Eisenhower responded. "Only time for weeks I got a decent cup of coffee."

"The general is so kind," the orderly continued, completely unabashed. "I got talking to some of our British friends. Strange little watering hole called the Ferret & Firkin. I never did figure out what the 'firkin' bit was."

"This story'd better be good, Mickey, or I'll have your balls on toast," Eisenhower chuckled; the orderly's calculated impertinence was beginning to work its usual magic.

"There's these two Brit quartermasters ferretin' and firkin' and feeling pretty relaxed about the whole thing. Seems they were just about to join the fun here in Europe, when most of their unit got orders to ship north, to York-Shire or wherever." He managed to make it sound somewhere beyond the Arctic Circle. "So this pair were left waging war with a mountain of supplies and equipment, while the rest of their buddies were off opening a new battle front."

"New front?" Bradley inquired.

"Well, General, I'm not supposed to breathe a word. Honest to God, they swore me to secrecy . . ." Mickey's eyes wandered theatrically around the room in search of eavesdroppers. "But it seems like there's been a big breakout, a whole prison camp full of Germans on the loose, with half the British army in hot pursuit. Sounded like the biggest roundup east of the Shenandoah, 'cept nobody's supposed to know a thing about it . . . Cream, General Bradley?"

But the two generals had lost interest in the coffee. "Could it be, Brad? Could it really be so cretinous?"

"A breakout?" Bradley sucked thoughtfully at his teeth. "What would we do in the same circumstances? I guess we'd want to keep it quiet. Hell, if we'd lost a whole campful of prisoners, Montgomery'd be on every radio broadcast, braying like a jackass and offering to help sweep up the mess."

"But to hold back an entire division from Europe at a time when Churchill is screaming for more action, just to cover up their own blunder . . . ?"

"Politics, Dwight. Capital 'P'. This whole damn war is growing to be all about politics."

Eisenhower's easy mood had vanished, steel reentered his voice. "That's no excuse for incompetence and duplicity, not when the lives of my men are at stake. Check this story out for me, Brad, see if it's true."

"And if it is?"

"Fight fire with fire. Take on the politicians at their own game." The lucky pennies jangled into the palm of his hand, where he gripped them tightly in a clenched fist. A tight smile of determination and of decision broke on his face. "You know, Brad, maybe Mr. Churchill could do with some help rounding up his strays. From some of the drovers in our press corps . . ."

He hadn't realized how cold he had become until the petrol ran out. He'd shaken the machine to slop every last drop from the tank into the fuel line, and it had given him a few extra miles, but then it had started coughing once more, slowed, and died. It was only then, as he tried to dismount, that he discovered his fingers, clamped firm and senseless around the handlebars, wouldn't move, frozen solid by the hours of forcing his way through the clinging mid-English damp. At first all he could manage was a spastic twitching of a little finger, and it took him several agonizing minutes before the rest had followed and he had loosened his grip. Then he discovered he couldn't stand straight. His clothes were drenched to the skin, his back locked as if he were still thrusting his way forward in the saddle, his eyes scraped raw by the night air. And it got worse.

After he had dumped the bike, he knew he would have to quit the roads and try his luck cross-country. South. As long as he headed south he was getting nearer his goal. Yet cross-country was murder. By day he looked suspicious, an increasingly unkempt vagabond in military uniform, so he tried walking at night, but that proved impossible in the perpetually cloud-covered countryside. And he was getting weaker, less able to fend off the biting wind that drove the temperature down and flayed at his resilience. As dawn broke, a week after the escape, he knew it was time for taking risks. The spirit was stubborn but the body was refusing to respond. It needed food, warmth, rest.

This was farming country, mindless miles of hedgerow and ploughed mud, across which a few homesteads and primitive cottages lay scattered like grains of discarded wheat. He had passed a small farm about half a mile back; there had been wood smoke curling from the chimney, and the low of cattle at milk coming from the shed to the rear. Too much life; he needed something altogether more quiet. Ahead he could see but one house, of pale yellow stone like so many of the rest, nestling beside a meandering lane but set well back up its own track. He could see no sign of activity. It would have to do, but not up the track where he could be clearly seen from both house and lane. It would have to be once more cross-country, even though that would turn the few hundred yards to the front door into a mile or more, skulking behind hawthorn bushes, hugging the trees, trying not to startle and scatter the sheep. He was shivering.

By the time he approached the house the trek across ploughed fields and through damp hedgerows had drained what little strength he had left. It had started to rain again; he thought he couldn't get wetter until he'd slipped and rolled into a mud-filled ditch. The once-clean Canadian uniform was now a sodden, filthy mess, as was the man inside. And he had stopped shivering, he was too cold even for that. What if there were someone home? He knew he should think of some passable excuse for his appearance, but his mind was numbed along with the rest of him, and he could find no answers, only a desperate need to find warmth and rest. The cold was making him impatient as well as slow-witted. The prison camp seemed a lifetime ago.

He broke cover from the apple orchard behind the house, and stumbled across the lawn toward the kitchen door, a spring shower lashing at him like a devil's whip, and he still couldn't stand up straight. He'd tried to slap his face into alertness but his wits had slowed; despite long minutes of close inspection which had revealed nothing, as he drew closer he saw something move in the window. Despairingly, he threw himself low and to one side, falling clumsily, his left boot submerged up to the ankle in a small ornamental fish pond, until he realized he had been jumping at his own reflection. His brain was too frozen even to curse. He made the last few yards to the kitchen door practically on all fours, tripping over a bicycle as his legs buckled in protest. He was kneeling, catching his breath, finding comfort in the solid appearance of the door — no scratch marks, no sign of a dog. Perhaps it would work out after all. He had to claw his way upright, each movement of his frozen muscles requiring a separate and specific command, until he was leaning on the door and trying to peer within. All seemed quiet and empty. He stepped inside.

At one end of the kitchen stood a wood-burning stove. The warmth cascaded over him as though he had thrown himself headlong into a bath. The room was large and low, with a great oaken table in the middle, and a rough staircase climbing the far wall, beneath which an open door led through to a tidy but undersized sitting room. The stove drew him like a magnet; he crossed the stone-flagged floor and sat on a hearth stool — not the comfortable rocking chair, too much noise — and began searching for signs of occupation. But there was no kettle on the stove, no sign of crumbs from an early breakfast on the table, no plate draining beside the sink. It took several minutes before the heavy pulse bombarding his temples began to subside, and he could listen properly for any trace of noise, but he found none. At last he began to relax, prizing off his boots, peeling down to his underwear, allowing the heat to replenish both body and spirit.

He shook his head violently. The heat was beginning to play tricks with him, tempting him to close his eyes, turning from ally to enemy. He couldn't afford to sleep, not here at least, for warm kitchens are not left empty for long. He glanced around, perhaps some food might help, and soon he had found bread, cheese, jam and apples — and butter! Real butter! When had he last tasted butter? It was rock hard and tore the bread to pieces, but after prison camp rations the taste was electrifying. It was as he was licking the final smears of strawberry jam from his fingers that he heard it: a noise from the direction of the stairs, a noise that banished the last traces of drowsiness from his mind and left him coiled inside like a spring. The noise of wood creaking beneath someone's step. As he looked up he saw a woman in her sixties, no taller than five foot two, wrapped in a white cotton dressing gown, and with a face like an apple wrinkled from winter storage. The hair was steel gray and sported a patchwork of hair clips, the eyes were cold and blue and were staring angrily at Hencke from above the well-oiled twin barrels of a shotgun.

"And don't for one moment think I won't use it."

Hencke could sense she was not bluffing. The suspicion in the eyes, the stiffness of her lined and leathery cheeks, and the way the thin lips were drawn down to form an ugly, uncompromising gash reminded him of his aunt, and his aunt had never uttered empty threats. The promise of a beating had always meant a beating, often two, until he had grown too big and she had been forced to lash him instead with her tongue, inflicting far more torment than the hand. It had been a cruel weapon, always questioning, prying, demanding explanations for any form of absence, refusing to accept that the boy was growing to manhood and independence and was no longer hers. That he was forming loyalties to others. His explanations had never been sufficient then and, as Hencke looked at the mess of crumbs on the table and the pile of steaming clothes lying by the stove, he knew that no explanation would be good enough now.

"I . . ." But he didn't bother to continue. He just shook his head and methodically began to wipe his fingers on his vest.

"Don't move!" The voice was shrill as his hands moved down from the table. "Push the knife away!" It was only a butter knife, but she was taking no chances.

He managed a smile. "Don't worry. I'm not going to argue with a loaded shotgun."

"And who might you be? Some sort of foreigner by your accent." She stepped from the bottom stair into the kitchen, chin up, prominent nose moving ahead like a ship's prow, waving the shotgun with menace. He raised his hands.

"My name is Peter Hencke. And I am sorry for the mess. I meant no harm."

"We'll let the police decide that." She took another step into the room, reluctant to come any closer. Her eyes kept darting from Hencke's face to the wall behind him, where he knew was the telephone. She needed it, but could take her time, working her way step by step round the room, keeping the barrels fixed firmly on him, until she had reached the telephone. One call and he was done for. One sharp move and he was dead. He had to gamble, to rattle her, throw her off-balance, and quickly. Who knew how long it would be before a husband, postman, friend or farmhand appeared? Time was not on his side.

"It is a special day for you. I am German. An escaped prisoner of war. I think you will find the police very happy to receive your call. Perhaps there will even be a reward."

He could see her eyes grow wild from the mixture of fear and excitement, and he could sense her finger tightening on the twin triggers.

"I'm not a fool; I'll cause no trouble." Hencke raised his hands still higher above his head and with great caution stood up from the table, stepping back out of her direct line to the telephone. "Your wretched English weather is enough to defeat anyone."

The attempt at humor was lost on her. Instead she waggled the shotgun with new fervor. "Back! Step back! Right away from the telephone."

Hencke took three deliberate steps backward. The shotgun waved, and he took another. He was a clear five yards away from the phone, and she began her advance across the room — but he was on his feet, not pinned against a solid oak table.

"Keep staring at these barrels," she snapped. "So much as breathe heavily and I'll use them, don't think I won't. An escaping Bosch, dead or alive — I'll maybe get a medal as well as a reward."

Hencke remained silent and motionless until she had reached the telephone. She was there, had offered no chance of surprise, was reaching for the phone, now was dialing. Yet in order to use it she had to take one hand off the gun and both eyes off Hencke. Her aging solitary arm found the gun too heavy, and as the dial clattered around the barrels began to droop toward the floor. It was the moment he had been waiting for. Hencke sprang.

Even so she had time to see him coming. "Why you . . . !"

She leaned backward, trying to force up the gun barrels and pulling the trigger as she did so. No, she was not bluffing, but in her weak grip the shot went wild and Hencke was upon her. She screamed and they both fell to the floor, ripping the phone from the wall as they did so, with Hencke landing heavily on top of the old woman and the shotgun wedged between them. She was still fighting and spitting, scrabbling once more to find the trigger for the second barrel, when Hencke wrenched it out of her grasp. The solid wooden butt flew away from her scratching fingers and caught her on the temple just above the left eye. Her head fell back sharply against the flagstones, hitting them with a loud crack. She lay still, breathing heavily.

Unsteadily Hencke pushed himself away and gazed down upon the unconscious woman. Eyes shut, mouth open, gasping — snoring, just as he remembered his sleeping aunt. The adrenaline that had revived him had as quickly evaporated, leaving him weak and trembling once more. He slumped back into the chair, the shotgun on the table in front of him, leaning on it as he stared into the battered face of the old woman. He had hit his aunt, too, that last time. Not for what she had said, it had been no worse than any of the taunts she had hurled at him since puberty had snatched the child from her and turned him into yet another deceiving, unworthy man. He had remained at university one vacation, preferring to spend his time with books and fellow students, and she had pursued him there, making such a scene of sobbing accusation and hysteria in front of his few close friends that he had felt humiliated and forced to do what he had vowed not to, and return home with her. No sooner had they stepped inside the front door than the tears turned to taunts and recrimination. Accusations about his special "friends." His loyalties, his obligations to her. His right to be his own man. "I made you, and what you are. Never forget that!" she had screamed.

And he had slapped her. Once. Full across the face. He

wasn't quite sure why. Not just hate, nor simply frustration. Perhaps because what she said was true, she had made him, uncertain and unsure, a man with no family and no experience of love, perhaps not a full man, perhaps incapable of love. If he were ever to find out, to discover what sort of man he truly was, it would have to be without her. And he had slapped her because that was the only way he knew to put an end to it. To go beyond the point of no return, to walk away, never to look back.

But as Hencke looked across the kitchen at the old woman he couldn't stop himself from looking back, reliving it all, losing himself in the mists of his haunted memories.

Why on earth had they been painted red? Some Bolshy bloody painter, he supposed. Maybe he should have them repainted blue, a good Tory color, and ignore the bleatings he would get from the two Labor members of his War Cabinet. Still, it scarcely mattered anymore. The war in Europe would be finished with soon, the bombardment of London by Hitler's rockets finished with even sooner as their launch sites were overrun, and then he wouldn't have to use this subterranean rathole any more. Oh, to be in fresh air once again . . . He leaned back in his chair and blew a cloud of smoke toward the low ceiling and its huge steel girders, painted as red as traffic lights, which had captured his attention. According to the engineers, they were strong enough to bear the collapsed weight of the entire building underneath which the wartime Cabinet complex had been built. "Has anyone told Goering?" he once inquired skeptically. He always felt uneasy under here. It was not that he was afraid to die, his contempt for his personal safety had been proven on battlegrounds throughout the British Empire during his younger years as a soldier. But that had been in the mountains of India's North West Frontier, on the Sudanese plains or the open veldt in southern Africa. Not cooped up in a sewer. He felt claustrophobic, uneasy, and the damp wormed its way into his bones. His bad shoulder was acting up again and he tried unsuccessfully to massage the ache from it. Not much longer, he sighed, as he watched the cigar smoke being caught in the draft of a wall fan and dispersed to the far corners of the small room among the fifteen other people attending Cabinet.

Churchill was distracted. The First Lord of the Admiralty was droning on about shipping figures, a matter that had ceased to interest Churchill since Admiral Doenitz's U-boats had lost control of the Atlantic and stopped sinking merchantmen by the score. At that time, it had been a matter of finding enough food to eat and oil to fuel the Spitfires and Hurricanes. Now it was all about tonnages of this and tonnages of that, and how the fishermen were demanding the return of their boats requisitioned for war duty. Statistics. Bloody statistics. He had no mind for them anymore. Some people wanted to fight the entire war with statistics, but war wasn't about desiccated figures; it was about men, real-life flesh and blood men, and hopefully more of the other side's flesh and blood than your own. He dragged his thoughts back down from between the bright red rafters as the First Lord came to a close.

"Well, gentlemen, I think that concludes the business on today's Cabinet agenda. Thank you for your . . ."

Before he could finish there was a waving of a hand somewhere on his left side. Churchill turned to peer over the circular frames of his spectacles and spotted Ernest Bevin gesticulating for his attention. No interruption from Bevin was ever welcome. The Minister for Labor and National Service had done a grand job squeezing every last screw, brick, and bullet out of the factories while heading off any serious strike activity, no one could deny that. But he was a died-in-the-wool, red-blooded, black-hearted, callus-handed Socialist, and the sooner Churchill could dispense with this wartime coalition and throw the Socialists out of the Cabinet, the better.

"Prime Minister, not yet if you please," Bevin insisted, a quizzical, lopsided expression stretched across his leathery face, giving the impression of his being slow and dogged, like a rumpled bloodhound searching for a lost trail. Every syllable betrayed his West Country origins, but that hadn't stopped his climbing out of the gutter and ascending very far — as far as Churchill's left hand. "I've 'ad some disturbing news this morning. I was called up at 'ome by a journalist from America's CBS..."

Churchill frowned disparagingly, making no attempt to hide his view of anybody who made himself available to journalists at home in the morning.

"Talked of reports about a great POW escape in Yorkshire last week. The details were sketchy, but the 'ole rotten camp got out, 'e said." There was a slight pause while he considered how to frame the question before deciding, as he normally did, that bluntness was better than politeness. "What about it? What's going on, Prime Minister? Is it true? What 'ave you been 'iding from us?"

It was too much for Churchill. He was tired, very tired, and despite his ministrations the pain in his shoulder was getting worse. He'd been looking for someone to lose his temper with all morning, since Clemmie had started up again with her endless nagging about his "extravagance" and worrying about how they were going to pay for everything from his cigars to the new drains at Chartwell. With his wife he had a lifetime's practice of closing his ears and gritting his teeth; with Bevin he could find no cause for self-restraint. With alarming abruptness the PM's fists beat upon the makeshift Cabinet table. His pen flew from the blotter and performed a full somersault, while the lid of the red dispatch box in front of him came down with a crash.

"How on earth are we expected to run a war when we are bombarded with questions like that? Whose side is your reporter friend on, for God's sake? Hasn't Hitler made our lives difficult enough without half the American press corps snapping at our heels?" Churchill's shoulders were hunched and rounded, his solid forehead thrust forward like a bull about to charge, an impression made all the more acute as, in the surge of excitement, his glasses slid to the end of his nose to reveal his furious red eyes.

There was not a sound from within the room beyond the exertions of the Old Man's breathing. The Cabinet Secretary had stopped taking notes, while most of the others in the room found things at the edges of their blotting pads that required their urgent attention. Only Bevin seemed unperturbed.

"For the record, Prime Minister, the man's a journalist, not the Gestapo. And I'd like an answer to my question. Seems simple enough to me. If any of what 'e 'ad to say is true I think the Cabinet 'as a right to know." He returned the glare.

Churchill needed to play for time to recover his composure. It was all very well losing his temper, but only if it had a point and gave him an advantage. There was none in this.

"Has anybody else picked up this sort of gossip?" He made it sound disdainful, as if he were making inquiries about a venereal disease. He glowered around the room, finding little response until he lit upon Beaverbrook, his close friend and Minister for Production, who was clearly agitated. Beaverbrook had tried urgently and unsuccessfully to catch him before Cabinet but, as usual, Churchill had been late and in a rush — delayed by Clemmie's damned nagging. Had Beaverbrook been trying to warn him? Beaverbrook knew all the gossip running around Fleet Street — hell, he owned half of it — and now he was nodding his head as if to confirm what Bevin had said. He looked forlorn, biting his bottom lip, implying that even with his immense grip on the media there was little chance of bottling this one up. But he remained silent, and Churchill was grateful for that, at least; it helped give him a means of escape.

The Prime Minister coughed to break the awkward hush. "Very well," he said. "I'm glad such inaccurate reports have not yet been widely circulated, because it gives me the opportunity to tell you the facts. This is a serious security matter, which is why it has not been included explicitly on the Cabinet agenda, although it had always been my intention to raise it today under 'Any Other Business.' " He shot a venomous glance at Bevin, daring him to challenge the lie, but all he got back was an inscrutable stare from behind pebble glasses.

"There was indeed a large escape last week from a camp in Yorkshire," Churchill continued, the flush slowly disappearing from his cheeks, "not, I hasten to add, as large as the wild rumors we have just heard might indicate." He took from within his ministerial box the note which Cazolet had prepared for him on a daily basis since the breakout. Statistics. More damned statistics, but he was grateful for them now. "Ten days ago there was a mass escape from Camp 174B — a camp guarded by Canadians." Nice point that; colonials were to blame. "A total of two hundred and forty-seven Germans were involved."

"That's the biggest blinkin' breakout of the war . . ." There was a gasp of astonishment from around the table as the scale of the fiasco sank in.

"The Cabinet will appreciate, I am sure, what impact news of the event might have had in the wrong hands. It might have caused panic among the public and could have given succor only to the enemy. As it is" — he scanned the note — "two hundred and eleven of the prisoners had been recaptured by seven o'clock this morning. The incident has been contained, almost snuffed out, and the damage it might have done has been avoided. Only thirty-six remain at liberty, by this evening that figure will be lower still."

Only thirty-six. The man had nerve. He made it sound like a triumph. At any other time the news of so many escaped POWs would have seemed like a national humiliation, heads would have rolled. But in Churchill's hands, and now, as victory approached . . . ?

"It is a glowing tribute to our security forces that the escapees have been rounded up so quickly. In spite of the initial misfortunes of our Canadian cousins, the incident has proved a testament to the success of the police, the armed services and, of course, this government in coping with these unique and unforeseen circumstances."

"Hear, hear," Beaverbrook growled, setting aside the temporary embarrassment of his Canadian birth.

"So I was right," Bevin snapped, sniffing the air as if trying to scent the weakness in Churchill's explanation. "Why didn't you tell us right off about this? Why did we 'ave to smoke you out? You know what you've done? You've given 'em time to get away."

"It was merely a tactical security matter, nothing more."

"You call the largest POW escape of the war a 'tactical security matter'?"

"To the extent that there were any security implications involved, I, as both Prime Minister and Minister of Defense, was kept constantly informed. The constitutional requirements have been fully satisfied."

Churchill felt more relaxed, he was regaining control. He had always planned to make an announcement, but later, in his own time, when the figures of those still at liberty were even smaller and more manageable, less likely to create silly sensationalist headlines. And if it gave one or two escapees a little more time, well, it was a price he could live with. His hand had been forced, but once it was out in the open it wasn't half as bad as he had feared. And Bevin had lost the floor; someone else was raising a question.

"But what of the remaining thirty-six prisoners? And are we to allow the country to hear about this through CBS?"

Churchill smacked his hand decisively on the dark blue velvet of the Cabinet table. "I think you will all agree, gentlemen, that we have reached an entirely appropriate stage at which to seek the public's assistance in rounding up the thirty-six strays and stragglers."

"So we'll no longer 'ide it, we'll make a full public announcement?" Bevin pressed.

"I agree with the Minister. It's time the people heard about this most recent British success."

There was a snort of ridicule from Bevin, but no more. It had been a close thing, and Churchill would dearly love to have the individual who leaked the news dangling by his balls from a bomb bay at 30,000 feet, but that, for the moment, would have to wait. For now the chase was on in earnest.

When Hencke opened his eyes and lifted his head from the shotgun the old woman had gone. He'd fallen asleep, lost in his recurring nightmare of memories and pain as the cold, sluggish blood had drained into his exhausted muscles, denying his faculties. Asleep! Only for a moment or two, perhaps, but it had been enough. Maybe she had gone for another phone, the police might already be on their way. His mind was still numb, disorientated. How much time did he have? Which way to run? Was there any point?

Then he heard it again, that same noise, coming from the stairs. Turning, he found her descending, still dressed in the white cotton dressing gown, a large darkening lump above her left eye, her eyes filled with hate. And she was holding another shotgun.

"This time, you bastard," she breathed in a quavering voice, and started to raise the gun to her shoulder.

Later Hencke would find many justifications and different crumbs of logic for what happened next. She intended to kill him, of that there was no doubt. Even if there had been doubt, he would never find another opportunity to escape. And the benefit of his succeeding far outweighed any cost. That war was filled with such calamities. He even wondered, very privately in those dark spaces within, if it was because she reminded him too much of his aunt, that he had woken in the middle of a nightmare to see this old woman, shriveled with hate, come back to haunt him. He was not certain of the reason, only that he had no time to resolve uncertainties. As the barrels of the old woman's shotgun rose inexorably toward him he felt the other shotgun beneath his hands. It was the work of a moment to swivel the stock around until the weapon was pointing in her direction, quell the doubts, ignore the screaming inside his head, pull the triggers. One barrel exploded and a damp, dark patch appeared on the woman's dressing gown just by her left breast. The look of hate on her wizened face turned to surprise, a slow, stupid look, as she was plucked from her feet and deposited against the wall several steps above where she had been standing. The patch on the pure white cotton had turned to sticky crimson and the blood began to seep down the front of her body and through her inquisitive fingers to gather in a pool on her lap. She died where she fell.

Hencke remained still. He sat staring at the body, juggling the justifications, arguing with himself, contradicting, unable to move. His body felt distant, separate, as though it belonged elsewhere. A battle developed within his gut as the guilt and vomit fought against resolution and excuse, tangling his emotions, and leaving his mouth soaked in bile. Then he stopped. He didn't need alibis, even to himself, so he said. It had happened, an accident, unintended and unwanted, but it couldn't be changed and there was no point in futile analysis. It was a fact of — a fact of death, like so many others in this war, and there was no time for grief or regret. He had learned in the ruins of his classroom that war leaves no neat divide between the warriors and the innocent, that no one could escape this game which others had begun. But he would finish it, if he could.

He rose and with great care mounted the stairs, stepping past the body with its arched, sightless stare of incomprehension, not daring to glance back. When he descended many minutes later he was clean and dressed in a complete change of men's clothes found in a bedroom cupboard. And outside he had a bicycle, or perhaps even something better in the garage. He stopped beside the damp tangle of Canadian and POW uniforms which still steamed beside the stove. If they found them near the body there would be no place for mercy in the hunt, any more than they would show a rabid dog. They would know that at least one escaped German prisoner of war would stop at nothing to get back to the homeland. They would know it, the whole world would know it. And eventually they would know it was he.

Hencke stepped over the pile of clothing, and closed the kitchen door gently behind him.

CHAPTER 4

London was hell. When Hencke first arrived, by fortune he had found himself immersed and anonymous in a sea of humanity. The capital was teeming — with soldiers on leave, with homeless persons bombed onto the streets and scratching around for a place to shelter, with refugees from occupied Europe. None of them seemed to belong anywhere, none could be easily traced by the authorities and, most helpful of all, many of them were foreign. Hencke could slip between the folds, unnoticed. It had kept him going for several days while he tried to focus on what he should do next. He'd slept on the platform of Swiss Cottage underground station, crowded with others who had nowhere else to go or who were simply unwilling to risk the attentions of a V-1 or V-2 while sleeping in their own, unprotected beds. It had been like a Tower of Babel built beside railway lines, with a cocktail of foreign tongues stirred vigorously by European Jews, Poles, Greeks, Hungarians, even a sprinkling of Yugoslavs, alongside resident Londoners and itinerant Scots and Irish. He got little sleep in the fetid atmosphere but it had been warm and even welcoming; his strong accent was unlikely to arouse suspicion among the cosmopolitan crowd. There had also been food, queued for at the soup kitchens or begged from American GIs, all of whom seemed to have a pocket stuffed full with oranges, chocolate, and cigarettes and who were constantly surrounded by groups of youngsters clamoring for gum. As the war moved closer toward its end there were too many people wandering the streets of London with no background and no permanent residence for one more disheveled foreigner to arouse much suspicion and, anyway, people were tired of suspicion. It had worn them out over all these years, and it was a relief to be able to relax, to let the guard down, to smile once more.

Then news of the escape had broken. And the hunt was on. At every street corner a newspaper billboard proclaimed it, in every soup kitchen queue people discussed it. Twenty-one still free! Within three days only a dozen left at large! Then but three! Hencke could feel eyes everywhere, probing, questioning, demanding to know who he was and why he had no money to buy food. It was his imagination, of course, but the sea of humanity in which he had been able to swim seemed to have become unsettled and full of menace, threatening to swallow him at any moment. He knew it was only a matter of time before his luck disappeared, before he was caught out, when someone asked an impossible question or his nerve broke and he gave himself away.

The day had come when the billboards screamed *"One More To Go!"* He was the last one. He was on his own. There was no more time.

For the previous three days he had been keeping watch on

the Spanish Embassy early in the morning, then around lunchtime, and again in the late afternoon, always from a different position, constantly on the move to avoid rousing the suspicions of the police guard, but studying everyone who entered and left. He was looking for the diplomatic staff, trying to recognize those who passed through every day and guessing which of them could be trusted and might help. Spain was nominally neutral, yet had been friendly toward the Axis ever since the fledgling Luftwaffe had helped Franco bomb Guernica and the Spanish Republican movement into rubble. In spite of their neutrality, someone might remember, and might be willing to repay the debt. But which one? How to tell a man's motivation from the way he dresses, from the turn of his collar or the crook of his nose? To distinguish a brave man from a coward, or a potential friend from somebody who wanted simply to play it by the rules? Yet Hencke had to try.

It had to be today. He had begun to take chances. His nerves were frayed and his hunger was beginning to burn in spite of the handouts, and the previous night he had fallen into conversation on the underground station with a married couple who had offered to share their Thermos of coffee with him. What did he do? How long had he been in England? He reminded them of their son, whom they hadn't seen in six months while he had been battling his way up the backbone of Italy. Why had Hencke been exempted from military service? Why wasn't he out there fighting? Within five minutes he had contradicted himself twice and their generosity had turned to resentment and suspicion. They thought he was a draft dodger, and it wouldn't be long before someone came to the correct conclusion. So it had to be today.

The embassy was a square-built Victorian affair, solid rather than pretentious, tucked away in the corner of Belgrave Square. It had a large portico that seemed to be the only entrance, and through which every visitor and staff member had to pass. Immediately outside stood the police guard, checking credentials. It had been doubled since news of the escape had leaked. So Hencke walked around the square, sat on a park bench, read a newspaper, and did his best not to look suspicious, all the time feeling as conspicuous as a Boy Scout in a convent. The man in the trilby and trenchcoat had entered the embassy shortly before eight o'clock and, if he followed the pattern of the previous two days, would be out for a stroll through nearby Hyde Park at twelve-thirty precisely. But what if he changed his plans? If he decided to take an early break? If he weren't a diplomat, after all? To curb his anxiety, Hencke was back waiting on the corner near the embassy shortly after eleven A.M. He had to dispense with the newspaper; it was shaking too much in his unsteady hands. His impatience meant he risked the attentions of the duty policemen; but it was time for taking risks.

The man appeared precisely on time. His collar was up and the trilby pulled down firmly over his head against the squallish wind, but there was no mistake. Hencke hurried on ahead, taking the opposite route around the square, relieved to see the other man pacing along his accustomed route, briefcase tucked under his left arm. By habit he would stop at a bench overlooking the lake in the park and produce sandwiches from the briefcase, munching through them before throwing any remnants of crumbs and crust to the sparrows. He liked birds, perhaps that was why Hencke had decided to trust him. His own father had been an avid ornithologist, so his aunt had told him. That was all he had of his father, a scrap of information about his hobbies, and a much worn but greatly treasured photograph, taken a few days before he left for the trenches, and which had been lost in the charred ruins of the schoolhouse. So the Spaniard liked birds, too? Perhaps it was an omen.

While the first sandwich was being extracted from the briefcase and consumed, Hencke took the opportunity to scout around the area of the park bench, checking whether there were any watchers hidden behind the bright spring foliage of the trees or bushes, trying to control his anxiety. By the time the second and final sandwich had appeared he knew he had to make his move.

Hencke sat down at the opposite end of the bench. "Please, do you have a cigarette?"

The Spaniard turned toward him. He was in his early thirties, with dark skin and a long face from which protruded a sharp, aquiline nose. The expression behind it was not friendly. Hencke was by this time peculiarly disheveled. He hadn't shaved for four days, his once-glossy black hair was matted and the stolen suit of clothes had become grubby and unkempt. There was an unhealthy flush across his lean face and a wild look in his eyes; Hencke thought he was developing a fever. He probably smelled, too. The Spaniard stared, examined the crumpled man who had accosted him and, without offering a word, returned to his sandwich.

Hencke clenched his fists. Perhaps he had made a dreadful mistake after all. The diplomat proceeded to scatter crumbs on the ground and attract the attentions of sparrows and pigeons. Even the ducks on the lake were beginning to honk their appreciation and clamber out of the water toward him. Within seconds he was festooned with birds, and in the distance Hencke could see two nannies with their broods of children advancing toward them with the intention of joining in the fun. Soon he would be surrounded.

"You're from the Spanish Embassy, aren't you? I must speak with you."

The man turned to stare once again. "Who are you? What do you want?" he demanded aggressively.

Hencke drew a deep breath. The nannies were only yards

away. It was now or never. "I'm German. The escaped prisoner of war. I need your help."

The Spaniard turned pale beneath his olive skin and shot to his feet, standing erect as the last of the breadcrumbs were scattered on the ground. Feeding time was over and the birds fled; at least it had the advantage of deflecting the two advancing nannies.

"You must be mad! Why on earth do you think I should help you? What on earth can I do?" The diplomat looked around him anxiously, whether to guard against approaching danger or to summon the nearest policeman Hencke could only guess. "The whole country is looking for you. You're the most wanted man in Britain, in God's name why pick on me?"

At least he was not screaming at the top of his lungs for help, thought Hencke. He was just plain scared. "I picked on you because I have nowhere else to go. I must have your help."

"Don't you realize there's nothing I can do? Spain is neutral, it doesn't get involved in this war."

"Germany got involved in your war. Or have you forgotten that already?"

"That was nearly ten years ago. This is preposterous . . . I must be off." The Spaniard began to brush the final crumbs from his raincoat in order to depart. It was almost over for Hencke.

"But you must help . . ."

"No. I can do no such thing. Neutral. Don't you understand?" He glanced around him once more. "If you continue to pester me I shall call for the police. Look . . . I'm sorry, but you don't realize." His tone softened slightly. The initial shock and panic had gone, but the deep unease remained. "You are the hottest target in the whole of London. You must believe me. Every embassy is being watched, our telephones are being tapped, everyone is on the lookout for you. It's impossible for anyone to help you and it would be madness for anyone to try."

He reached into his pockets and pulled out a couple of crumpled notes and a handful of coins. "Here. Take some money; you look as if you could do with something to eat. But that's all. There's nothing more I can do."

"Wish me luck, eh . . . ?" Hencke muttered bitterly, glancing derisively at the few pounds in his hand. It was all going wrong.

"Not even that. *Neutral.* Don't you understand?" The Spaniard was becoming agitated again, wondering whether he had already gone too far. He began striding away, wishing to put as much distance as possible between himself and this nightmare that had been thrust toward him.

Hencke made after him, but all he could see was the man's back. "One other thing you can do for me? It won't hurt . . ." He began to raise his voice as the diplomat's figure receded into the distance. "You have the means. Get a message back to Berlin for me. From Peter Hencke." He had to shout now. "Tell them I'm coming back!"

The diplomat didn't falter in his stride. In a moment he was gone.

Hencke was left alone, defeated. His fever was getting worse, he had nowhere to go. He looked ravenously at the complaining ducks.

"I find it so difficult to believe, Willie."

"Seems little doubt, Prime Minister. A farmer's widow, living on her own. They found her with half her chest missing, a shotgun on the kitchen table and a pile of prisoner's clothes on the floor. And none of those we've recaptured seem to have been anywhere near the area. The one out there is our man." He looked quizzically at Churchill, who appeared more affected by this news than even by the initial reports of the mass escape. The Old Man sat brooding.

"I suppose . . . I suppose I, too, might have killed. If necessary. To gain my own escape."

"Not a defenseless old widow, you wouldn't. That's sheer bloody murder."

"Murder? Self-defense? A casualty of war? Who knows, Willie, what each of us is capable of." He shrugged. "It will at least give us an excuse for hanging on to that division of troops."

"An excuse?"

"A bargaining chip, perhaps. I'll not hand them over until I can be sure I can send them to Berlin."

"I . . . don't understand. You're using the troops against the Americans? I thought they were supposed to be used against the POWs."

"We must make the appropriate noises over the escaped Germans, Willie, but they are as nothing compared with the opportunity of reaching Berlin. I would willingly set free a thousand Germans and, yes, sacrifice a thousand innocent widows if it would give us Berlin."

"But there is no connection . . ."

The Old Man sat silently gazing through the window.

"I fail to understand, damned if I do." The tone was angry, hurt. "All the way through you seem to have had" — he picked the word with care — "almost a sympathy with these escapees. Almost as if you identified with them. Excused them." Even murder, he thought, but did not say so.

"I was once on the run myself, remember?"

"Even so. This one's a murdering war-trained Nazi, you can't possibly identify with him. I still don't understand." Or care for this, his tone implied.

"There are many things we don't understand, yet which have their purpose." And after that he would say no more.

* * *

They were overhead again tonight, as they had been for nights innumerable and ceaseless, wave after wave of them on their way to Leipzig, perhaps, or Hanover, or most likely Berlin. Down in the tiny cellar it was impossible to tell if they were British Lancasters or American B-17s, since the throbbing of heavy bombers sounded much the same when you had buried yourself as deep beneath the ground as you could go, but the two elderly women held each other's hands for comfort and hoped the planes were British. The Americans were more trigger-happy and careless — or was it just plain skittish? — and liable to unload their bombs anywhere. The small town of Friesenheim had for centuries nestled comfortably in the security of the valley carved through Westphalia by the headwaters of the Ruhr River, but the valley ran west to east from what was left of the industrial complexes concentrated along the Rhine, and acted as a highway for Bomber Command right into the heart of Germany. Friesenheim was on no one's list of priority targets, but that hadn't prevented it from being hit several times in the last month, as bomber crews got into trouble, got into a panic, or simply got it wrong. In places like Friesenheim there was no such thing as the skill or the art of survival, it was nothing more than a matter of fortune. You crept into your shelter and stayed there for days on end until the weather was bad enough to keep the bombers away, not knowing how long your meager food supplies were likely to last, sharing everything with the rats, your nerves shot to hell as the walls closed in, and praying that you would be one of the lucky ones who wouldn't die in this hole, or be buried alive, or be drowned as the sewers burst and flooded into your hiding place.

You spent a lot of time praying, because prayer was all you had to defend yourself, yet frequently even prayer was not enough. A few nights previously a rogue 10,000-pounder, which had become stuck in its bomb rack, was dislodged and dropped over Friesenheim by a U.S.A.F. crew on its way home. The townsfolk were well sheltered and one hundred thirty-three of them, mostly women and children, had been packed into the ancient crypt which acted as an air raid shelter underneath the Evangelical church. The pastor had been conducting, encouraging all present to sing at the top of their voices in the hope that it would drown the noise of battle overhead. His wife scurried around serving ersatz coffee and comforting a baby born four days previously.

No one heard the bomb. The walls of the church were thick and the crypt deep, as was the fashion in the *Mittelalter* days during the long and glorious reign of Charlemagne, when the first foundations had been laid. But there was a grille set in the ground at the back of the nave that was used to facilitate the passage of heavy objects such as coffins or casks of wine in and out of the crypt. It was only a small grille, but the bomb had struck the grating at an angle, bouncing down the chute and into the crypt, where it exploded in the middle of the pastor's choir practice. A fluke, a million-to-one chance, but in the confined space the devastation was appalling. Only twenty-three had been pulled alive from underneath the collapsed church, and several of those had died in the days since, the local hospital long ago having run out of anesthetics, of antibiotics, of trained doctors, and of hope. Of the pastor, his wife and the baby there had been nothing left but a memory.

The two elderly women found it hard to change the habits of a lifetime so, in spite of the evidence of the crypt, they huddled in their cellar and continued praying and hoping, smoking cigarettes made out of dandelions and listening to the radio. They found the radio of most comfort. It was their link with sanity, letting them know in the middle of the darkest night that life still went on somewhere outside their tiny, fear-filled world. Otherwise it would be easy to imagine that they were the only people left alive, that the rest of humanity had killed itself and they were left in the darkness as the last survivors of a mad, suicidal world.

Only the radio and the next wave of bombers brought them back to reality. And reality tonight was another interminable broadcast by Goebbels. As always, it brought news from the war front, and a call for still further sacrifice to resist the criminals threatening the homeland, larded with vituperative attacks on the nameless Jewish conspirators who had promoted the war and sought the extinction of the German race. Although it was clear to most listeners that in recent weeks the emphasis of the news had changed, with reports from the battlefronts becoming briefer and more vague, while the denunciation of those responsible for the growing calamity grew ever more fantastic. Yet tonight there was something different, a new element in the formula. News of a massive breakout by German prisoners of war in England, "a powerful illustration that the spirit of our fighting men is not broken and clear proof of how vulnerable our enemies still are, even in their homeland. The British Tommies scurry around after escaped prisoners, when the whisky-sodden war criminal Churchill would have them butchering German women and children. Even without their weapons, the unquenchable determination of our German soldiers is continuing to resist the onslaught of our enemies, and helping to defend the Fatherland. Resistance, in all manners, at all times, must be our watchword!"

One of the women held a piece of bread and hard cheese in her hand, all they had left until the bombing stopped and they could forage for new provisions. Tears were trickling down her cheek and falling on to the stale, dark bread, but she seemed not to notice. She was staring into another world that she remembered from long ago, one which had long since been destroyed and which she knew she would never see rebuilt.

"The British are sparing no effort to recapture our escaped German soldiers, but even after many days they have not succeeded. The entire country is on alert, looking out for one brave German whom all the might of the British cannot seem to apprehend. My friends, a new German hero has been born, a man who singlehandedly is defying thousands of British security men and tweaking the bulbous nose of Churchill. Even when thrown into one of the British torture camps he refused to submit. He continued to fight. His courage and devotion to duty never wavered. His resolution should be an example to us all. The whole of Germany salutes one of our bravest men. Peter Hencke!"

The woman wiped her nose with a small embroidered handkerchief she took from her sleeve, but the tears continued to flow. "What's the use? Why run? Why resist anymore? Haven't we done enough already?" The words were soft, scarcely audible, directed more to herself than the other woman.

"Frau Deichsfischer," the other muttered, "you mustn't give up hope."

"I've given up everything else . . . A husband. My sons. Two brothers. How much more do they want from me? What else do I have to give?"

They lapsed into silence as the crackling voice across the radio continued its address.

"Peter Hencke has set the historic example demanded of us all by the Fuehrer. Resist! To the bitter end! Knowing that the National Socialist spirit will survive and outsmart our enemies. Even now our Fuehrer is working in Berlin on plans which will bring new victories to our German armies and exhaust the Allies' will to continue the fight. Even in these dark hours we must not forget that victory can still be ours, so long as we remain determined to keep the faith and never to give in. Long live the German *Volk*. Long live our beloved Fuehrer, Adolf Hitler! Death to the Jewish conspirators! My friends, keep up the good fight!"

The strains of the national anthem blared out across the cellar and Frau Deichsfischer reached out to lower the volume. As she did so the bread, by now thoroughly soaked with her tears, crumbled in her hand and fell to the floor. She looked at the crumbs in despair. "In God's name, why do they want us to go on? What can be worse than this?"

"The Russians, Frau Deichsfischer," the other whispered. "The Russians."

The transcript of Goebbels' broadcast lay on Cazolet's desk. As was the custom with Goebbels' lengthy ramblings, the important sections had been highlighted in pen and he scanned them quickly. He arrived at the references to Hencke and rubbed his tired eyes, in a futile attempt to persuade them they had made a mistake. How on earth had Goebbels discovered the identity of the one remaining escapee? Without a name, he was just a statistic, a single digit in the vast lists of war; with it he became human, could be touched and sensed, and Goebbels was transforming him into the torch carrier for the entire German war effort. "Bloody hell," was all Cazolet managed to say before placing the transcript on top of the Prime Minister's dispatch box. The Old Man wasn't going to like this.

"The Fuehrer will not permit it, Erich, because I will not permit it. I hope I make myself clear?"

There was no response, only a look of defiance on the other man's face.

"Erich, your son's there, isn't he?" Dr. Josef Goebbels, Reichsminister for Public Enlightenment and Propaganda, held up his hand to stifle the other man's protests. "Look, I know you're not arguing for a withdrawal on personal grounds, but since your son *is* there let me explain why it's imperative we hang on to Prague as long as we can. No matter what the cost."

From an immaculate silver case he offered a cigarette to Major Erich Hirschfeldt, one of the longest-serving members of the FBK — *Fuehrerbegleit-kommando* — the hand-picked SS detachment that acted as the Fuehrer's personal bodyguard. The major's hand trembled slightly as he took the cigarette. His hand hadn't shaken, Goebbels reflected, at any other time during all the years in which Goebbels had known him, when Hirschfeldt had led the street gangs that had split so many heads in the early days and had suffered so many casualties themselves, when he had personally executed dozens of men at Hitler's order after Stauffenberg's failed assassination plot, or even a few weeks ago, when he had clawed his way out from under the collapsed roof of the Reich Chancellery's east wing after being buried for almost five hours. Yet that was all gone. He was no longer a fearless defender of the cause, but a simple German father, scared about his son, needing a shoulder to cry on.

"He's . . . the only son I have left, Herr Reichsminister," Hirschfeldt stammered as he tried to light the cigarette.

"I can understand how you feel, Erich. Remember, I have a son and five daughters myself." Goebbels smiled reassuringly. He hated playing father confessor, but he couldn't afford to have Hirschfeldt falling to pieces. The impact on the others would be appalling. It was bad enough that, day by day, they were being forced to retreat out of the sunlight and magnificent edifices of the Reich's *Hauptstadt* into the underground cellars with their bare concrete walls and atmosphere of catacomb decay; they couldn't survive the collapse of discipline too. Goebbels had to hold on to them all, everyone in Berlin from the Fuehrer and Hirschfeldt, all the way down to the telephone operators and drivers because, if they fell apart, everyone in what was left of the Third Reich would know about it within hours and it would all be finished within days. He must get them to hold on, for just a little longer.

"I know things look grim but all is not lost. Think, Erich, think of what might still be salvaged. This coalition between capitalists and Stalinists — how long can it last? Every day as their armies draw closer across the battlefields it becomes more likely that this bastard alliance will break apart and they will fall upon each other. Churchill hates Stalin, Stalin loathes Churchill and that sick old man Roosevelt understands and trusts neither. We only have to hang on a little longer, Erich. Give the damned alliance time to disintegrate, that's all we need." His voice was soft and encouraging, full of confidence; it was confidence not yet shared.

"But do we have time? Will there be anything left to save?" The agony was chiseled into Hirschfeldt's face. Once he'd had a faith built of steel which could withstand any number of blows; but Hirschfeldt had watched incredulously as his own faith had rotted and rusted away beneath the tears he had shed for his son. He would have condemned other men for it — *had* condemned many for much lesser offenses in the earlier years of glory, but now it had taken over his entire being and he felt unable to resist.

"They will go for each other's throats — believe me," Goebbels said with passion. "In months, maybe only weeks. That's why your son and Schoerner's army must hang on to defend Prague as long as possible; they cannot be allowed to withdraw or capitulate. Will your grandchildren forgive us, Erich, if we surrender our armies on foreign soil without a fight? Did we forgive our fathers' generation for the humiliation of 1918? I have no intention of surrendering our armies intact so they can be dragged off to prison camps, while our enemies march across our undefended frontiers to pillage their way through our womenfolk. Think of your wife, Erich, is that what you want for her? Schoerner must hold on in Czechoslovakia as long as possible. If it means more sacrifice, it is a price we must willingly bear."

He studied the major closely — the drooping head, the hunched shoulders, the once-immaculate black uniform grown dusty and tarnished, the boots unpolished, the dark rings around the eyes supported by a two-day growth of stubble. Goebbels was a master with words, but he also realized that words alone were not always enough. They hadn't worked with Hirschfeldt.

"Look, Erich, perhaps you need a change. This scurrying around like troglodytes is enough to depress anyone. If you really feel it's so important, I could get you transferred to Prague, to be with your son. How better to take care of him . . . ?"

And, he thought, how better to take care of you, you miserable bastard, whose long face and doubting eyes are in danger of infecting everyone around the Fuehrer? As if the Fuehrer didn't have enough doubts himself. So off to the Eastern Front with you, Fritzi, and a chance to die usefully for your country instead of living miserable and contagious here in Berlin. And by your death allow Goebbels the chance to create another heroic myth, of a man at the right hand of the Fuehrer who insisted on defending the Reich to his last breath. Hirschfeldt had been a good servant, up till now. He deserved the opportunity to die a hero.

Hirschfeldt looked up with exhausted eyes. He had been around the silver tongue of Goebbels long enough to know what he really meant. "I'm sorry, Herr Reichsminister. I love my country . . ." He took a long pull on the cigarette and tried to muster a smile, but it didn't carry much conviction. He nodded in resignation and acceptance of his fate.

"You'll be all right, Erich. Trust me," Goebbels said, gazing at the wreck of a once-mighty man in front of him. The spectacle started him worrying. He began to wonder whether Peter Hencke had a family . . .

* * *

A special observation post had been erected overlooking the river on a hill above Xanten, complete with camouflage netting, mobile caravan and a host of junior liaison officers who hung around chatting in the background. From their vantage point they could see the broad sweep of the Rhine as it unfolded in front of them, a great ribbon of water disappearing northward like a winding road into the early morning haze which still clung to its edges. To their left lay the ruins of Xanten, the spire of its church savagely torn off, the town emasculated, while above them scurried squadrons of fighters, like swarming bees on a ceaseless mission through skies beginning to turn crystal blue as the sun burned off the mist. It was a good day for dying, and there would be plenty of it before nightfall.

Churchill, in a bulging uniform of the 4th Hussars which he chose to wear on his visits to the front, clapped his hands in excitement as he turned to Eisenhower. "My God, but this makes the blood run thicker through the veins!" There was strong color in his cheeks for the first time in weeks, and the sparkle had returned to his eyes. "How I envy you fighting men. In my lifetime, General, I have seen war grow steadily more murderous and awesome, and perhaps I should be condemned for finding any glory in such a deadly clash of wills, but this" — he waved a gloved paw across the panorama in front of them — "this is so exhilarating! You know, the easiest way of telling the true character of a man is to study his response to the call of the bugle — does it fill his guts with fire, or render them liquid with fear? That's when you know his real worth."

Eisenhower, who hadn't heard a bugle sounded in anger since reveille at boot camp, nodded and said nothing. He hadn't wanted the Old Man here at the battlefront, but Churchill had insisted — and Eisenhower knew that as usual he would try to interfere, throwing off an abundance of homespun military theories and anecdotes with all the energy and subtlety of an exploding catherine wheel. As if launching the major Allied crossing of the Rhine wasn't going to present him with enough difficulties... For a short while, however, Eisenhower would have no reason to worry; further conversation was made impossible, as the massed guns below commenced their barrage of the German positions on the opposite bank, filling clear skies with the menace and anger of thunder. They watched, mesmerized by the pinpricks of fire from nearly two thousand artillery barrels and the great plumes of smoke and destruction that erupted seconds later on the far bank. In response there were but a few tiny flickers of resistance from the positions facing them.

As instantly as it had begun the shelling ceased, as though the film they were watching had been pulled from its projector. There was silence, more deafening in its way than the sound of the guns, a stillness which surrounded them like a cloak, making the moments seem like hours and sending a shiver of anticipation through the tiny group. Eisenhower consulted his watch. "Time for the drop."

Yet they were not to have it all their own way. No sooner had he spoken than, away in the great distance, a thin white trail of smoke or condensation began to climb slowly into the sky.

"Hell fire," Eisenhower muttered, the satisfaction gone from his voice. "A V-2, on its way to London, I'd guess."

"No, General. Remember your Bible, when Moses led his tribes across the Red Sea. There was a pillar of smoke then, too. We have God's blessing this day."

"Unfortunately, in my experience the Germans are very bad at reading smoke signals," Eisenhower responded caustically. It was all very well for the Old Man to come and make speeches from the hilltop, like a new Sermon on the Mount, proclaiming his belief in God, but they were Eisenhower's men down there about to die, and after all these years of war he found death a more concrete concept than the Hereafter.

Then the Dakotas came, wave after wave of them, flying low and in tight formation, with their fuselage doors open and men standing in the doorway, ready to jump. They had all but disappeared into the mists across the Rhine when the group on the hilltop began to see the parachutes open, falling gently as seed might be scattered on the ground. And there was reaping along with the sowing; soon the Dakotas returned, many in trouble and some on fire. The far bank was not going to be vacated by the enemy without a struggle. And the German guns seemed to have gained strength, pouring a hail of shells across the river and into the Allied positions. Soon a salvo of enemy shells began to creep toward the hilltop, gouging out a crater of earth and destruction as each shell stretched ever closer. Junior officers rushed forward to hustle the Prime Minister and the Supreme Commander back toward safety, but Churchill ignored them, stepping forward as if to meet the challenge head-on, oblivious of the danger, seeming to show supreme faith that this was not his time to die. Eisenhower, embarrassed by the older man's bravado, brushed aside the protests of his staff and stayed out in the open. He was damned if he was going to be shown up by a seventy-year-old civilian.

Soon the moment had passed, the shells were gone, and Eisenhower was left with a feeling of deep irritation at the stupidity of it all. He didn't share the Old Man's direct line to God, and the moment of danger had left his mouth dry. It would have been a pathetic way to go, the Supreme Commander and the Prime Minister swept away just when the victory was theirs to claim, all for a moment of petty playacting. Heaven rid him of meddlesome politicians!

Churchill's face was glowing when eventually he turned away from the view. "Marvelous! Marvelous!" was all he could say. As he stepped closer to Eisenhower, however, his face took on a more considered expression, a scowl of concentration seeming to split his forehead in two. Something was bothering him.

"My dear General, you have done a magnificent job today. I have no doubt that by nightfall we shall have achieved our objectives and another great step taken toward final victory."

The old bastard's buttering me up, Eisenhower said to himself. What does he want?

"Seeing the valor of our troops and the selfless way they are willing to lay down their lives for that victory, it makes me more certain than ever that we have no option, in honor, but to ensure that their courage and sacrifice are not offered in vain."

So that's it! He never gives up . . .

"We cannot afford to win the war yet see the peace we have worked so hard to build thrown away. We must push as far east as possible — surely you must see the sense in that?"

"As far as Berlin, Mr. Prime Minister?"

"At least as far as Berlin . . ."

The American shook his head, slowly and deliberately. He had guessed this would come, they had told him Churchill was as hard to shift as a mule in mud; but now he felt almost relieved that he had taken so badly to Churchill's vainglorious defiance of the German shelling. It made him more determined than ever to get this over and done with, and if it meant some plain speaking to the Old Man without any of the diplomatic niceties, well — sure as hell he was in the mood for it.

"It's too late. Over. Done with. Let me make this clear, Mr. Churchill. Berlin isn't going to happen."

The Prime Minister was taken aback. He wasn't used to such outspoken defiance. "No" is not a word used between allies, not baldly and up front like this. "But surely that is mistaken . . ." He bit his lip. His lisp became much more pronounced when he was off-guard, and his choice of words was clumsy. "General, we could be in Berlin inside a fortnight. You cannot possibly pretend it's too late . . ."

"Mr. Churchill, believe me, it's too late. I've already been in contact with Marshal Stalin. And we've agreed. Berlin is his."

Churchill's lips pouted incredulously like those of a hooked fish, then his jaw dropped until it sagged onto his chest. The exhilaration drained from his face, and he began to search for his words with uncharacteristic diffidence. "You . . . have taken it upon yourself . . . to communicate directly with the Russians? Without any reference to me? Or President Roosevelt?" Churchill could scarcely believe the words, even as he found them. "In God's name, General, what the devil do you think you're playing at?" he shouted, loudly enough for the aides to wander discreetly a few steps farther away. "You can't go round making deals with the bloody Russians!" He thrust his walking stick into the soft ground, like a medieval knight planting his colors.

Eisenhower did not flinch. "On military matters, indeed I can."

"This isn't military. This is high politics. And to my mind, high bloody treason!"

"Prime Minister, politics may be your game but the military conduct of this war and the defeat of the German armies is *my* responsibility as Supreme Allied Commander. My conversations with Moscow have been entirely nonpolitical."

"Nonpolitical! With Stalin?"

"With Marshal Stalin as Supreme Commander of the Red Army. Yes."

The aides of both men had begun to shuffle closer once again, anxious not to be completely out of earshot. This was going to be one for the grandchildren.

"You have stabbed me in the back. Ruined everything I and my country have fought for all these years."

"That's rot. Berlin's of no military consequence. It has no

great defense industries, no strategic significance. Only piles of smashed coffee shops and hordes of civilians, many of whom are going to be slaughtered no matter who takes Berlin."

"It is of supreme political importance, General Eisenhower..."

"That's one for the politicians, sir. Not for me. I'm concerned solely with the military aspects of this war which I want to finish with as little loss of Allied life as I can manage. For that it's essential I come to tactical battlefield agreements with the Russians. That's all I've done." There was a small, insincere smile playing around Eisenhower's lips. He had the argument rehearsed word-perfect, including all that crap about it having nothing to do with politics. He was a military man but he was beginning to learn about politics. Fast.

The two men stood on the bare hillside, silhouetted against the panorama of the Rhine and its military activity, with all the passion and hostility of the thousands of men below seemingly concentrated in the few feet between them. One aide later said it was like watching an old-fashioned duel, the weapons being words instead of cocked pistols.

"Be in no doubt, General, that I shall contact the President. Immediately. This decision must and will be overturned. And if it means your removal or even court martial, then so be it!" Churchill pushed one foot forward toward his adversary, as if preparing to fire.

In contrast the American seemed to relax, shrugging his shoulders, already confident that the threat would miss its target. "Think, sir. Think very carefully before you rush into that. You know just how sick the President is. Frankly, he's been incapable of handling any serious paperwork for several weeks. He's dying, that's the view of those around him. And he's certainly not fit enough to handle matters like this. Any decision will simply be shunted back down the line. Probably right back to me. And it's inevitable there will be some considerable delay, by which time" — he shrugged — "it will all be history."

Churchill began to feel he was being outmaneuvered. He waved his hands as if to imply that the issues were much broader than Eisenhower could possibly contemplate, his voice booming in an attempt to bully the American into submission. "War should be a building block, not just a mindless system of destruction! Politics must have its place in the way a war is fought."

"Like the sort of politics you've been playing with my reinforcements?"

"What on earth do you mean?"

"The several thousand troops who should be out there now, winning the war" — he jerked his thumb in the direction of the great river behind him — "instead of scurrying around Britain searching for one escaped prisoner. What is the world going to think, Mr. Churchill, of a leader who publicly urges a bloody advance toward Berlin, while at the same time privately denying that effort its necessary reinforcements? People might conclude you've been playing politics with the lives of tens of thousands of innocent soldiers. Seems to me it's not just my job that's at risk here . . ."

Churchill's complexion had become suffused with the heat of anger and indignation. "You are threatening me, General!"

Eisenhower returned the challenge with steady, ice-cool eyes. "Oh, no, Mr. Churchill," he said softly. "I'm just calling your bluff."

Goebbels watched the broken figure of Hirschfeldt shuffle out the door. The condemnation of a friend who had served the cause faithfully for so many years left no trace of emotion in his face, it was just another sacrifice required by war. He had long ago learned to compartmentalize his emotions, not to allow them to get in the way of doing his job. And he was very good at his job.

Almost before the sagging back of Hirschfeldt had disappeared the doorway was filled with the figure of Captain Otto Misch, also a member of the FBK, immaculately suited in his Waffen SS uniform, complete with death's head insignia and slashing shoulder flashes. Misch was tall, blond, sinewy, every inch as if he had stepped straight out of a recruiting poster, although the three fingers missing on his left hand and the Iron Cross pinned at his neck declared that he was no paper hero. He had seen action, and reveled in it. That was why he had been selected for the elite. Although a veteran, Misch was young, still in his early twenties and, beneath the veneer of the uniform and medals, was still callow, with little experience or confidence outside his military life. Ruthless, unquestioning, indefatigable, dedicated to ensuring that his leader's will was done, but immature and in complete awe of Goebbels — in the Reichsminister's mind it was an exemplary combination of qualities, which was why he had chosen Misch as his ADC. It had the added advantage, Goebbels mused, that the captain would not dare to respond to the advances that his wife Magda offered so freely to any good-looking young man who came within her orbit, particularly a specimen who, like Misch, made up for his intellectual and social inadequacies with the physical frame of a stallion. The cow always chose someone as different from himself as possible . . .

And the choice was enormous. It was a deep sadness to Goebbels that National Socialism had attracted over the years so few people of intellectual quality. That hurt. But there had been no time for persuasion and argument, to employ the tools of discussion and debate, in the rush to build the Reich. Perhaps if they'd been able to give themselves a breathing space, if they hadn't invaded Russia so soon . . .

The click of Misch's polished heels interrupted Goebbels' reflections. "You called, Herr Reichsminister."

"Hirschfeldt. He's being posted to Prague. Effective immediately. I want that son-of-a-bitch out of here within an hour. See to it."

"*Zu Befehl!*" Misch responded, but made no move to leave, as Goebbels indicated he had something else on his mind.

The Reichsminister rose from his chair and began to pace the small room, trailing one highly polished boot. He'd been born with a club foot that he had dragged behind him all his life, the reason why he had always taken care not to be forced to march swiftly in public, and to ensure that the cinema newsreels hid the impediment and made him look as whole and manly as the others. It was why he could never be a leader in his own right, and perhaps why he had been attracted to Hitler from the first. The Fuehrer never marched briskly, but always adopted a strolling swagger; it made it easy for Goebbels to keep up without embarrassment. Yet the days spent in claustrophobic underground shelters, with the excursions outside becoming increasingly less frequent, had aggravated his leg. The fuggy atmosphere seemed to stick in the lungs, the blood circulated less freely, the damp seemed to worm its way inside his foot, and the dull ache stretched from his toes to every other part of his body and soul. He rubbed his thigh, trying to force the blood to circulate some warmth, but it was no good.

"Let's get out of this sewer, Misch. Christ, I need some fresh air."

Without a word the captain followed him through the door, where they turned right and immediately began ascending a long flight of bare concrete stairs. They proceeded slowly, one step at a time, since the brace on Goebbels' leg made using stairs difficult. There were lifts, at least when the power supplies were operating; but only a few evenings before Goebbels had been stuck in a lift, after one of the first bombs of the nightly raid had fractured a main power system. He had been forced to linger for more than two hours in a lightless, tiny steel box which at any moment threatened to become his coffin. He had needed all his considerable mental powers to control his mind, let alone his bladder, as he waited, powerless and trapped in the dark, to die. It had given him nightmares, a hatred of being stuck underground in these wretched bunkers, and an overwhelming, animalistic desire to die out in the open, not in a hole in the ground. So Goebbels didn't use lifts anymore.

Soon he and Misch were in the gardens of the Reich Chancellery. He stood for a while, allowing the daylight to replenish his energies, breathing in air which bore no taint of the gas filters and oily air conditioning. The Allied raids had reduced much of the once ornate gardens to a rubbish heap, yet the daffodils were in bloom and he plucked one, savoring its faint scent and admiring the luster and bright color. The flowers would be blooming in the Alps by now, he thought. The narcissi, the alyssum, the whole mountainside would be bursting with life, and hope.

"Before the daffodils fade, Misch. We must be ready before the daffodils fade," he muttered after several minutes.

"Yes, sir!" Misch responded, with as little comprehension as if the Reichsminister had been discussing the finer points of Nietzsche.

"I must buy time!" He would trade half his remaining panzer divisions for the few more weeks required to prepare for the Alps. "Misch, what does the twentieth of April mean to you?"

"The Fuehrer's birthday, sir."

"Exactly. Less than a month. We must be ready by then. We won't have another chance. When they all gather to honor the Fuehrer I want the occasion to be a celebration, not a damned wake. We need something special, an omen, a symbol, something that will turn the gathering into a revival of the German fighting spirit, and give us the time we need." His eyes burned and his scrawny neck strained like a greyhound in the slips. His thin fingers with their finely manicured nails closed clawlike around the daffodil until it disappeared.

"Misch. We need Peter Hencke!"

The bloom fell to the ground, crushed.

"I will not submit to your blackmail, General!" Churchill clenched both his fists, as if he were ready to take a swing at Eisenhower should he come a few inches closer.

"No blackmail, Prime Minister. Only facts. Hard and cruel, perhaps, but facts you can't avoid." Eisenhower had taken out a cigarette and was lighting it carefully. He needed one, to be sure, but more importantly he wanted Churchill to see his steady hand, how much in control he was.

"What *facts* are these?"

"The fact, Prime Minister, that after this shooting match is over, there's going to be only two great powers in Europe. The Americans and the Russians. Germany and France are defeated. Britain is exhausted. Don't get me wrong, I take no pleasure in it. But my admiration for what you and your countryfolk have done can't change the fact that you're down on your knees."

Churchill was flexing his bottom lip as if chewing Eisenhower's words in preparation for spitting them out, but for the moment he held his peace.

"You can't duck it, you can only pick sides. American or Russian. It may not be fair, but Britain has no other choice."

"What sort of choice is that?"

"Not much of a choice, I admit. A power from halfway around the world, which left Europe to rot after the last war, or a bunch of Communists led by a ruthless son-of-a-bitch who'd slit his grandmother's belly just for the practice."

"Then why, oh why, give him Berlin?" The tone was almost pleading.

"Because Berlin is of less military importance than cutting

Hitler off from his hideaway in the Alps. And because it's my duty to see that the piles of dead which get left behind in the rubble are Russian rather than American!" He drew long and thoughtfully on his cigarette. "Time to choose, Mr. Churchill."

There was a long silence. Less than a mile away, a Dakota returning from the dropping zone came down in flames, the explosion as it hit the ground emitting a deep roar and sending a ball of fire and black smoke many hundreds of feet up in the air, but neither of the men noticed. They were busy deciding the future of postwar Europe, two elderly and overweight men stuffed uncomfortably into khaki uniforms.

Eventually Churchill broke the silence. "What is it that you want of me?"

"I want you to stop fighting over Berlin. Not another word, a sigh, no raised eyebrow or even an impatient puff of cigar smoke. For me it has become an article of faith that you accept my judgment on this matter and we put it behind us. Or else."

"Or else what?"

"Or else I'll let Stalin know you're trying to fiddle him out of Berlin. If he knew, he'd tear up every bargain he'd made with you British, and he'd never let you near the negotiating table again."

"You would do that?"

"If you force me, I'd even let the Labor Party know. Wouldn't look too good in the run-up to an election, would it? Cheating Stalin out of Berlin and me out of my troops."

"You would go to such lengths . . . ?" A timbre of uncertainty had begun to infect the voice.

"I don't want to, believe me I don't. You and me, we've always worked so well together. More than allies, I thought; friends. I know how passionately you feel about this, but it was you who raised the stakes. You've lost. Now it's time to pay."

Churchill swallowed deep. It was sticking in his maw. "How?"

"I want an end to the games you've been playing. Not another step toward Berlin. Above all, I want those troops."

"But I need the troops to prevent Hencke getting back to Germany. He would be such a prize for them. And he killed a widow, you know . . ." It was a weak card, played with an uncharacteristic lack of vigor, but it was the only one Churchill had left.

"Then there's only one solution. Do your job. Get Hencke!"

In the garden of the Chancellery, the crumpled daffodil lay at Goebbels' feet. "So that's your task, Misch. Hencke is our talisman, our good luck charm, the one who can rekindle the German will to resist and buy us time. This may be our last chance, the only thing standing between us and total annihilation. Find him, whoever he is, wherever he is, before the Allies do, and bring him to Berlin. If it's the last thing you do, you must bring me Hencke!"

Churchill stood on the hilltop — his Golgotha as he later came to call it — where Eisenhower and his aides had left him alone with his misery. It was a long time before Cazolet dared disturb him.

"It's over, Willie. We've lost. We shall not have Berlin now. He wants the troops back in the front line. And he wants Hencke's head on a plate." He wiped his damp eyes with a huge linen handkerchief. "To win the war, Willie. To win after all the toil and bloody tribulation, yet to lose the peace, to have it thrown away at the last gasp. Will they ever forgive us?"

"Defeat is but a state of mind, Prime Minister."

"Who said that?"

"You did. Back in 1941."

"The whole of the world is turning on its head, Willie. We went to war to prevent Germany moving east; now the East is about to come to us." He blew his nose in one final, huge, tempestuous gesture. "Ironic, isn't it? Eisenhower insists I destroy Hencke, and in doing so I shall only destroy myself."

"You mean . . . because we will lose Berlin?"

"More than that. Much, much more than that. Hencke has become the most devilish and dangerous man in Europe." He looked at Cazolet through bleary eyes. "And it's all my fault."

PART TWO

CHAPTER 5

Hencke shivered uncontrollably, feeling more wretched and forsaken than a fox before hounds. Even on a bad day a fox has some chance, he mused. Hiding in a copse, doubling back to confuse the pack, taking advantage of sudden bad weather which might deter his pursuers and take the sting out of their efforts before the light fades and they eventually tire or get bored and go home. But he would get no such chance. He had become the most wanted man in Europe. Every hour of every day, in any hiding place he chose, he would be hunted. They would never tire.

He was hungry, and was sheltering in a doorway of a back street in Cricklewood. The despicable rain — that most underestimated of English weapons — had scarcely ceased bombarding him since he had left the camp, and he had no idea where to turn. Prompted by the couple who suspected he was a draft dodger, many pairs of eyes had been turned on him in the Underground, eventually forcing him out of his shelter. The money thrust at him by the Spanish diplomat had largely gone to buying a hot meal and a fresh set of clothes, to make him look less conspicuous. But now the second-hand suit was little more than sodden rags clinging to his back. Thoughts of failure were beginning to invade his mind. It was the easy course; the more wretched his physical condition the more attractive it seemed. Just to let go, to sink gently back into the relative warmth and comfort of captivity, to stop running.

But he couldn't; he owed too many people, had too many memories to stop. His aunt had always said he could never make it on his own, that without her he was nothing. She'd been wrong then, and he wasn't going to prove her right now, not after all this time. He'd drown in this damned English rain first.

He huddled in the recesses of the doorway, flinching every time someone passed by, wondering how soon it would be before a policeman found this vagrant and demanded to see the identity papers that didn't exist, and realized that he had stumbled upon the most important prize of his career. Hencke had discovered, during the last few days of wretched weather, that doorways were not all the same. Some gave better protection, deeper shadows, warmer corners. Others gave easy access to a maze of back streets, into which he could disappear given half a head start. This doorway was different; it gave him a view. Across the street there was a pub, with a fresh supply of beer and with the noise and jostle of ordinary people enjoying themselves. Somewhere inside a piano was being played, not very well but with a captivating enthusiasm. At that moment Hencke needed the sight and sound of people more than a four-course meal, to be reminded that there was a world outside his life of fear and flight, and to cling to the hope that some day he might be allowed to return to it.

Cricklewood was the Irish quarter, poor, rundown, dirty, like all immigrant ghettoes. Yet, perhaps because of their deprivations, the moments of relaxation were embraced by its people with more vigor and genuine relish than were found in less grubby areas of London, particularly on a Friday night. And although Hencke was losing track of time, and didn't know it, tonight was Friday. The piano beat out song after Irish song, the laughter was as coarse and disrespectful as the conversation, and Hencke longed to be part of it. He dug into his pocket and pulled out the few coins he had left. Eight pence. Enough for a small glass of beer. He hauled himself out of the doorway and stepped toward the pub.

Inside the lights were bright after the darkness of the street, and it made him conscious of the bedraggled state of his clothes. He needn't have worried; most of the men were still in their working clothes and, judging by the amount of paint and cement dust on their trousers and mud on their boots, they had come straight from a building site.

The cursory glances thrown at him through the smoky atmosphere were warm and friendly; fate had chosen his pub with care. He bought his small glass of beer at the brightly polished bar without problem. In spite of indications around the pub that the English — or Irish, at least — had a seemingly infinite variety of beers from which to choose, there was only one on offer this evening. He settled into a corner and soaked up the warmth.

He didn't rush his beer; he wanted time to relax and, in any case, the beer tasted awful, with a sharp, bitter tang. He put it down to wartime shortages. All around him the conversation was of home, of Ireland, conducted in broad accents difficult for him to follow. Most people seemed to wish themselves in a different place, "across" as he heard them refer to it; he identified with their longing and understood. It was a different world, like the one he could remember from many years ago, before the time when all conversation became dominated by the war, when men still joked about tomorrow and complained about their work and their wives. There seemed to be little talk about the war, and in their tales and reminiscences he could detect no sympathy for the British. At the next table two young women were talking about "the boys" and "the struggle" but it was clear they were not referring to the battle with Germany. He sat back and let their conversation drift over him.

He soon realized he had made a dreadful mistake. While the chatter washed around him and he listened to nostalgic talk of times past and a homeland far away, his own memories came flooding back. Of the happiness he once enjoyed in a homeland he had loved, of the bright faces that used to smile at him before they were riven with pain and death, of the love that he had shared and which had been shattered by shrapnel and taken from him by the men he would hate forever. Normally such memories made him hard and determined, but he was weak from exposure and hunger and the mouthfuls of beer were beginning to have a soporific, sentimentalizing effect. He felt the resistance ebbing away from him; he wanted to curl up into a ball, to cast the world aside, to forget and to sleep forever.

But the world had other ideas. As he felt himself floating off and the atmosphere of the pub stripping away his defenses layer by layer, he picked up the conversation of the young women at the next table. Of Patrick, who would be out in another eight months. "And never any chance of parole. Mind you, there was never much chance of his giving them any good behavior." Of the different ways in which a coat might be refashioned. Of the longing to be back home, with a job and a husband. Of the bitterness at having been forced by poverty to exchange the open rolling pastures of Donegal for a flea-bitten bed in Cricklewood which three people used in shifts. Of the offal which could be bought off-ration and disguised as food. And of "that little German bastard who's got the bloody Tommies on the run. Mother preserve him!"

It wasn't a choice, more an instinct grown mighty with desperation. He had no one else to trust and nowhere else to go. He'd run out of ideas, money, and strength. As the piano struck up a new tune and the men in the bar began to sing in deep, sorrowful voices the words of an Irish Republican battle hymn, Hencke reached across and touched one of the women on the arm.

"Excuse me. I'm that little German bastard. Would you help me, please?"

They looked at him in a mixture of astonishment and alarm, unable to utter a word, their world stopped. He wondered what they would do when they recovered — cry out in alarm? — yet in his exhaustion his worries had a distant, almost academic air.

Base reality came flooding back as the door of the pub burst open to reveal eight London policemen, truncheons drawn. They stood blocking the entrance, staring around, while silence and resentment descended between walls which a moment before had been ringing with gaiety. For one interminable moment nothing moved except for the eyes of the policemen as they roved around the pub. Hencke felt his mouth run dry. One of the bobbies was looking straight at him.

She could find no fear in his expression, it was all too sudden for that, but she couldn't fail to see desperation and defiance. It was a look she knew well. She had seen it in Paddy's face when the army came for him, and again when the judge had sent him down. She'd seen it in her mother's face when they told her that her husband wouldn't be coming home again, ever, not with all those bullets in him. In the depths of Hencke's steady, dark eyes she could see memories of pain and anger, and she knew about those, too. She had little time for the Germans and their violence, but she had no time at all for the British, and she would do almost anything to get her own back. Yet hadn't she troubles enough without walking into new ones in the pub?

The girl sat wrestling with the contradictions, not knowing if she wanted or would be able to help, until one of the policemen began beating his truncheon up and down in the palm of his hand, slowly thumping out a message of menace and hate. It was a message she knew all too well, and it was enough. She leaned across to two men at a neighboring table and whispered urgently between their lowered heads. Just a few words, but there was a nod of understanding, the briefest pause, before the two men stood. It was the first sign of any response to the unwanted invasion, and all eyes were upon them. They stood staring at each other, no more than a foot apart when, without exchanging a word, one clenched his fist and struck the other full on the chin, sending him sprawling across a table and knocking glasses everywhere. A neighbor retaliated on behalf of his fallen friend, and in an instant a volcano of commotion had erupted in front of Hencke. The pub became filled with a pandemonium of shouts, curses, waving arms, smashing glass, women's screams and breaking furniture. A jacket ripped, a lip was bloodied. Then the truncheons started flying. Hencke scarcely had time to witness one of the policemen succumbing to an assault by two elderly and determined women armed with heavy handbags before he felt an insistent tugging at his arm. It was the girl.

"Come on, Adolf. Time we left." She clasped his hand and dragged him, stumbling and uncomprehending, toward the rear of the pub. As they passed the bar he heard her shout, "Turn off the bloody lights, Harry!" He ducked as a glass crashed off the paneled wall above his head, and shattered into a hundred fragments. Still shaking the shards from his hair, he was dragged through a door and into the women's toilet, a dim and squalid little place with a cracked and badly stained basin but, to his relief, another door. He found himself in a dark yard surrounded by a looming wall; but piled against the wall, forming stepping places, were several crates, and already the girl was scrambling up. Peering cautiously over the wall, she urged him on. "It's clear!" she shouted, before disappearing over the other side.

Hencke followed. Behind him the noise of battle inside the pub was beginning to subside; even the most determined of opponents were having trouble sustaining a good fight in total darkness. He threw himself over the wall. His jacket caught on something, there was a tearing sound and he felt a burning sensation across his forearm, but before he knew any more he was in a cobbled back street with the girl screaming at him to run. He had landed heavily and was winded, but it could be only moments before the police found the back door and were upon them. Stumbling through the puddles of rain, he followed the flapping tail of her raincoat into the night.

They ran until they were both exhausted, through dark streets, avoiding the lights, alert for the sound of pursuit, until they could run no longer. Their lungs rasped from the effort, the rain trickled down their foreheads to mix with the sweat, their energy gone.

"I think we've done it, Adolf," she panted, looking up at him through strands of russet hair which had hung in long tresses before the rain turned them into a soaking mat.

"My name . . ." he muttered doggedly between great gulps of air, "is not Adolf. It is Hencke. Peter Hencke."

"OK, Peter Hencke. Any ideas what we do for an encore?"

She wrapped her raincoat around her, tying the belt tightly. Her efforts served to outline her slender waist and hips, while beneath the clutter of damp clothing her struggle for breath emphasized the shape of her breasts. She was young, less than twenty, he guessed, on the verge of full womanhood, with a handsome oval face and healthy skin which shone translucent in the rain. What the hell was she doing here, he began to wonder, before deciding that he was too weary even to speculate.

As a fresh squall of rain hit them they heard the bells. A jangling alarm began to sound on all sides, approaching, growing louder, bells of warning, bells — so the sudden look of fear on her face told him — of authority. They were near, just around the corner, accompanied by much shouting and noise of commotion. His mind recognized peril, demanded action, but his body was confused with exhaustion; the louder the bells grew, the more distant and infirm his legs seemed to become. Hencke glanced desperately down the street, searching for some source of salvation, but all he could see was the unmistakable sight of a police car rushing through the night toward them. He might have run but it would have served no purpose. He couldn't outpace a car and, anyway, he was drained, no reserves left. He leaned back against the wall, his eyes closed, waiting for the inevitable.

When he opened his eyes he found himself staring into the face of a policeman who was studying him with great interest. Hencke's coat was torn to ribbons by his leap over the wall, the burning sensation on his forearm had turned out to be a throbbing pain from a deep cut, with blood trickling down his fingertips, and the look on his face told its own story of agony. The policeman was reaching for him.

"You all right, sir? Had a close shave by the looks of you. Still, quite a number of others not so lucky, I'm afraid. You and the lady come with me, we'll get you fixed up . . ."

Uncomprehending, speechless, Hencke was led around the corner. The spectacle that confronted him was so overwhelming he all but stumbled in alarm before the policeman caught and steadied him. They were in a street more brightly lit than the one they had just left, with tall rows of houses stretching on either side. The street was residential, not very salubrious, with the worn-down air of a shoe which has had too much use. The buildings were tenements, normally crowded with people, many of whom were at this moment spilled along the street. Immediately in front of Hencke there should have been a solid frontage of brick; instead there was a hole some forty yards across, filled with rubble, smoke, smashed wooden beams, splinters of steel and teams of men clawing away with their hands at the ruins.

"You live there, did you?" the policeman enquired solicitously.

Hencke shook his head.

"Oh, passing by, were you? Bloody V-2s. Can't hear them coming, not like the doodle-bugs. First thing you know is when it's hit. Too late by then, usually. You're lucky, really lucky, believe me. Still, you and the lady must be badly shocked. Come on, let's get that arm seen to and find you both a cuppa . . ."

They were led along a street full of fire tenders, dust, ambulances, air raid wardens, rescue squads, housewives dispensing blankets and sympathy, doctors and nurses tending the injured, and policemen. Lots of policemen. And bodies. In a quiet corner there were already a dozen corpses covered by blankets. A woman's feet stuck out from under one blanket, a child's hand from beneath another, tightly clutching a teddy bear with one arm torn off. And the memories came flooding back . . .

Neither he nor the girl said anything while his arm was tended, the Red Cross nurse used to dealing with patients in shock and happy to do all the chattering herself. It appeared the rocket had fallen some fifteen minutes earlier, about the time the pub fight started. Perhaps that was what had masked the sound of the explosion. The section of the street which had disappeared into the crater normally housed over a hundred people, the nurse said. She hoped that most of them had been out enjoying their

Friday evening. But many clearly had not, and the row of bodies being assembled under the blankets grew longer with every passing minute. She would like Hitler and all the rest to be brought back to London and a German hanged on every site in the city where a bomb had fallen. Her fiancé had been captured in Singapore and was still, she believed, a prisoner of the Japanese, and the same went for that lot too. She wanted Hencke to go to hospital for stitches — the wound was deep — but he refused, so she disinfected it and bandaged it tightly.

"Just keep it quiet for a couple of days and don't do too much running around, love," she advised. "You'll be as right as rain."

With that they were packed off for a cup of tea from the mobile canteen.

The girl had wanted to forgo the tea and sidle out while they could, but Hencke shook his head. "Wait. We're all right for the moment. Take the tea." He was trembling from the shock and the cold, and he needed time to recover.

But there was something else. In the shadows behind the canteen the line of bodies was still growing. Distraught men and women would occasionally walk over to turn back the covering blankets and search for a loved one. No one interfered; death like this had long been routine in London.

It was after their second cup of tea, drunk without a word, that he took her firmly by the hand and led her toward the line of blankets. He avoided those which obviously covered women or children. But the others he began to turn back, staring at the dead, holding on to his companion's hand as if they were a couple seeking mutual comfort. He found what he was looking for underneath the eighth blanket. A man's body, you could tell that by the trousers and the hair on his chest. But of the face there was nothing other than a mass of angry bone and flesh in no recognizable human pattern. The girl drew back in horror, but Hencke knelt down close, as if grieving. Another couple passed by giving them a wide and sympathetic berth, leaving them alone in their sorrow. The Irish girl watched transfixed as Hencke removed an oval dog-tag from his own neck and placed it around the neck of the corpse, before standing up in apparent distress.

"It might confuse them for a while," he whispered, "buy us a little time."

"Now can we get out of here? Or do you fancy hanging around a little longer, just in case the Prime Minister decides to pay a visit?"

She grabbed his hand and was dragging him away when they passed by the body of the child clutching the mutilated teddy bear. Hencke stopped and stared. Tears filled his eyes and his lips moved in agitation, whispering silent words of anguish, remembering. He fell to his knees and began to pray.

"Holy Mother of God," the girl snapped in exasperation, looking around for the posse of policemen she expected would descend on them at any moment. "Can't we do our praying later?"

But he would not be hurried. He finished, oblivious to the bustle of the street, before leaning down and taking the child's tiny hand. With great tenderness he prized the armless toy away from her. "For luck, Little One," he whispered, and gently covered her hand with the blanket.

When he rose he stood tall, shoulders braced, and for the first time she saw what a powerful frame he had. The shocked and crumpled man of moments earlier was gone. In his eyes burned the glow of a bitterness and a determination which she understood well.

"Let's go," he said grimly, tucking the bear inside his shirt. "There's still much I have to do."

* * *

The Old Man was sitting on his own, in the gloom, with just a small table lamp to cast light. Had he been paying attention to the box of papers at his side he would undoubtedly have suffered severe eye strain, but the papers lay untouched. Churchill was alone with the thoughts that had preoccupied him ever since his return from Germany. He could have been excused a moment of exhilaration, the first Allied political leader to set foot on enemy soil, but there was no zest in him. He had been brooding — sulking, some were saying — and had neglected not only his official duties but also the normal civilities that attend governmental life. Even Clemmie had taken umbrage, deciding on the spur of the moment to visit relatives in the country for a few days rather than indulge in yet another heated and utterly pointless exchange with her husband. She was used to his moods and tempers, but she could see no reason for this bout of petulance. It was not as though he had lost a battle — or so she thought.

Only Cazolet had shown any inclination to indulge him, and the rest of the Private Office had been more than content for him to shoulder the burden. Cazolet had sat for many hours, ignoring the barbs and the criticism, showing indifference to Churchill's irascible accusations of disloyalty aimed at those around him, even offering a rebuke when the Old Man had gone inexcusably far. Cazolet considered he was overreacting, and told him so. Yet, self-inflicted or not, the pain was real. He resembled a great old oak, now dying, the ancient limbs sagging under their own weight, the sap no longer rising. Instead of thrusting for the sky he seemed to be slowly falling apart.

As Cazolet entered, the Old Man looked up. There was no friendly rustle of leaves, no welcome in his eyes. He was swathed in his favorite silk dressing gown whose rich brilliance he usually outshone; but tonight his garb seemed oddly out of place.

"They've got him," Cazolet said. "Or at least they're pretty sure it's him. Ironic. It was a V-2 the other night. They pulled him out from under the rubble."

There was an involuntary gasp. "What do you mean — 'they're pretty sure'? Is it him or isn't it, for God's sake?" There was a petulant, unsteady timbre in his voice.

"Not much to identify, that's the problem. Just a man's body with its head blown off and a German identity disc around the neck."

"Prison camp records? Size? Weight? Hair color? Isn't there something else? We must be sure!"

"That will all take a little time, I'm afraid. The state of the camps, particularly for transit prisoners, is pretty awful. The whole system's been swamped and the records are all over the place. It'll probably take a couple of days before they're sure . . . But how else could Hencke's ID end up on a body underneath tons of rubble?"

"I don't know. I really don't know . . ."

Churchill's eyes were closed, as if in prayer. For several minutes he scarcely moved, he might have been asleep, but Cazolet could see the occasional agitated shaking of his head, the only sign of some inner turmoil. When at last Churchill looked up, Cazolet saw the change in the eyes. The emptiness had gone, in its place was a spark of emotion — not release, certainly, more grim resolution, but a spark nonetheless.

"Great turning points in history are usually marked by death, William. I never guessed it would be Hencke's."

"We don't know for certain."

"He's dead. He must be dead, don't you see? It's as if he has been holding up the onward march of history, and history cannot wait. There is a great war out there which must be finished, one way or the other. Events have moved beyond my control, and I must follow in their wake, whether I like it or not." He took a deep mouthful of brandy. When he spoke again there was resignation in his voice. "Get me General Eisenhower on the phone."

"But we can't be sure . . ."

"The war isn't going to wait around for your doubts, Willie!" he snapped, unwilling to brook any delay now his mind was made up. "I need to get hold of Eisenhower and tell him that one more soldier is dead and he can have his damned division. There's nothing to be gained by holding on to them any longer."

"It's nearly midnight, two in the morning at the general's HQ," Cazolet protested. He could no longer be certain whether the Old Man was thinking straight. "To be honest, I'm a little confused . . ."

"I, too, am confused, William. Last time I inquired I was His Majesty's First Minister and Secretary of State for War. I don't recall having laid down either of those heavy burdens. Which gives me the right and you the duty to get the good general on that bloody phone without further prancing around. Or would it make it easier if in future I gave you orders in Swahili, as the King's English seems to be something of a problem?"

Damn, but the Old Man was in a foul mood. Swallowing his doubts and irritation, Cazolet picked up the telephone and tapped to attract the operator's attention. "See if General Eisenhower's in the land of the living, would you, Grace? The Prime Minister would like a word . . ."

It was miserably uncomfortable and the smell appalling. That's what made it such a good hiding place.

After they escaped from the bomb site she had dragged him through the shadows of yet more anonymous back streets, pausing only to make a hasty telephone call before arriving at an unkempt boarding house set back from the road behind a bushy, secluding hedge. Their reception lacked any trace of enthusiasm. Behind the front door hovered a small and wiry man who appeared greatly agitated and whose polished bald head was flushed and sweating profusely in spite of the cold. He wore an unironed shirt and an unwelcoming glower, closing the door quickly before rushing them into a back room with curtains tightly drawn. Hencke was instructed to wait in the sparsely furnished bed-sit, with its squeaky floorboards and discolored sheets, while she busied herself with the proprietor. They obviously knew each other well, but that didn't prevent her frequent disappearances from the room to consult with him turning into a running battle conducted in voices which became increasingly heated. He didn't seem pleased to see Hencke.

"Don't worry about Uncle Billy. He's a miserable sod with a nervous disposition, but he'll do as he's told." She said it with such authority that Hencke never doubted her. It was during a pause in the ongoing argument, held just outside the door, that Hencke first learned her name. Sinead. No other name. He also discovered her secret. "You'll guess this much anyway before this is over, so I'll tell you now and you'll get very little else. So don't go asking bloody stupid questions which I can't answer." She lit a cigarette and offered him a whisky, but he declined. He remembered how quickly the half pint of beer had begun to affect him after so long without a drink.

"We're Irish. Nationalists. You mustn't believe everything you've heard about us," she hastened to add with a nervous smile. "We're nice people really."

Hencke declined to mention he'd scarcely heard anything about Irish Nationalists, although what little he had heard was none too complimentary. But then, what must she think of him, a widow murderer? War makes strange companions.

"The British occupy half our country. We want it back," she continued. "And we're willing to fight for it, if necessary. Fortunately for you, it's meant getting our boys in and out of London without the police knowing, and that's what we'll have to try with you. Get you to Ireland. There you'll be safe — and halfway home."

Hencke sat quietly, saying nothing, trying to figure her out. She had an open, honest face, a natural smile and full lips which belied the uncompromising tone of her words. The scattering of freckles across the bridge of her ski-slope nose and the healthy bloom in her cheeks gave her an aura of innocence, yet once she had taken off her raincoat there was no denying her womanhood. As she felt the pressure of his steady gaze she lost her sense of authority and began to feel awkwardly girlish. She lit another cigarette, her lips closing nervously around the tip, like a young girl at a village dance waiting for her first date. He could see she had poise beyond her years in dealing with him, yet a touching naïveté about herself. Though her large hazel eyes bubbled with enthusiasm, already there were the first crinkles of maturity appearing at their downcast corners. Something in them suggested a sadness which tinged her ebullience, marking her, while not yet scarring. Her initial appearance, he decided, was misleading. This was no ordinary Friday-night girl in a pub. He had already learned not to make the mistake of patronizing her.

"So, how will you . . ."

"No questions, Peter Hencke. This could all go wrong and they might get their hands back on you. I don't want you giving away our whole game. So keep your eyes closed and your mouth shut and we'll be getting along just fine."

"One thing I must know, Sin . . . Sinead." He was unused to the name, and had to wrap his Middle European lips carefully around it. "One question. Why did you decide to help me?"

Her brow furrowed. "The most difficult question of all. That's just what Uncle Billy's been bellyaching about. And I can't say I've got much of an answer." Self-consciously, she twisted the bracelet on her wrist. "You looked so pathetic in the pub, starving and wet, and that always appeals to an Irish girl's heart.

Then I had to make up my mind — you or those bloody bobbies. Not much of a choice, really. You could be Attila the Hun for all I care, you'd still be preferable to those black-hearted bastards. Anyway, you've lovely eyes. They sort of glow. Like my brother's."

"Patrick?"

"How do you know?" she shot back, suspicion creeping into her voice.

"The pub. You were talking about him in the pub. And Donegal. And home."

"We thought you were asleep. So you were eavesdropping?"

"No. Just identifying with someone who wanted so much to be home."

There was an uneasy silence. The conversation had become very personal, and here she was sitting on a bed swapping intimacies with a stranger.

"How long will it be before we can get to Ireland?" he asked.

"Depends. Our group's been in hibernation since the war began; for some while your lot was doing a much better job of getting at the British than we could ever hope to do. So it may take us a few days to get hold of the right people. With luck less than a week."

"How?"

"I can't tell you."

"Secret?"

"Not really. It just depends who we can find at a moment's notice after five years. We'll have to blow away a few cobwebs."

"I don't get it. Five years . . . you must have been still in school."

A flush of embarrassment came to her cheeks.

"How many men have you smuggled out?" he demanded,

but her only answer was downcast eyes. "Don't tell me I'm your first?" He couldn't disguise his incredulity.

"My family's been part of the struggle all my life," she said fiercely, fighting against her own awkwardness. "I was there when they arrested my brother and locked him away. I sat holding my father's hand on the night before they killed him. Three Orangemen who found him in an alleyway called him the father of a Republican pig, and shot him where he stood. Not even executed him. They blew his kneecaps away first, then put two into his guts so that he would die, but not too quickly. They made sure he'd suffer first. And made sure my mother would suffer, every day and every night for the rest of her life. Mr. Hencke, I know as much about this business as I need to!"

There were no tears, but she was shaking all over. Hencke reached out and held her hand to stop it trembling. "I've already seen what you can do, Sinead No-Name. Believe me, I've got no reason to complain. I know. I was there, remember?" His words thawed through her blushes. Anyway, where else did he have to go? "Do your best, that's all I ask."

Her best, two nights later, proved to be a dilapidated truck carrying sacks of vegetables and empty fish crates to Liverpool. The sacks gave reasonable cover behind which to hide from prying eyes, the sour smell of fish offering added discouragement to anyone venturing too far into the entrails of the load. But for Sinead and Hencke, hiding in a small compartment crafted out of crates and sacks deep inside the lorry, it meant a night of bone-bruising discomfort. Their hiding place was claustrophobic and dark, and every jolt of the old axles seemed to transmit itself directly through the hard wooden floorboards, in spite of the small mattress thrown on the floor. They lay on the mattress, trying to brace themselves against the incessant jarring as they drove through the outskirts of London onto the main Liverpool road. The noise and discomfort made conversation difficult and the enforced intimacy left them both feeling awkward, so they settled back as best they could, bathed in the glow of a flashlight which gave their faces a ghoulish, melodramatic cast.

They were making steady progress north on the A5 through the suburbs of Birmingham when they hit the potholes. They were driving along a stretch of road that had received attention from a Focke Wolf's bombload in the early part of the war. The surface damage had long since been repaired. But, underneath, the Victorian sewers had leaked and grumbled and groaned and, finally, had collapsed. The lorry's front wheel sank into a deep hole, the steering wheel spun from the driver's hands and the vehicle was sent skidding across the road before coming to rest, front fender buckled, against a brick wall. From their hiding place they heard one burst of profanity from the driver before other voices crowded round. This was not the first vehicle to come to grief that night on this stretch of road; and with the wartime spirit of camaraderie abounding there were plenty of voices to offer consolation, and many hands to help. The tire had punctured; it would have to be replaced and the crumpled front fender bent out. "Should only take us twenty minutes," they heard one cheerful voice saying.

They were still feeling their bruises when someone climbed into the back, flashing a torch around in search of the spare wheel. "I'll do it!" the driver exclaimed, an edge of panic in his words. But already it was too late. While Hencke froze, the girl wriggled as close to him as possible, trying to burrow into his overcoat and make their profile as anonymous as one of the sacks of vegetables. Moments later the beam of a powerful torch began to probe around them, licking like a lizard's tongue into the corners, bouncing off sacks and trying to peek through the gaps between the fish crates. She squeezed ever more tightly into his body as the light swam around and above them, her body taut, holding her breath, feeling her heart beating like a tattoo against his chest. Then the light disappeared. The tire had been located; their hiding place had worked.

The repairs, as the helpful stranger had predicted, did not take long. Soon the lorry was ready to proceed, but there were new agonies as they heard the muffled sound of not one but three men climbing back into the cab. God, surely the driver wasn't offering lifts! It was not until much later they discovered that two soldiers on leave had asked to be taken on to Liverpool, and the driver, anxious not to create suspicion by refusing, had been forced to agree.

It was as the lorry was drawing away that they became aware of a more subtle predicament. The load had shifted. Only a little, but as they relaxed their grip on each other and tried to regain their original positions on the mattress they discovered there was no room left. They were stuck, face to face, unable to move because of the load, and unable to talk or call for help because of the presence of strangers just feet away. Even the flashlight was too great a risk. They continued on in darkness, every muscle tensed, their only means of communication being through the touch of their bodies.

They were so close she could feel every part of him — the bristles on his chin and neck, the muscles on his sinewy shoulders, the heaving of his chest as he breathed, even the sharpness of his buttons and the bulge of the child's toy stuffed inside his shirt. Their enforced intimacy had caused his legs to entwine involuntarily with hers, his breath wafted through her hair and down the back of her neck. Every move of their bodies, every bounce of the truck, brought them into fresh contact, and she knew there was no part of her own body which he couldn't feel or sense. They were close enough to smell each other.

She might have expected him to be frozen with embarrassment; she wouldn't have been astonished had he become aroused and immensely masculine, but all she could sense was self-control. His body was there, beside her and upon her, with a muscular thigh stuck between her own, but it was as if he were merely an observer, treating her body with the curiosity characteristic of a surgeon, or a sommelier examining a wine with a sense of professional detachment, without any intention of drinking. She tried to wriggle to get herself more comfortable, to let him know she didn't mind. Several of the boys she knew would have given anything — and had frequently promised to do so — for the chance of being in contact with her like this. But Hencke, as she already knew, was different from other men. He offered no response. He seemed to have built a protective shell around himself and he wasn't going to break it open for any young girl in the back of a lorry.

They lay like this for another hour, he silent, she lost in the tingling of her senses, before the lorry stopped again to disgorge its unwanted guests. A few minutes later they reached their destination in a quiet siding where the driver was able to remove the press of sacks and crates to release them. As Sinead clambered down she was trembling. From stiffness. From the excitement which the warmth and pressure of his body had aroused within her, and the feelings of guilt which that had caused. From curiosity about this strange man. And, even more, from curiosity about herself.

"Say, Beetle! Where's the place we liberated, the one with all those salt mines stuffed full of booty?"

Lieutenant General Bedell Smith entered Eisenhower's room with as much haste as the dignity of his rank would allow. "D'you mean the place near Merkers? The Third Reich seems to have been using it as a bank vault. Not only crates of gold and silver plate, but there's also a collection of art looted from all over Europe. Half the Louvre seems to be there in wooden packing cases; we're already getting telegrams every hour from de Gaulle claiming most of it. Then there's at least two huge halls full of nothing but bank notes. Don't know yet whether they're duds or the real McCoy . . ."

"Yeah, but wasn't there a mountain of wine crates — claret, brandy, that sort of thing?"

Bedell Smith checked his list. "Right. Historic vintages mostly, intended for Goering, so the locals are saying. We also found a whole batch of papers which we thought might be vital to the war effort. Just got the translations in. You want to hear? — 'The delicate smell of the fruit is just slightly obscured by the nutty transformation of the oak tannins . . . the length and elegance of these delicious cognacs compare so favorably with the pretty Parisian girls . . .' Turns out the friggin' things were some vintner's tasting notes."

"OK, OK. Get a crate of the brandy. Send it to Mr. Churchill with my compliments and some sort of message about it being from one Napoleon to another. You know the kind of thing. To get back on track with him."

"Good idea. There's lots of it. One crate enough?"

"I want to show there are no hard feelings, Beetle. Not suggest I'm in love with him. For Chrissake, the idea's to keep him quiet, not to give him any encouragement. Anyway, the old bastard drinks too much as it is. Wouldn't want him getting carried away and coming up with any more of his bright ideas. Would we?"

The three-star general winked mischievously, offered a smart salute, and hurried on his way.

CHAPTER 6

Liverpool tasted different. Instead of London's choking fog there was the sharp tang of salt air, with many fewer military vehicles roaring down the streets throwing diesel fumes at him. People on the streets hurried along, keeping their heads low, bending into the breeze that blew off the Irish Sea, the distant sounds of a railway station traveling on the wind. A cinema was turning out its patrons after the last show, nearly catching Hencke and the girl in the rush. "Trampled to death by Noël Coward. My father would never forgive me!" Sinead had joked before she remembered that she probably shouldn't joke about her father, her mother would not approve.

It was a long walk before they entered a cul-de-sac at the head of which stood a tall, imposing house of four floors, in darkness except for a porch lamp making circles of light in the stiff breeze. They stopped under a tree, like any courting couple in no hurry to find their way home, while Sinead made a careful inspection of the house and its surrounds. She was uneasy — something was not right — and they moved on, back to the streets, taking a cup of tea at a late-night canteen near the docks, never lingering too long in one place, anxious to avoid inquiring eyes, shivering as the damp sea air turned colder with the night, tripping over dustbins and piles of rubbish in dark alleyways that served as homes to bad-tempered cats. Hencke was wrung out from the ceaseless walking, but it was not until the first hint of dawn that they were back in the cul-de-sac facing the tall house. This time, after a brief inspection, Sinead seemed to have found what she was looking for and hurried him toward the door. Someone opened it without her knocking.

The someone turned out to be a tall and exceedingly handsome woman in her late forties, perhaps past her prime but with much femininity still, and great, possibly excessive care taken about her appearance. She closed the door quickly behind them while Hencke blinked in the blaze of light that lit the interior. As he looked around he could not hide his astonishment. There were other, younger women standing to the sides of the large hallway. He blinked again to make certain but there was no mistake. He hadn't been told, and in a thousand lifetimes would never have guessed.

"Well, I'll be . . ."

"Later, dearie. Anything's possible if you behave yourself, but for the moment let's get you safely tucked up out of the way," the woman responded.

"A brothel . . . ?"

"Where else would a good Catholic girl take a man like you?" Sinead chuckled mischievously. "But there's no time for gawking. Come on with you."

The house was quiet but not asleep, as if pausing to catch its breath before the night shift clocked off. Sinead led him past a broad, gilded staircase which swept to the upper floors, past chaise longues tastefully covered with brightly patterned upholstery and adorned with women in even more brightly patterned costumes that decorated without denying what lay underneath. None of them looked up or appeared to take any notice, burying themselves in magazines or relaxing with cigarettes protruding from extravagant holders. Everything glittered without being truly gaudy, was orderly, in its carefully chosen place, and there was little room for doubt that the madame ruled with an iron fist inside her elbow-length satin gloves.

He was hustled through a down-to-earth kitchen where a pot of coffee bubbled away on the stove, and one counter stood crammed with bottles of varied colors and kicks, then up bare wooden stairs which in earlier times servants had used to clamber from the scullery to their attic rooms without disturbing the family, until eventually he was led through a brightly lit corridor and into a room where the door was locked securely behind them.

Sinead waved her hand to preempt the inevitable flood of questions. "Before you start, you've got to believe me. This is the safest place in Liverpool for you."

"A brothel?"

"This is a high-class establishment, the best there is. And the finest safe house on the road back to Ireland. The British would never raid it; they'd be terrified of how many chief inspectors and judges they'd unearth."

A look of amusement crinkled the edges of his eyes, and for the first time since they had met she thought he was smiling, although it was difficult to tell. The scar on his upper lip twitched occasionally, yet she could never be sure.

"And a wonderful place, no doubt, for picking up all kinds

of useful information across the pillows," he suggested.

"But you catch on fast, Peter Hencke. And, my God, you seem to recover fast, too!"

Hencke had walked over to a small table laden with two plates, food and drink, and was already ripping and chewing his way through a cold pork chop. In a stride she was beside him, snatching hungrily at her own meal. The food was like nothing either of them had eaten for months. Pork chop, cheese, chicken, butter, even fresh fruit, nothing which could be found off-ration, a feast which could only have been obtained at considerable expense under the counters and behind the curtains of the black market. They tore at it.

"They seem to like you here," he spluttered through a slice of chocolate cake.

"The woman at the door, she's my father's second cousin," she replied with a mouth equally full. "I told you. This is a family affair."

They were smiling at each other across the mouthfuls of food. They couldn't easily sit down — there was only the large brass bed — so they stood and stuffed until, overcome by the delight of rare indulgence, they had entered a race to see which of them could finish first. She won, by a short biscuit.

"You bastard. You let me win," she accused him gaily.

"Nothing so gallant," he shook his head. "Do you realize I've just eaten the equivalent of a month's rations in the prison camp? I think I may be sick." As if to give weight to his words, he stretched out unsteadily and sank onto the bed. For the first time since their departure from London she looked at him closely. He was exhausted. The lean face had grown gaunt, the cheeks hollowed, the scar about his mouth carved more deeply into his skin. His eyes had sunk into dark pockets, yet they still held that glow of defiance which so intrigued her. Once again she wondered what drove him onward while so many others had given in.

"Here. For medicinal purposes." She uncorked a bottle of Scotch and handed him a large slug in a tall tumbler; but even as she reached across to him she saw he was already asleep. "The first friendly bed you've slept in for a long time, Peter Hencke. Enjoy it." She sat on the end of the mattress, looking at him.

When he awoke it was dark still — no, that couldn't be, it had been dawn when they arrived. Had he slept the entire day? The only door in the room apart from the entrance had been left open, leading to an extravagantly decorated bathroom full of mirrors and tiles and polished brass, with a pile of fresh cotton towels at the foot of an ornate cast-iron bath. The water was hot, and soon he was soaking up to his neck, having laced the water with scented salts he found in a glass jar. He tried to remember the last time he'd had a bath. He couldn't. Then he felt a cool draft across his chest and arms as the outer door opened and someone entered the bedroom.

"By the sounds of all that splashing I suppose it's a silly question to ask if you're dressed yet? Do you know that wartime regulations allow us only a couple of bucketfuls of water in the bath? You'd best be careful. Be pathetic if someone turned you in for a criminal waste of water."

"At the moment they would certainly find me unable to put up a great deal of resistance."

"Then you'd better make yourself presentable. There's a robe hanging from the back of the door. Throw me your clothes; I'll get them cleaned."

In a minute he was out, toweling his hair until it was again dark and sleek, trying to make himself look respectable in a cotton robe that was pink and too short and exposed the smooth, hairless skin of his chest. She tried hard not to stare.

"Good morning. Or is it?" he inquired.

"It's eight P.M. You've been asleep fourteen hours."

"Tell me, how much longer will I be here? I hate to complain, I suppose it's every man's dream to be locked inside a brothel, but after the prison camp I can do without being locked up anywhere."

"Can't tell, maybe not long. But Aunt Mary . . ." She twiddled her fingers nervously, not wishing to look at him. "She said she'd like to help. Not personally, of course, but . . ." The young girl inside her was babbling a little. "She said she'd be happy — you know — to send along one of the girls. On the house, so to speak."

At last it was blurted out. He began to laugh. "That's . . . very nice of your Aunt Mary but . . ." He shook his head. "I don't think so."

She blushed. "A man of principle, Peter Hencke?"

"No, Sinead. Don't make me what I'm not."

He could sense her relief and thought he understood. He was hers. This was a great adventure for her, and he, or at least his safety, was her prize. The stories that would be told by her friends and family for a long time to come would be her stories, no one else's. She didn't want some tarted-up part-time hooker spoiling it with tales about him she couldn't possibly hope to match. He smiled at her secret, happy to play along.

"Don't you know that Nazis are supposed to drink babies' blood and screw nothing but young virgins?"

"What! And go to bed only with teddy bears?" she chuckled. "What sort of Nazi are you, Peter Hencke, sat here wearing a fluffy pink dressing gown and nothing else beyond a smile?"

They both began to laugh, from relief, from the bond of growing friendship and shared secrets, from the fact that neither had found much to laugh about for so long, until they both collapsed on the bed, sobbing with the effort.

They were still laughing when they heard the commotion

downstairs. The banging of doors. The raised voices. Feminine screams of surprise mixed with male shouts of authority.

"Holy Mother, it can't be! A raid?" she gasped.

"I thought you said the British . . ."

"They never have . . ."

The door was flung open. One of the girls stood panting, her ample chest heaving beneath a flimsy covering of lace. "American MPs! Looking for one of their sodding sergeants," she shouted before disappearing to warn others.

Hencke's eyes searched desperately around the room, for a way out, a means of escape. He didn't need to say anything.

She shook her head, her face pale. "There's nowhere to run, Peter."

"Then I am lost."

She bit into her lower lip. "I won't have it. No!" In one action she kicked off her shoes and scrabbled at her sweater, tugging at it until she popped out. "We've maybe one chance." The zipper was undone, the skirt already falling to the floor, with the petticoat following. "You're not American. You're a civilian having some fun in a brothel." Stockings, garter belt. "If they believe that, maybe they'll leave us alone." She tore at the straps of her bra with a ferocity that caused something to give. Then it was her panties, and she was standing there naked, glowing. "So pull your bloody finger out and get into bed!"

She had rushed across and was leaning over him, pulling at the robe, when the door burst open once again. The form of a young military policeman filled the doorway, all metal helmet, armband, white webbing, razor-sharp creases and polished boots. He had a nightstick in his hands and a nervous tic in his left eye, which was trained on Sinead and had to be torn away before finally settling on Hencke. The soldier took one step into the room.

"So, what's going on here?" His voice was youthful, light on the authority of age and experience, and lacking totally in any sense of occasion.

Before he could move farther than a pace Sinead was in front of him, blocking his path, hands on the curve of her naked hips, her full breasts bouncing with indignation as she faced up to him.

"What's the matter with you stupid Yanks? Never seen a woman getting laid before? If you're here for lessons you'll have to wait your turn like all the rest. In the meantime just bugger off, and let a girl get on with a night's work!"

The tic around the MP's eye seemed to double in intensity. He made no attempt to move farther into the room, which he could only have done by touching Sinead. He seemed embarrassed to be confronted by a woman, stark naked, and a good twelve inches shorter than himself. It hadn't ever happened to him before. Not a completely naked woman, not under any circumstances. Never.

"Christ, Peterson," a voice called from down the corridor. "What the devil are you up to? Is he goddamned there or not?"

The soldier looked up nervously from his inspection of her bright red nipples and glanced again toward Hencke, studying him for a fraction of a second before looking back down at Sinead and her nakedness.

"Er . . . no, Sarge! Not in here."

"Are you certain, asshole?"

The MP was looking distinctly uneasy, and beginning to sweat. Sinead, confusing him by switching her tactics, had hold of his nightstick and was stroking it tantalizingly between her breasts.

"Come back later, soldier, when I'm through with this one. Let's have some fun," she whispered.

He shot another nervous glance in Hencke's direction, comparing his profile with the description of the errant soldier they were seeking. There was real anguish in his eyes. He was mortified while he looked at Sinead, yet he couldn't bear to take his eyes off her. "No, definitely not here, Sergeant," he croaked.

"Then what are you waiting for? Get your butt up to the next floor," the disembodied voice of authority came back down the corridor, just as Sinead's fingers reached in the direction of the soldier's shirt buttons.

"Yes, Sergeant," he whimpered, and was gone.

Sinead closed the door quietly before she turned round. She had a brave half-smile on her face which she tried desperately to turn into a convincing look of triumph; but the lower lip began to wobble, and in a moment the resistance was gone and tears were flooding down her face. She threw herself into Hencke's arms and sobbed great tears of tension and relief. She was still crying when she lifted her head and began kissing him passionately, her salty tongue probing between his lips.

He did not respond, just as he had failed to do in the lorry, but she was making all the advances. Her body was warm from the nervous energy, her nipples burned against his body, her tears turning to sighs of passion.

"Peter, in this world it may be our last time. Please!"

Something told him that for her it was also the first time. She was so young, scarcely older than some of his pupils. He was confused, uncertain, the self-righteous moralizing of his aunt ringing in his ears, but his indecision was overwhelmed by Sinead's insistence. In the end he had little real choice but to join in and, if not exactly enjoy it, at least to take comfort in her gratification. She knew what she wanted, instinctively, even if she wasn't totally clear how she wanted it. The raw energy more than compensated for her youthful ignorance. It wasn't great sex, but for her it would always be special.

When she had finished she lay back to catch her breath, coming down to earth, her whole body tingling, feeling places within for the first time. She knew it was a moment she would never be able to forget, or to repeat, no matter how many years she might live. Not even with Hencke. It was a long time before either of them spoke.

"You have someone back home?" Perhaps it wasn't the most tactful question but she couldn't help herself; she didn't have much experience at this. She had to ask. She felt now she had the right.

"No. Not any more." His words were clipped, without any trace of self-pity, as if all emotion had already been wrung out of him. But in the gaze which held her she could once again see the fire inside, and there was pain.

"You lost someone, too?"

He didn't respond, simply nodded.

"But if they're gone, why are you so impatient to get back home?" She made it sound like a rebuke.

"Wouldn't you be?"

She propped herself on an elbow. "I'm not sure, Peter. Back to Germany? I don't want to take sides in your war, but over here we don't hear pleasant things about Germany."

"It's like many places. Some good parts and fine people. Many bad. Like most places. Like Ireland, I suspect." He was deflecting her questions, throwing the challenge back at her. "Why did they arrest your brother?"

She didn't reply immediately. "They claimed he left a bomb. There was a warning. But a policeman got hurt . . ."

"Did he do it?"

"I . . ." She pulled away from him and her face flushed with anger that he should dare raise the question; but his eyes were searching around inside her. He already knew. "I . . . don't know. In all honesty I truly don't know." There was great misery in her. "And I don't know why, Peter Hencke, but that's the first time I've ever said as much to anybody. Even to myself." He had penetrated more than her body, and with the admission, a little bubble of faith which had survived all previous doubts and assaults quietly burst within her.

"So he might be guilty?"

"The policeman didn't die," she began in mitigation, but she wasn't convincing even herself. Her head fell forward to hide her confusion, her long russet curls falling about the pale skin of her breasts. "He was crippled. He won't ever walk again."

"He had family? Children?"

She could do no more than nod.

"And friends, who were so filled with revenge that they shot your father. This is your 'family affair'?"

"I didn't start our troubles, Peter."

"You may not have started it. But who's going to finish it? That's always the difficult part."

Suddenly she resented the assault upon her integrity and ideals, and the way he was ripping her world apart. "I suppose you're going to tell me that it wasn't Hitler but Poland that started World War Bloody Two. And that you're going home to finish it!"

"I'm sorry, Sinead. I have no right." He paused, remembering the widow. "We all do things of which we are not proud, which we would change, if we could." He reached out to touch her hand, to reestablish contact. She didn't respond, but neither did she move away. "There are some things we would gladly die for, if we could change. Which means that others, too, sometimes must suffer. I know. I have my own 'family affairs' to see to."

"But why, Peter? You said you had no family left."

"I have memories. Sometimes all you have left are memories."

"And can you live just for memories?"

She studied him closely, following the profile from his high forehead down his long nose to the scarred lip and sharp, determined chin. He didn't reply straightaway. It seemed a lifetime since anyone had got close enough to ask such questions.

"I've tried. Yet . . . you spend your life looking back, and the farther you have to look back the more you die each day, little by little. No, I can't live for memories, no one can. You mustn't try."

"But you are prepared to die for them?"

She waited, but there was no answer. For all their adventure and talk together she still knew little more than his name. He was a man who kept his secrets wrapped tightly around him, a man with fire in his veins and steel in his bones, yet who could still cry over a little girl and her teddy bear.

"Why are you going back?"

He remained silent, unwilling or unable to say, staring blankly at the ceiling.

"Peter Hencke, I don't want you to be the last man to die in this bloody war!"

A wry smile began to play around his lips — or was it the scar? "No one wants to be the last man to die. Not in this war, not in any war."

"Does . . . that mean you'll be coming back?"

He turned to face her until she could see his eyes. He didn't want any misunderstanding.

"You mustn't hope for me to be something I cannot be. No, Sinead, don't think of it." He shook his head. "I won't be coming back."

CHAPTER 7

"Not too hot for you, sir?"

The only reply was a grunt.

At least he's not complaining, not yet, thought the barber. Doesn't mind me scalding my fingers raw, but let him feel the slightest discomfort from the hot towels and he'd let the entire bloody street know. After which he'd moan about his shave not being close enough. And he never left a tip, not even at Christmas.

"Did you see they got Hencke at last?"

"What, you mean that bloody German? Thought they'd picked him up a long time ago."

It was not an uncommon assumption. With so many stories queuing up to demand space in the news columns as the war drew to its climax, the coverage of Hencke's escape had rapidly disappeared from the pages. Even today's report had been restrained, wrapping up what editors decided was an old story.

"No. They found the blighter in Cricklewood — or what was left of him. Seems he'd been leading the police a right merry chase, then a couple of nights ago he got caught underneath one of their V-2s. Poor sod. Seems unfair somehow."

With victory within their grasp, the British sense of fair play was beginning to flourish once more. And since Hencke had a name he was no longer simply another bloody Kraut, but a real character, even an underdog, and the barber held a sporting regard for any underdog, particularly since he had done the decent thing and thrown himself under one of his own rockets.

"Serves the miserable Hun right," the customer barked from underneath the towels. "Should have shot him if they'd caught him alive. Probably a damned war criminal anyway; most of them are."

"Well, I don't suppose we shall be able to shoot them all."

"Damn it, but I'd like to try," the voice came back from within the fog of steam, as the barber tried to remember from behind which desk the customer had fought his war. "Particularly this one."

"Why him?"

"Most dangerous type of Hun. Doesn't know when he's beaten. Too stupid and arrogant to know when he's lost the bloody war." But it was more than that. It was his example, one lonely man — even a German — running around the country sticking his fingers in the face of Authority, an example which all too many seemed willing to follow. It couldn't be tolerated. These were difficult and unsettled times, when people needed to be reminded about their proper place and duties. There was more than one way to lose an empire. "And be damned careful how you trim the mustache!"

The barber stropped the razor and examined the customer's throat. One day, he promised himself. One day . . .

In Berlin the news that Hencke's body had been discovered was heard widely, even though it was carried only by the BBC, and listening to enemy radio was an offense punishable by summary execution on the street corner. The populace took comfort in the fact that the law was unenforceable; there simply weren't enough lamp posts. But in the bunker the news became available to very few; Goebbels saw to that. Hencke had been his prize. Great hopes had been raised upon the prospect — which many took as a promise — of a triumphant return to Germany; and he didn't like to disappoint the Fuehrer. Indeed, it was Goebbels' full-time task to keep the spirits of the Fuehrer high, to persuade him that salvation was still at hand, to find every omen, helpful horoscope or shred of encouraging news, and cling to it like a climber to an iceface.

Above all, however, Goebbels was a realist. That was why he was so useful to the Fuehrer. He wasn't a carpet-widdling spaniel like so many of the others. He told the Fuehrer what he wanted to hear, of course, but not to ingratiate himself and flatter, only to encourage and strengthen. If they were to salvage anything from the heap of scrap into which Germany was being bombed, they needed time and the undisputed leadership which only the Fuehrer could provide.

And they needed luck. It was ironic how, after all their planning and preparation and *putsch*-ing, all the great victories and still greater reverses, everything came down to a matter of luck. If only they'd invaded Russia a year later, after an armistice on the Western Front. Or reached Moscow a month earlier, before the snows. If only that oaf Goering had continued bombing the British airfields a few weeks longer, when the enemy had only a handful of aircraft left, instead of turning his snout to the blitzing of London. If only the Japanese hadn't bombed Pearl Harbor and brought the Americans rushing into the war. If only . . . It all came down to luck and fickle fortune in the end. That was where Hencke came in. Goebbels wanted him as his lucky charm, to dangle round the neck of the Fuehrer, to ward off the doubters and defeatists who undermined the leader's morale, and to give him back the resolve to continue for the few vital weeks they needed. With Hencke and a little luck anything would still be possible. Yet suddenly the luck seemed to have run out.

Hencke was beginning to feel that death might, after all, be a soft option. They hadn't been long in the rusty fishing smack, only a few hours, but the seas were rough and growing fiercer, and he was a rotten sailor.

She noticed the sudden sallowness in his complexion and the grimness about his mouth, the scar tugging at his lip. "Think positive. The weather makes it more difficult for the coast guard, too. Anyway, we've not long now," she encouraged.

No sooner had she spoken than through the low-hanging storm clouds on the horizon appeared the outlines of a rocky coast.

"What is this place?"

"Man. The Isle of Man, they call it."

"I thought we were going to Ireland?"

"One step at a time. The Isle of Man is in the middle of the Irish Sea, halfway there. All the direct routes to Ireland are carefully guarded. We're going to try to slip through the back door."

"As long as it's dry land I don't think I care any more . . ."

"You should feel at home. The island is full of Germans and Italians sitting out the end of the war."

"What?"

"It's one of the main internment points for enemy aliens and prisoners."

"You're taking me to an island the British use as one vast prison camp?" he groaned, trying to find the strength to raise an eyebrow.

"It's the Irish in me," she said, mocking him. "But don't worry. They're so busy trying to stop people getting out that no one expects anybody to try to get *in*."

Hencke had held out, against seemingly overwhelming odds, until they were approaching the relative calm of a small West-facing harbor called Peel, over which towered the crumbling red stonework of a ruined castle. He and Sinead had no opportunity to admire the view; they had been ordered into the hold to hide them from prying eyes. So Hencke had lost sight of the horizon, the only immovable and unheaving object to which his fragile senses had been able to cling, at precisely the moment his stomach was assailed by the overpowering stench of fish. His resistance came to a sudden end.

"And this is the secret weapon with which Germany is going to win the war?" Sinead taunted as he sat hunched over a bucket.

"If you have any mercy, shoot me."

"Too late," interrupted the skipper, clattering down wooden stairs which led from the deck. "Apparently the British government have just announced that you are lying on a slab in a mortuary somewhere in London. Officially you're dead already!"

Hencke thought for a moment about attempting a smile, but decided that triumphs could never be celebrated on a retching stomach. He reached for the bucket.

Any depression that Josef Goebbels might have allowed himself on hearing that his talisman had been found crushed under a pile of German-induced rubble quickly disappeared when he received the top-secret cable from the German Embassy in Dublin.

HENCKE . . . ALIVE . . . FREE . . . IN DUBLIN. HALFWAY HOME!

It was 10 April. Russians less than eighty miles east of Berlin, their advance troops already ripping through the outskirts of Vienna. To the west the Americans, Canadians and British, swarming across their bridgeheads on the Rhine, their vanguard almost as close to Berlin as the Red Army and making faster headway. The great Reich which had once stretched from the edges of Moscow to the Atlantic and from the northern tip of Norway as far as Africa, now reduced to a narrow ribbon a few dozen miles across, as the vast armies of their enemies pressed in on all sides. For a man whose task it was to manufacture propaganda, all that recent weeks had given him by way of raw material were bricks of straw.

But now! A saga of German courage, of triumph against seemingly insuperable odds, an epic example of endurance which showed that all was not lost, that victory could still be theirs! All they needed was time, a little more sacrifice from the German people, another burst of national resistance. If only Germany could hold on a few weeks longer, Stalin would go too far as he had always done, the West would begin to understand how wrong they had been to trust him, and how much greater was the menace of Bolshevism than any posed by Nazism. Then, perhaps, they could come down from their Alpine fastness . . .

If only Germany could hold on a little longer. If only the Fuehrer could hold on. And with the inspiration of Hencke's example, they both might.

He brushed aside the fine layer of dust that had already settled on the cable, savoring once more the most encouraging news he had received in months. More dust began instantly to fall. The Americans and British were bombing the capital around the clock, the last hope of German resistance in the air had already been blasted from the sky or reduced to matchwood on pulverized airfields, and even the bits of Berlin that had not suffered direct hits were being slowly shaken to pieces. It was April, yet scarcely a tree in the city bore any leaf, as if a Valkyrian whirlwind had stripped them bare. The skies above the capital were beginning to fill with the yellow, acrid smoke of cordite, soot, and dust that turned day into night and the eternal hope of spring into darkest autumn. Goebbels fanned the flames of hope among all who would listen, but he knew the odds lay heavily against him.

And all because of one man. Churchill. *Churchill!* The evil old drunkard who, if only he hadn't been so monumentally stubborn and shortsighted, could have brought the war to an end less than a year after it started, with Britain and its empire still intact, and Germany straddled across Europe. They could have shared the world between them. But in his whisky-sodden blindness he had thrown away the historical destiny of their two great nations, had bled them both dry, Winston Bloody Churchill, who had been biting their backsides for years. Well, perhaps it was time for him to take some of his own medicine. And the poison was here, in Goebbels' hand.

He knew he couldn't wait until Hencke was back. Hencke might never get back or, if he did, it might all be too late. Goebbels needed something *now*. Not next week. So he would announce Hencke's survival and escape to Ireland, and humiliate Churchill in his bare-faced lie, and hope to cause so much confusion that the world would never again believe a thing that the British leader told them, even if he had Hencke, his grandmother and his entire fornicating family on public display in London Zoo.

The lights flickered and dimmed as the blast from a nearby

explosion momentarily disturbed the smooth running of the generator. Another cloud of dust descended from the ceiling and fell around Goebbels. But in the half light, he didn't seem to mind. For the first time in days, he was smiling.

"I did warn you."

The old, baleful eyes turned, admonishing, but said nothing. Cazolet was right, after all. Damn him.

"Don't feel too depressed," the younger man continued, adopting a more generous tack. "It's not the first time Berlin Radio has accused you of lying."

"The great British public expect their politicians to lie," Churchill responded mournfully.

"So . . . ?"

"But not to get caught."

"They can't blame you."

"Willie, he is part of the biggest escape of the war. In response, we are forced to launch a nationwide manhunt. Then, with all eyes upon us, we announce his death. Yet within days Goebbels is able to tell the whole world I was lying. If he ever has the proof, if in spite of it all Hencke turns up in Berlin, we shall never hear the end of it. At best I shall look incompetent, as though I am losing my grip. At worst it will look as if I have been deliberately deceiving both our electorate and our allies to cover up my own inadequacies. Sacrificing the truth for my own squalid personal purposes — that's what they will say."

"What does one man matter? The whole world is changing, victory is within our grasp . . . Hencke is a mere drop in the great oceans swirling around us."

The Old Man looked up sharply. "Willie, you do not yet understand."

"You're right, I don't. I've always felt you had some sort of mystical attachment to this man, admiration for him, even. Solidarity among escapees."

"He is a brave man. And far from being a drop in the ocean he is of overwhelming significance."

"As you said, I do not yet understand."

Churchill shook his head sorrowfully, his fleshy jowls quivering in agitation. "It was all so simple when it started. Hencke seemed just another escaping soldier, of little consequence, the merest flicker of a candle in the darkening night of German defeat. But . . ." He sighed deeply. "He has changed, beyond anything we could have expected. He is no longer anonymous. Eisenhower chose to turn him into a token of his victory over me, now Goebbels has embraced him as a symbol of ultimate resistance. In every broadcast Berlin Radio will try to humiliate and destroy me. Through Hencke."

"Surely not . . ." Cazolet felt sure that Churchill was going too far in personalizing events, but the Old Man raised his voice to shout him down.

"Hencke is a remarkable man, a prize in anyone's army. Unique. Powerful. He has outwitted an entire nation." Animation had sparked within the Old Man, as if he were caught personally in the excitement of Hencke's adventure; he waved away the smoke that was clinging around his forehead in order to see Cazolet more clearly. "If he makes it back to Berlin, the only German soldier to do so throughout the course of this entire bloody war, Hencke becomes a mighty weapon. It has been inevitable since the moment he escaped."

"Then let us pray he never makes it back."

Churchill glowered. "Goebbels has stacked the odds so fearfully against him."

"Goebbels . . . ?" Cazolet was growing impatient. Churchill talked in such riddles, making no sense that Cazolet could discern.

"In order to use him as a weapon against me, Goebbels has betrayed him. He should never have told us that Hencke was in Ireland."

"But we can't touch him in Ireland. Can we?"

"Already he will have been smuggled out of Dublin, to somewhere safe, somewhere beyond our reach. But . . ." The lower lip quivered, the moist end of the Havana forgotten. "To accommodate his disastrous timetable, Goebbels has to get him from Ireland back to Germany in a fearful hurry. He cannot be smuggled through Spain or some other neutral country — it would take too long. He cannot be flown there, for we have total mastery of the skies. They have no ships left afloat which could make the journey. No. There is only one way. By submarine!"

Cazolet was nodding slowly; this much he could understand.

"And there is only one route, Willie! To run the gantlet of the English Channel, so full as it is of our frigates and patrol boats, would be suicide. A twenty-mile stretch of water without so much as a friendly rock behind which to hide. He couldn't escape detection if he tried to swim through! No, Willie, no. He must go the long way round, beyond Scotland and down through the North Sea. There he might hope to hide in the depths, to escape our attentions. Nearly two hundred thousand square miles of dark water. There he might stand a chance." Churchill had seemed himself to be caught up in Hencke's challenge, his cigar stabbing the air to leave a trail of smoky exclamation marks, but in an instant his demeanor changed. It was as if a string had been cut. He slumped back in his chair. "And it is *there* they shall stop him. Because of Goebbels' precipitateness and stupidity. The Navy are already moving everything they have to throw a gate across the North Sea so solid that even the fishes will have trouble penetrating it." The voice brimmed with anguish. "They will leave nothing to chance, Willie."

After many years spent so close to the Old Man, Cazolet was

accustomed to the sharply swinging emotions, his sudden tempers too, but never had he seen his mood change so quickly. One moment Churchill had been lost in self-pity, the next caught in the thrill of trying to outwit Goebbels and even his own sea defenses; yet now he was shedding tears.

"Goebbels has sacrificed him, to get at me. He could have waited, got Hencke back home before making his wretched announcement, keep us unawares. But he couldn't wait to humiliate me. Goebbels has betrayed him with the kiss of Judas. And so we must betray him also and nail him to a hard cross on which only brave men perish." His bottom lip quivered, the head fell forward, the tears began to fall into his lap, tears of sorrow, of pity, and of guilt. "We move great armies around the chessboard of war, knowing the battle will result in tens of thousands of deaths. When I went to thank the troops on the night before they left for the Normandy beaches, they cheered, even with the knowledge that many of them were shortly to die as a result of my orders. There will be death warrants to be issued even after this war is over, and I shall not shrink from signing them. The game of war brings death, and the devil has ensured that this has been a hellishly long game. But to conspire in the destruction of this one brave man, whose only crime has been to love his country and to show the most peculiar courage, to order him cast over like a pawn, is almost more than I can bear. For he is no ordinary man. The whole world has betrayed him, poor, poor man. And now it is our turn."

"How on earth can you betray a murdering bloody German?" Cazolet burst out in alarm, for the first time beginning to wonder whether the older man's logic as well as emotions were beginning to succumb to the strain.

Churchill reached over to grab the knee of his young companion, beseeching his understanding. "He is not just another bloody German! Haven't you realized yet? He is . . . Berlin! My victory! Or was, until Eisenhower intervened." He sobbed, his voice subdued in recognition of his own defeat. "The Alps . . . the idea was always ridiculous, so far-fetched . . . I wanted to make sure. And all I have done is ensure the needless death of one brave man, and now I dare not stop it . . ."

The sun was setting, a vivid cusp on the horizon, by the time they reached their destination. They had been traveling since morning, just the two of them in a battered Bedford farm truck, for the last three hours bumping along rutted tracks as they scurried, as rapidly as the conditions would allow, beside the bleak coastline of western Ireland. They had passed barely a dozen cottages and several of those had stood abandoned and roofless, their bare chimney stacks standing like gravestones, memorials to a past, better life. The way of life in this part of Ireland had scarcely changed since the Famine, she had explained, except to get worse. The scenery was green yet barren, and the rugged basalt coastline stood out like the craters of the moon, caught by the embers of the dying sun.

She parked the truck on the cliffs above a broad bay; there was no cover to hide the vehicle, no tree, no bush, only bare grassy slopes. Out to sea the final rays of the sun kissed the tops of low islands that guarded the entrance to the bay and kept its waters calm and smooth. All was still, the only sound the lapping of the tide and the mewing of gulls as they cartwheeled overhead and plunged into the sea in search of sprats. They trod carefully down a rocky path which he would never have spotted had he not been walking on it. They held each other's hands tightly. She led the way, while he acted as a great anchor to guard against the boulders and stones trying to trip them and send them stumbling, until they had clambered down to the narrow shingle beach below. The tide lapped gently across the stones.

"What do we do now?" he asked.

She checked her watch. "We wait."

They were the only words exchanged. They knew these would be their last moments yet neither could find the things to say. They stood side by side looking out to sea, still holding hands, losing themselves in colors which, in the final struggle of day, were swirling turbulently above the horizon. She felt the elements mimicking the turmoil inside her — happy that he was almost safe, feeling desolate that his salvation would make her miserable for the rest of her life. She thought once more of that night in Liverpool when, for a fleeting moment, she felt she had got close to him. But the feeling had never returned.

Then it began. The sea before them which had been peaceful and at rest started to lift and part, a fermenting brew of waves and foam that rippled out and filled the bay.

"Your lift," she said simply.

They watched as through the clinging beds of kelp rose the profile of a conning tower, its U-boat insignia still identifiable in the last light of day, and already there were men scuttling across the wave-washed upper deck, manning the anti-aircraft guns, and launching a small, collapsible rowing boat. Approaching the shore, its crew was alert and wary. Hencke and Sinead had only moments left together.

"Thanks," he whispered. He was still looking out to sea rather than at her.

"No thanks needed. I love you."

"Please, don't. Don't love me."

"But I do, Peter Hencke."

"You mustn't, Sinead. There's no future for us." Still he could not look at her.

The rowing boat was already beginning to scrape its way onto the beach, with two armed German sailors jumping out and taking guard against unforeseen danger.

"Kill hope, Peter, and you kill the heart. Don't take that from me."

"I know what you mean. Believe me. But I'm not coming back."

"The war will be over eventually . . ."

"Not even then. Not for me. I'm sorry."

She wanted to scream at him, to demand that he open the doors inside himself which he kept so tightly bolted, that he owed her more than "I'm sorry" after all she'd done, that the least he could give her was an explanation. But an officer was scrambling up the shingle toward them and was almost upon them.

"Captain Eling," he introduced himself with a salute. "My compliments! Please come with me."

She tried once more but the captain was glancing around anxiously.

"Please. We must leave. Immediately."

Only then did Hencke look directly at her, with that light in his eyes turned from defiance to a soft glow of comfort. "I shall remember you, always."

"Pity we can't live on memories."

"But at least we can live *with* them, which is more than many will be able to say after this madness is over."

"What will you remember?"

He smiled, and perhaps for the first time she felt the doors inside opening a little. "Someone who took my despair and gave me hope. Someone with whom I shared a special kind of love. Someone who, in a different world, could have become my dearest friend. And who knows, perhaps in the next world it might be."

"Then there's no need to be sorry, is there."

"No regrets?"

Hesitantly, reluctantly almost, she shook her head.

"I'm very glad to have met you, Sinead No-Name." And with that his hands slipped from hers and he was gone.

He didn't look back all the time the boat slapped through the water on its way out to the waiting submarine. As they approached, in the gathering dusk, he could see the crew lined up along the hull, watching him. He heard no one give an order, but as they drew near the men and officers raised their arms in salute. The final red and purple glow was fading into a dark sky; the submarine stood in silhouette, the last rays of day glinting off the conning tower and bringing an edge of fire to the dull and battered metalwork, making him feel as though he were in the midst of a timeless ceremony of champions, like a warrior being greeted on arrival in Valhalla.

He turned to the captain in puzzlement. "Why?"

The captain paused to consider his answer. He had several weeks' growth of beard, his white officer's cap was crumpled and the eyes beneath appeared haunted and exhausted. His face bore the marks of many missions. "Because we understand the meaning of duty, and know what it's like to risk everything to get home. A submariner is never captured, he never has the option, like so many others nowadays, of sitting safely on his ass and waiting in comfort for the end of the war. A submariner knows only one thing — to fight or to die. In our book, Hencke, you're one of us." The captain's hand came to touch the peak of his cap and offer his own respectful salute, one fighting man to another.

"They sent an entire submarine crew — just for one man?"

"Three crews of three submarines. Out there are two more U-boats. Me to take you. The other two to act as decoys. We have to assume that the whole British anti-submarine effort is waiting for us out there. It's going to be one hell of a ride."

"Decoys? You mean like decoy ducks?"

LAST MAN TO DIE

The captain gave a thin, humorless grin. "Something like that. Decoys who will fly off in opposite directions and hope to drag the British after them. Disperse their effort, create a hole in their defenses through which we may sneak undetected."

"But that's no better than . . ."

"War is a dangerous profession. We're used to it. At least with you aboard we'll be heading back home. If we have a choice, I'd rather be heading home, not buried along with the worms three miles down in some mudhole in the middle of the Atlantic. Feels better the closer you get to home, if you know what I mean." He sniffed the salt air with the intensity of a man taking his last breath.

"How many men on a submarine, Captain?"

"Like this? Around fifty."

"Times three. One hundred fifty men. To bring me back home." He nodded toward the crew waiting on the U-boat deck. "Do they know . . ."

"That's why they're all there. To see you. To honor you. To know what they might be dying for. That's all a soldier ever wants, isn't it, to know what he's dying for? I thought it only fair."

"And I have become their Angel of Death . . ."

They were bumping alongside the hull, the dark waters of the Atlantic slapping its side, throwing the tiny rowing boat around and making it impossible for him to keep his balance. But there were hungry hands stretching down to grab him and haul him on board. As he found his feet on the slippery wooden deck casing, he glanced around at the men who were facing toward him, still saluting. He tried to look everyone directly in the eye, relieved in the near-darkness that he couldn't. He stood to attention, but did not return the salute; he saw no point in saluting death, there had already been too much dying.

"Straight below, please. We're already taking more risk

than we ought to, sitting here. I think we've outstayed our welcome in Irish waters.''

It was only as they led him away that he turned for one final look at the shore and Sinead, but she was already lost in the descending night. He hoped she had already dried the tears and had gone.

CHAPTER 8

It was around first light on what looked like being a filthy day when the sonar operator aboard the frigate H.M.S. *Juno* picked up the fleeting echo. It was just as likely to be a shoal of cod as a 1,000-ton U-boat, he thought, but his was not to reason why. He informed the officer of the watch, a punctilious if unimaginative youth from Yeovil, a former corporate clerk made lieutenant who did everything by the book. The young officer had no hesitation in deciding to wake the captain; it was his first tour of duty as officer of the watch, and he was already mightily frustrated that the war would almost certainly be over before he had a chance to lob a depth charge in anger and play his own role in the annihilation of Hitler. He had no desire to add to that frustration by getting caught out, so he pulled his naval cap more firmly over his head, and blew down the voice pipe.

The captain didn't complain; he was too professional for that, but the croak in his voice betrayed the fatigue. They had just finished a particularly rough passage from the Arctic, and were about to finish a far longer war, and somehow the adrenaline wasn't pumping in the way it used to. He hadn't been in home port for more than three months — none of them had — and to be ordered to turn around just a day out, and take up position counting whitecaps off Rockall tested the patience of everyone. Yet even the suggestion of a submarine still caused the turbines to turn and the blood to surge. Through tactics and technology, the Royal Navy had largely won the confrontation with the U-boat packs, yet no commander underestimated the potential and the toughness of any U-boat crew, particularly one that had survived this long. The captain was on the bridge in less than a minute.

"Report, Mr. Ansell."

"Fleeting echo, sir! Indicating northerly heading. Trace very faint — sonar's trying to pick it up again," the excited duty officer sputtered.

"Steady on, Mr. Ansell, you've got time to take a breath," the captain counseled. "Now, no chance of it being one of ours, heading back home to Scapa? Don't want us snapping after our own tails, you know."

"Definitely not, sir," came the reply in a tone of hurt pride. "No reports of ours in the area, I've double-checked. I've also alerted the other ships in our group."

"Very well. We'd better try and pick them up again. Yeoman, form on a line bearing 270° — course 030° — ships two thousand yards apart."

"Further instructions, sir?"

" 'Tally Ho!,' Mr. Ansell. 'Tally Ho!' "

* * *

In the monochrome light that flooded U-494, the crewmen seemed already to be wearing death masks. There was a weariness about them even the tension couldn't disperse. Hencke discovered the crew had returned to Kiel after a grueling tour of duty in the waters of the Bay of Biscay, torpedo tubes empty, one victim claimed, nerves shattered and duty done, the crew desperately hoping that this was the end of their war, when they'd received orders to sail immediately for Ireland. They hadn't even finished handing over their craft to the maintenance crew before they were instructed to refuel and were turned around; many of the crew hadn't had the chance to set foot on shore. The days without sunlight, breathing air contaminated by diesel fumes, listening to the monotonous, maddening drip of condensation, having had no bath in fresh water for weeks, watching the food gradually mould, all left their marks on the faces of the submariners. They were haggard, bearded, dirty and scared. They had been ordered back to sea on a Friday, the thirteenth of April, and that was as bad a sign as an albatross building its nest in the conning tower.

Early on the first day out from Ireland they had been brushed by the tentacles of enemy sonar, but a sharp change of course seemed to have thrown that off. Perhaps they hadn't been noticed at all. On a normal patrol they would have taken a wide sweep round the Faeroes, to avoid their notorious minefields, before heading into the North Sea, but nothing was normal on this patrol. They had orders to take the short cut and risk the mines. It would save time. It might make them crab meat. But it also seemed to have fooled their pursuers. When finally they broke away from British coastal waters and into the North Sea the crew was allowed in pairs onto the conning tower bridge for a taste of night air, to recover from the putrid atmosphere created by the tension.

Eling had wanted to head for one of the U-boat bases in German-occupied Norway, or even one of the isolated fjords along the Scandinavian coast, but his suggestion had been rejected. The High Command didn't want Hencke in some distant outpost of the Reich, where their control was all but shot to hell, and with local resistance fighters crawling out from behind every rock. They wanted Hencke home, in Germany. Eling's orders were specific about that. So once in the North Sea they proceeded south, risking the surface by night, submerged by day, and hugging the deep trench off the coast of Norway where the darkest, safest waters of the North Sea were to be found. But they couldn't stay in the depths forever. Sometime, sometime soon, they would have to make a break for it.

"Then we're really going to find out how good a sailor our captain is," one veteran spat. "No torpedoes, no air cover, that stupid *Scheisskerl* Goebbels having told the entire fucking world what we're up to . . . Going to be a ride to remember, this one."

"To where?" Hencke had asked.

"Kiel. Wilhelmshaven. Bremen. Probably to Hell. Wherever's open. And if not . . . as close as we can get."

"He'll get us home? The captain'll get us home?" The voice belonged to a young sailor, on his first patrol, whose features had already been aged by the experience and the pale light as he sat in the shadows of empty torpedo racks.

The veteran offered no reply, preferring to study the dirt in his fingernails.

"I don't want to die," the youth continued. His words lacked pathos; he was making a statement of fact rather than a plea of self-pity.

"No one wants to die, you unwashed idiot. We don't get any choice in the matter," the veteran responded. His words were sharp, but his tone understanding.

"But not yet. Please God, not yet. I . . . I haven't even had a woman," he said. He was struggling hard to control the tremor in his voice, wanting to share. "I had it all planned for when we got back to port. A shower. A beer. Then a woman. I had it all arranged . . ."

"Shit, you'd deserve an Iron Cross after going with one of those raddled old whores. They say they've had the clap so many times it's incurable, nothing can touch it. The Bremerhaven burn. Rotten way to go."

It was coarse but not intended to be callous; the young seaman was now worrying about something other than dying at the bottom of the ocean, and anything was better than that.

"And what is it that you're so willing to die for, Hencke?" the veteran prompted, wiping the sweat from his brow with an oily rag.

"What makes you think I'm so eager?"

"You're going back, aren't you?"

"Only if you are."

"I didn't get a choice in the matter."

"Somehow war seems to take our choices and tear them into a thousand tiny pieces."

The veteran looked at Hencke caustically. He wasn't in the mood for someone who talked in poetic riddles. He turned back to his young companion, his thoughts wandering off to their favorite hunting grounds. "When we get back, son, I'll take you to a proper place, not one of those crab-infested whorehouses you'd end up in. A proper place, with real women, who understand what pleases a man. If you're going to die, that's the place to do it. A long, slow afternoon's screwing with some gorgeous blonde who knows what she's doing, her lips all over you, the fire stoking up inside you, then one great, fantastic explosion — and it's all over. What a way to go!"

"So we *are* going to get back, you think?" the youth asked eagerly.

Once again, the veteran didn't reply but the insistent question disturbed him. He wiped his hands vigorously on the rag, trying to rid himself of the frustration building up inside him, but no matter how hard he wiped it didn't work. His hands got grimier, his frustration grew. He threw the cloth impatiently into a far corner of the torpedo room and turned on the unwanted guest. "What the hell are you doing here, Hencke?"

Hencke looked at the anger in the other man's eyes. "Don't you want to get back to Germany?"

"You must be a brave man, braver than I am to want to go back. Or mad, like a lunatic trying to get back into the asylum. Maybe you've been away too long and simply don't know what a bedlam our beloved Reich's turned into," he continued bitterly. "Each time we come back from a patrol everything's changed again. The buildings and bars you used to know have gone, half your friends dead or disappeared, nothing works anymore. You try to find out if your family is still alive, but it can take you days to do that, by which time you're out to sea again on another patrol. The orders get crazier, the odds get more ridiculous, half the damned torpedoes won't fire, while the medals on the chests of those shit-eating Nazis get bigger and bigger. That's not the Germany that I signed up to defend!"

"But it's home, the only home you've got."

"And we were there! A spit away from dry land. It would have been the end of the war for us. Then *you* came along. If it weren't for the fact that we're *Kriegsmarine* and we'd follow the captain to the other side of damnation, you'd still be sitting on some potato pile in Ireland and we'd both be on our backs getting laid." He shook his head bitterly. "I really wish you weren't here, Hencke."

"Don't expect me to apologize. I didn't ask to be here either."

"I don't want an apology, I don't want anything from you.

All I want is half a chance of getting out of this tin can alive, and you can't give me that."

Before he could continue, all conversation throughout the boat came to a stop. The submarine had changed course; it was noticeably bow-up — beginning to ascend. They were climbing out of the depths. Heading home.

"Message from Admiralty. They've established contact."

Churchill looked up from his chair in the Library. He had been in there an hour on his own, surrounded by the great men and events of history, wanting to be in touch, to draw strength, feeling at home among the memories. He had asked not to be disturbed unless it was important, and Cazolet knew that this was important. Yet the Old Man appeared not to have heard him. He sat in the light of a single green-topped table lamp, poring through the pages of an old book bound in cracked leather.

"Carlyle," he explained. *"History of Frederick the Great.* D'you know, Hitler is a devout follower of the old Prussian king. Almost mystical about him. Thought I might find some clues, some insight."

"And . . . ?"

"Frederick waged war against all his neighbors, his armies rampaged throughout the land. He won great victories yet he reduced Prussia to poverty and starvation. And he took off his boots only once a year — on his wife's birthday."

"So what clues do you find in that?"

"None, dear boy. Absolutely none. But there is more. There came a time, in the middle of a long winter, when he found himself surrounded by a great coalition of his enemies. Winter of '62 — 1762. There appeared to be no salvation. Frederick himself was besieged in Berlin and considering taking poison, so desperate stood his cause."

"That does sound familiar."

"But then, *then* the miracle happened. At the height of his peril, his enemy the Czarina died, the great coalition ranged against him fell apart, and the sun shone on his endeavors once more."

"A fairy tale."

Churchill shook his head as though it were a huge effort, weighed down by nearly two centuries of history. "It means I was right. He will never give in, Willie. He will live in hope of salvation until the day he dies. And this war will not stop until Hitler is dead. He will put his trust in ghosts rather than those who would urge him to give in, to bring the slaughter to an end. It must be by his death, Willie. Nothing else will do." Churchill closed the book reverently, as if closing the pages on his own life. "He'll never leave Berlin. Eisenhower was quite wrong to worry. If only . . ."

He couldn't finish, he didn't have to, not for Cazolet, not any more. Cazolet knew, shared the pain. And the guilt. There was a long period of silence between the two men.

"The submarine. They've made contact with the submarine," Cazolet began again, but Churchill was waving his hand to cut him off.

"No, Willie. No more reports. Not until it's all over."

As Cazolet left he could see the tears back in Churchill's eyes.

There was neither time nor opportunity for finesse. The odds against them were overwhelming. There was little opportunity for surprise, and the forces crisscrossing the sea and skies above them would react quickly and expertly, as they had learned to do in grinding the once insuperable *Kriegsmarine* into defeat. They would have only one moment in which to grasp the initiative; after that it would be simply a matter of time and great torment before their luck finally ran out.

The plan was simple, for simplicity is born of desperation. The captain had explained it to every man in the crew over the intercom. "We've come this far together; you have a right to know what to expect." They would be rendezvousing with the two other U-boats — if they weren't already at the bottom of the North Sea — just off the southern coast of Norway. It was Germany's doorstep; there was no other route home, and that's where the British forces would be waiting. At first contact the two other boats would go to full speed and head south and west, crossing wakes to make false echoes which might confuse the enemy, while U-494 slipped slowly south-south-east through the small hole in the net which the other boats had torn, hoping to get away before the deception was discovered, and the hole was closed, and their last chance gone. It was suicide, of course, probably for all three craft, and certainly for the two decoys, but the fear was not new. Scarcely one in ten of their colleagues with whom they had started the war was still alive. They had been living on borrowed time for as long as any of them could remember.

U-494 hung back, electric motors turning the screws slowly, allowing her sisters to make the running and to drag off the cover. They were blind but for hydrophones, eighty feet down; but sound travels a long way under water, and the hydrophone operator could follow the trail of battle as clearly as if he were a spectator in the arena. It began with the thump of screws as the two sister ships began forcing their way through the cold waters of the North Sea, followed only minutes later by the high-speed whine of surface turbines, alerted by their own hydrophones, and giving chase like greyhounds in the slips. The first submarine could be heard zigzagging, changing course, trying to find shelter in the underwater thermoclines, which might hide and confuse the pursuers. But soon they could hear the *crump* of falling depth charges. You didn't need a hydrophone to pick up their unmistakable sound. That was when U-494 began to put on a little speed, hiding behind the noise of battle, slipping through the gap they hoped had been torn in the defenses.

There was nothing for Hencke to do, there was nothing for anyone to do, but pray. He tried to concentrate on distractions, even embracing his memories to stave off the fear and the tomb-like claustrophobia, while the sweat poured down his face and splashed onto the bare metal plates beneath his feet.

The second submarine was being attacked now, but all the time the sound of combat was drifting farther away. And still no one had picked them up.

"God help those poor bastards," the veteran muttered through clenched teeth as the cacophony of underwater explosions increased.

"But save a little for us," whispered the youth.

In the control room the hydrophone operator was reporting the action of battle. "Submarine engines stopped . . . can't tell whether they've been hit or are trying to shake them off . . . more depth charges . . . engines started again at full speed . . . more depth charges, there seem to be at least three of the bastards circling above . . ." He tried to clear the grit from his voice and swallowed his words along with it. But there was little need for his commentary; every man on board could hear the steady, insistent clamor of depth charges far away. When at last he looked up at the captain, his anguish told the story. The U-boat had been hit. Its race was nearing its end. "Sounds like one of the engines has stopped . . . tanks being blown . . . they're trying for the surface but . . ." He could hear the futile, ragged whine of the U-boat's screw, more depth charges dropping on and around the stricken craft and, with an awesome finality, the sound of the pressure hull being crushed. He shook his head.

"OK," cut in Captain Eling. "Time to get out of here. Bring her up to snorkel height and engines to full!" he commanded.

The air-breathing snorkel broke surface, allowing the powerful diesels to kick in, and there was an immediate surge of power as the *Diesel Obermaschinist* threw the lever that poured fuel down the throats of the engines. There was a pounding from the propeller shafts, the boat vibrated, even the crockery rattled. The pretense was over.

Eling flicked a switch above his head and spoke into a mouthpiece. "This is the Captain. U-909 is gone." A slight pause. "Good luck to you all."

"You marvelous diesel-brained idiot!" the hydrophone operator exclaimed. "Oesten's boat. He's making enough noise to wake the *Bismarck!*" He bit his lip to control his uncharacteristic excitement. "He's doubled back, bearing north-west."

The captain had grabbed the hydrophone headset, listening for himself. "He's trying to draw them off and give us as much cover as he can," he said, sharing with the rest of the crew. But quickly he grew silent as, above, the sacrifice was offered up and greedily accepted. Eventually he muttered between clenched teeth, "They're on to him, caught him in their sonar. Two, maybe three of them." The *crump* of depth charges was faint in the distance, scarcely audible above the sound of the stretched engines. More minutes passed, until he had heard enough. Reluctantly he handed the headset back to the hydrophone operator, and moved across to the intercom. "Gentlemen, we're on our own now."

They had no time to grieve. It was precisely four seconds later when they heard the sound of sonar *ping*ing across the steel hull of their craft, reaching out for them, grabbing at them, pouring ice into their hearts.

Josef Goebbels sat stroking the blonde hair of his youngest child, Heidi, not yet six. She had fallen asleep in his arms as he told stories of fiery dragons and shining knights, and she lay with a look of sublime peace, oblivious to the noise. Across the room her five brothers and sisters, directed by the eldest, Helga, were singing to the accompaniment of an accordion, and as their treble voices rose higher and higher the faces of their parents glowed with pride. The mood of celebration was being matched at many points around the bunker and Reich Chancellery, although nowhere with such simplicity or innocence.

"They sing like angels," he whispered.

"Didn't you once write that children were the bright ideas of God?"

He looked up to share a momentary smile with his wife, a rare event nowadays. They had long since ceased sharing anything of personal value, beyond the children. And their devotion to the Fuehrer. It was that which had kept them together — or, more accurately, his explicit refusal to allow them to part and his instructions to continue with their hollow form of marriage. He couldn't afford a public scandal among the Party leadership. So their spats and screaming abuse and infidelities had been covered up — after all, who better than the Minister of Propaganda to ensure not only what was printed, but what was left out of the newspapers. It had always been an unlikely alliance, the diminutive stump-legged academic with the crooked teeth, pinched face and a body which looked as if it had been squeezed in a vise, matched against the highly-strung society beauty in expensive silks from the finest Italian couturière. But there were the children, it hadn't all been wasted.

"Josef, there can be no doubt, can there?"

They broke off to join in the singing of the chorus before he answered her.

"No, Magda. I heard it myself on the BBC, and the news has been repeated for several hours. The American radio is playing solemn military music. There's no shred of doubt. Roosevelt is dead."

"The Fuehrer is so happy, and I am so happy for him . . ."

Goebbels had heard the news driving back from an inspection of the front. He had immediately telephoned the Fuehrer, only to discover Magda already with him, celebrating. She often saw as much of the Fuehrer as he did, and had always had a more personal relationship. Again, as he had many times over the years, he wondered whether they had been lovers. He had once overheard an adjutant in the Reich Chancellery joking that he could hear Magda's ovaries clanging every time she entered the same room as the Fuehrer. Goebbels had the adjutant posted to the Russian front, but he couldn't dispose of his own suspicions so easily. On another occasion she had come back from one of the intimate tea parties — just the Fuehrer with Magda and one of the secretaries — and she had been flushed with pleasure and physical energy. She had insisted they make love, and had been drenched in her own excitement before she had even taken off her clothes. And she had always been viciously jealous of Eva Braun.

But, no, decided Goebbels, it was probably not so, just an affair that had never grown beyond the idea and the wish. In any case, what did it really matter, when he and the Fuehrer were building the greatest Reich Europe had ever known and when, at their desperate hour of need, fate was once again smiling on them?

"It is a sign, I'm sure," he continued. "Roosevelt choking on all the blood he's spilled. And Hencke, a German hero about to become folk legend, on his way home. Death and Deliverance, the two mightiest weapons of war, all at once thrust into our hands."

He looked at his wife. She was no longer the beauty he had married; the war and childbearing had taken their toll on her nerves, which had never been robust. The pencil-thin eyebrows were now just other lines on her face, the soft hair that had lain on so many pillows was dull and brittle, and the lips had begun to sag. They had all of them become old and wrinkled, of course, but somehow in women it carried less well. No, if *Der Chef* wanted her, he was welcome to her.

"What was the Fuehrer doing when you left him?" Goebbels inquired, as the children struck up a new tune and Heidi stirred. He placed a gentle finger on her lips to soothe her back to sleep.

"He was reading a book," his wife replied. "Something about Frederick the Great, I think . . ."

They were almost home. Only a few hours' sailing from the safety of the mainland and its air cover, when the final bombardment began. They had been fortunate up to that point, driven along by the twin screws and their fear, every change in sea temperature and salinity confusing the enemy sonar, throwing the pack off-balance for a few miles more, slowly eating up the distance between themselves and home. Somehow they had survived, the screws had kept turning, and for a couple of hours they had thought the sacrifice of their compatriots might be enough. But, deep down, they had always known it was hopeless. They couldn't elude the most experienced sub-hunters in the world, not forever. The nearer they got to home, the shallower the seas, the closer they were forced to the surface, and so their last hiding place disappeared.

The captain had ordered both engines to low revs, in order to kill any trace of noise from the submarine, but U-494 had been caught in coastal waters, with nowhere to run. Their hunters were getting closer, the insistent noise of sonar mixed with the thumping of turbines and propeller wash, to form a cocktail of madness which each submariner feared would strip him of his courage and make him run screaming through the craft. But no one did — this was Eling's crew. So they waited to die. There was a crescendo of noise, a lip bitten to flesh, and the hunters were overhead and past. A whispered prayer. Could they have missed? For a moment without end there was stillness. As one, the crew took a sharp inward breath, knowing it might be the last. Instinctively, hands reached out for support, a stanchion, a pipe, an instrument panel, anything that might brace them and help guard against the blow. Then it struck.

Hencke was thrown aside and his arms all but wrenched from their sockets as two hundred fifty pounds of amatol exploded twenty feet above the rear torpedo compartment, forcing the stern down savagely toward the bottom of the North Sea.

"It's OK," shouted the veteran, clinging to a bed frame. "Most of the force goes upward. It's when they explode underneath that you kiss your ring goodbye . . ."

But already, above the relentless and chaotic singing of sonar, they could hear the splashing of further depth charges being thrown at them. And in spite of the captain's maneuvering they were getting closer. Hencke heard one canister bounce off the outer hull with a dull echo, as though someone were knocking on a coffin lid. They were at 93 meters. The depth charge was set for 105. It detonated directly beneath U-494's engine compartment. Even so most of the plates and valves held, but at 93 meters most isn't good enough. The blast caused the craft to heel violently, ripping away Hencke's purchase on the torpedo rack and lifting him bodily, before throwing him across the oily floor. Dials shattered and bulbs smashed as the pressure hull bent inward, plunging the craft into complete darkness, and there was a ringing in his head so loud that for a moment it was beyond his brain's ability to comprehend. His ears felt as if someone were trying to drive six-inch nails into them. When the auxiliary lights flickered on, he found himself staring at the lifeless eyes of the young submariner, blood trickling slowly from the corner of his lips, from his nose, and from his ears.

In the control room a few yards away he could hear the

captain screaming for a damage report; feet began to pound along aluminum gangways; from above came the fading noise of the hunter completing its first pass. But there was another sound, as unmistakable as it was insistent. The sound of the craft dying. The savage hissing of gas escaping under pressure from somewhere nearby, the crackle of flame as smoke billowed from a control panel where the electrical circuit had shorted out, the explosive sound of bolts shearing, a raised voice reporting irreparable damage to two hull valves, mingling with the cries of the injured and the hammering of tools on paralyzed controls. And beneath his feet Hencke could hear the terrifying noise of water beginning to slop its way through the bilges.

But he could hear no shouts of terror and panic, as he might have supposed. Instead there were only shouts of instruction and command as the submariners, fear tempered by years of experience and discipline, scurried to salvage their crippled craft. Men began hurtling like acrobats along the gangways and through the small circular hatchways, there was the sound of banging metal as leaking seals were retightened and closed, and within seconds he could hear the drubbing of hammer on wood and steel as a team struggled to shore up buckled plates and stem the flood. Already the water was bubbling above the metal floor grille on which he was standing, and the submarine had adopted a strange, unnatural posture, leaning to one side. Then another lurch, gentler this time, accompanied by the sound of compressed air being forced into the tanks as the screws beat desperately to gain purchase and force the submarine upward, but the hydroplanes had gone.

For an agonizing time the boat seemed to hang suspended as the upward thrust of the engines was canceled out by the weight of water pouring into the hull. Hencke's lungs were frozen, his body was no longer his possession and belonged to some other entity that was deciding his fate. And it seemed to be an age making up its mind. Slowly, imperceptibly at first, then with painfully increasing confidence, the craft gained stability as the nose of the boat forced its way upward. They were going to make it after all! The tension in Hencke collapsed and he began to breathe in deep relief, but he saw the veteran still clinging like a man possessed to the bed frame. He was shaking his head. He knew what was yet to come.

Perhaps the captain of the frigate was a touch too eager. Had he waited a few seconds longer there could have been no doubt; but, in his anxiety to ram the submarine, he hit her just before she was fully surfaced. The bow sliced across the forward hull, tearing a great gash, but the submarine bounced rather than being ripped instantly in two. She would die, of course, but slowly rather than in a moment.

Through the pandemonium Hencke could feel the craft rapidly beginning to settle, bow-down. And still the water rose, up to his calf now, pulling at him and the others, trying to drag them under.

A face forced its way through the hatch that led from the control room. It was a sub-lieutenant, with blood running from a gash on his forehead.

"Hencke to the control room!" he screamed. "And secure all watertight doors!"

So that was it. The bulkheads were being sealed, the six compartments, around which U-494 was built, were being shut off from each other, transformed into their own private coffins. The most experienced hands prayed she would flood quickly and put an end to their inevitable agonies, the less experienced with their naive hopes of survival hoped it might flood more slowly, but everyone knew it was only a matter of time. Yet still the order of duty and command prevailed. The veteran grabbed Hencke by the arm and thrust him toward the hatch. Unceremoniously he was bundled through, smacking his head against some sharp metal edge, and as he picked himself up and turned he could see the veteran about to close the bulkhead door, with water already beginning to spill over the sill. The submariner's eyes were raging with anger.

"I wish to God you hadn't come," he swore.

Then the steel door slammed shut, the wheel securing the watertight seal was being turned, and he saw the veteran no more.

Inside the crowded control room Eling was standing by the intercom, barking instructions, eyes fixed on the dials and gauges as he listened to replies. But already he was giving instructions to sections of the boat from which no reply was forthcoming. As the chief engineer shouted in his ear that both aft torpedo hatches were flooding, water began seeping down an instrument panel and there was the unmistakable sound of the electric motors complaining, complaining again, and falling silent.

"Engine room! Report!" Eling shouted into the mouthpiece, but there was no response. He looked imploringly at the chief who stood soaked in a torn singlet beside the far watertight door, shaking his head.

With the dying of the engines and the closing of the hatches, a relative quiet descended over the craft. Metal was still pounding against metal in a distant forward compartment, but soon that also stopped. The craft was settling nose-down in the water, and they listened to the submarine's death throes. A groan here, a creak there, the crying of tortured metal, the cracking of the internal wood fascias as they buckled and split, and always the slow, deadly sound of gurgling water. But from the crew there was only silence, the silence of men fallen to despair. The captain's gaze was fixed unblinkingly on the depth gauge, watching its hypnotic fall, great beads of perspiration trickling down his forehead. Then there was a heavy bump, hands once again reached out for support, and the submarine settled on the bottom.

The captain tapped the gauge. "One hundred twenty meters," he announced, his eyes glazing. "Could be worse . . ." There was silence as everyone calculated the odds. "Chief! Damage report," the captain instructed.

"Engines dead, rear compartments flooded. I can't raise the forward torpedo compartment. The bilges are flooding, so the batteries are gone, and if they've not yet drowned they'll be choking on chlorine gas in next to no time . . . Sorry, Captain," the chief apologized as Eling's stare gave him silent rebuke. This was still the *Kriegsmarine*, and there was a proper way to die. "The control room is the only watertight compartment. For now."

"How many men do we know for sure are still alive?"

"Just what you see, Captain." It made a total of fourteen. Fourteen out of fifty. No, out of a hundred and fifty.

"Looks like we have them surrounded, eh?" Eling said grimly. He turned to Hencke. "I'm sorry, Hencke. It seems we failed. I've got a dead craft and fourteen men left. As far as we can tell all other compartments are flooded, which means that anyone behind those doors is already dead. I *am* sorry."

Hencke marveled at this man who had been ordered to sacrifice his craft and most of his crew in order to bring one passenger home, yet who still felt the need to apologize.

"Is there anything to be done?" Hencke was surprised at how calm his voice sounded, betraying none of the turmoil and twisted nerves within.

Before Eling could answer, from no great distance away came the echoing sound of an explosion, not a depth charge but something big. A grim smile of satisfaction flickered around the captain's mouth. "So the dying's not yet done, and maybe the surviving too . . . That was a mine. One of ours. Ripping the bottom out of a ship. One of theirs. I took us into a minefield," he explained. "Seems to have paid off."

"What will happen now?"

"They'll have trouble locating us on the bottom with all the junk and other wrecks around here. And now they've lost one of their own . . . ?" He shrugged. "They'll probably call it a day. They won't want to thrash around in a minefield, particularly when they know there's a ninety-five percent probability they've sunk us already."

As if in confirmation, from nearby came the explosion of a clutch of depth charges, one final gesture from the Royal Navy, planted along the huge oil slick which was forming on the surface and which they hoped marked the tomb of another U-boat. One for luck, and farewell. The violent rocking cast the craft into darkness yet again, and when at last some source of light was restored, even the rueful smile which the captain had managed to manufacture had been wiped away.

"Further damage report, Chief! Chief?"

But the chief did not respond. He was staring transfixed at the cabinet where the emergency breathing gear was kept. "They're gone. There's not a single one left . . ." And with those words, each man knew, had disappeared their last chance of survival. The chief turned in desperation toward the captain. "The maintenance crew, at Kiel. They were stripping the boat down for overhaul, started here in the control room. They were unloading everything. Then we got orders to turn around, I threw them straight off board . . ."

No one spoke. What was there to say? In spite of the angry looks cast in his direction, it wasn't the chief's fault. On arrival in Kiel after weeks at sea they hadn't even had time to break wind, let alone check stores, before they were ordered back out to sea. How could anyone have reckoned on some half-witted fitter forgetting to replace the breathing gear? On all the emergency supplies in other compartments being cut off behind flooded bulkheads? On being caught out playing taxi at the bottom of the North Sea?

As the silence dragged on, Hencke could feel the eyes of some of the crew, particularly the younger ones, latching on to him, piercing him with accusation. The one who had brought them here. The one who had caused all this. The passenger . . .

"Do we have any prospects?" he asked the captain.

"Staying here and slowly choking to death," responded Eling grimly. "Or trying to escape without breathing apparatus from one hundred twenty meters and probably drowning. Take your pick."

"It's no fun dying slowly, Captain."

"I do so agree." He gave a small Prussian nod of respect. At least the bastard wasn't panicking and screaming his head off; Eling couldn't have stood that. "So. We make ready to abandon ship! Chief. Chief, where . . . ?"

The chief had disappeared head first through a service hatch in the floor. When he hauled himself back up he was coughing, and his eyes were full of terror. "Chlorine!" he gasped. "Chlorine!"

Sea water was leaking into the huge batteries that powered the electric motors. The result was a chemical reaction that produced a gas as deadly as that found in any trench of the First War. And it was seeping uncontrollably around them.

"For God's sake flood the compartment and let's get out of here," pleaded one of the younger ratings.

"Can't," the chief sputtered. "Won't be able to open the hatch until the air pressure inside has equaled the water pressure outside. One hundred twenty meters. At that pressure the concentration of chlorine in the lungs will kill us in seconds."

"But it'll kill us anyway!" the rating responded. "We stay, we die. We try to leave, we die. What have you done to us,

Chief?" The edge of desperation in his voice was beginning to infect the others around him. It wouldn't be long before there was a general outpouring of panic which would overwhelm them all.

"There's one chance." It was Eling who spoke, very quietly, to reassert his authority. "One chance, perhaps. Above our heads in the conning tower. There's room for one man. We close the hatch between the control room and conning tower, he floods the conning tower like an escape chamber, he opens the exterior hatch, and escapes."

"But what about the rest of us?" pressed a petty officer.

The chief interjected, desperate to offer hopeful tidings for a change. "The first man closes the exterior hatch from the outside, we drain the conning tower, we do it all over again. Fourteen times." But he didn't sound as if he had convinced even himself.

"No, Chief. It won't work. Not at one hundred twenty meters." It was Eling. "In order to shut the hatch from the outside he'd use up so much oxygen he'd never make it to the surface. If he forgets about closing the hatch he's got a chance. A small one. One man. That's it, and that's all of it." A stillness of crushed hopes and despondency settled among the men. "I'm sorry, gentlemen," Eling continued. "You deserve to know."

"So which of us is it to be?" a voice inquired.

"Not I," stated the captain.

"Nor I," whispered the chief.

"Then who?" insisted the petty officer. "Who's going to play God and decide which one of us gets it?"

"*Meine Herren,*" Eling commanded sharply. "If there has to be an end, let us make it a good one, one worthy of the *Kriegsmarine.*"

"I've got a wife and five children," the petty officer said. "My end is no bloody use to them, good or otherwise."

"You knew what your fate would be when you started on this war. The only thing you didn't know was how or when," the captain responded, staring into their eyes. "So — now you do."

"But who is to get the chance? I've got five children too . . ." another seaman lied.

"Let's draw lots," another suggested.

"Call yourselves submariners," the wretched chief engineer cried, almost in tears. "Flood the whole damn boat and let's get it over with!" He lunged for a valve.

"No!" Eling instructed. "Chief — *take your hands away!*"

The chief looked at his captain through red eyes, and slowly withdrew. There was still too much discipline in him, he couldn't refuse his commanding officer, not at the last, not after all this time.

"I cannot play God," Eling continued in a low voice, forcing them to listen in silence, "but in the *Kriegsmarine* we don't rely on luck or divine intervention, certainly not on the wisdom of our political leaders, but on *duty*. You've all followed that sense of duty from the moment you stepped on board this submarine, and that's what has got us this far. Through the ice pack off Murmansk. And the convoy escorts off the Azores. And back to homeport time and again when other U-boats weren't so lucky. So our luck's run out. But we are still submariners! We started this mission with orders to do everything we could to get this man" — he waved at Hencke — "back home. We still have those orders. You all know who should get the chance."

"His life means we all die," the rating said.

"Whoever gets out, the rest of us are going to die. Our only choice is whether we die like men or like rats. Not much of a choice, I agree. But it's the only one we've got."

No one moved. It was the truth, they knew it, but no one wanted to accept it. Surely there was some other way? Then the chief stepped forward and stood by the conning tower hatch. He offered the captain a crisp salute. In turn, the captain faced slowly toward Hencke. He had bloodshot eyes; Hencke could see close up that he was scared.

"Do one thing for me, Hencke. Just get back. Make all this worthwhile."

Hencke nodded. He said nothing; words would have been inadequate, even insulting. He placed his foot on the first rung of the ladder into the conning tower and began to climb, assisted by one of the men.

As he disappeared what was left of Eling's crew came to attention as the captain barked the final order, "Chief. Secure the hatch!"

"Thanks for agreeing to see me at such short notice." Eisenhower's hand shot out from a crisp cuff and grasped the pudgy fingers extended toward him at the door of Number 10 Downing Street.

"Your visit comes as a welcome distraction, General — particularly when the matter sounded of such urgency." Churchill led the way across the famous threshold, trailing cigar smoke. "I have to admit, now our armies are ploughing remorselessly through the remnants of the Wehrmacht, that time seems to hang heavy. Not so long ago — do you remember when we were planning the invasion of Europe together? — every hour seemed filled with suspense and the need to take mighty decisions. Today I find that matters for my attention are brought to me not by great commanders bearing brave ideas, but by bureaucrats who bear nothing but endless mountains of paper. I do battle with what they call postwar projections. It is an unappetizing struggle." There was a weariness in the Old Man's voice, an emptiness inside where once excitement and intrigue had burned.

He set a desultory pace as Eisenhower followed him into the secluded garden, where the mellow red-brick wall was covered with climbing plants, and the lawn liberally sprinkled with daffodils and early tulips in abundant bloom. The cherry tree would soon be in blossom, encouraged by the unseasonably warm sunshine. Churchill had put on a floppy Panama hat which he used while painting, to guard against the sun, and beside the cherry tree stood a table with comfortable wicker chairs and two large china cups.

"And coffee. Scalding hot. Just as you like it," Churchill commented as a secretary brought out a steaming jug to stand beside one of the cups. It was accompanied by a more modest pot of what Eisenhower concluded could only be that piss-tasting English tea. They busied themselves with the formalities of pouring and stirring, using courtesies to avoid serious discussion. It was the first time they had met, even spoken directly, since that morning above Xanten; both were taking care not to scratch at half-healed wounds. It was only when they had settled and the wicker creaked and complained beneath them that Churchill decided the time had come.

"Your message was intriguing, General. "Face to face . . . not to be entrusted to any other means of communication." I have to admit that I have turned every corner of my mind to discover what could be of such magnitude as to bring you hurrying here, but to no end."

Eisenhower sipped his coffee carefully, watching over the rim of the cup as Churchill slurped away unselfconsciously, wiping a dribble of tea from his chin with the back of his hand. He waited until Churchill had replaced his cup in the saucer.

"It's about Berlin. And the redoubt. I felt I had to come and tell you personally."

The Old Man's eyes were instantly alert, the glaze of weariness gone. They reflected disquiet, and anger. The hurt of their last encounter had not yet died, but he said nothing, waiting.

"You know, I've been a military man all my life," Eisenhower continued as though telling tales around a fireside. "And I'm pretty damn good at it — one of the best. But the military is all about manpower and firepower and beating all kinds of hell out of the other guy's army, and how you do it is almost secondary. That's why I've never been able to understand why you seemed so . . . passionate about getting to Berlin and rejoicing in the ruins."

Churchill was about to intervene to protest that he had never described his ambitions in those terms, but held back. He wanted to hear what Eisenhower was trying to say. Anyway, it was true.

"But I've begun to realize that in one sense you were right. You can't judge an enemy solely by the size of the barrel he's got pointing at you. There are more ways to die in war than simply getting blown to pieces . . ." The folksiness was gone, a sadness crept into his voice. "You know the reports we've been getting out of Poland of camps full of prisoners and bodies? I don't know about you; I always treated the reports with a touch of caution. Those camps weren't military targets, they didn't affect the way the war was being fought. Anyway, there was always the suspicion they were exaggerated by Stalin's propaganda machine. Deep down, perhaps I didn't want to believe."

"The reports have been insistent, and growing in frequency. I dread to imagine what we might discover when the final curtain is drawn back on the Nazi stage."

"No need to imagine any more. Four days ago I went to a place called Ohrdruf Nord, just outside Gotha, which we captured last week. The local divisional commander called me direct. Said I must come. He was almost in tears. Believe me, it's all true and more." He moistened his lips, his mouth felt parched, like the taste of vomit not yet gone. "I saw bodies lined up in great avenues, hundreds of them, stacked one upon the other, just cast-off pieces of bone and skin lying out in the open waiting to be burned. Men, women, even children. The scale of what has happened passed anything I could comprehend. I thought they had brought me to the gates of hell, yet by the day we are discovering more camps, places like Buchenwald and Belsen. As we drive deeper into Germany they're getting bigger and far, far worse. Seems the Germans are running out of time and furnaces to cover their tracks, they simply can't dispose of that many corpses quickly enough . . ."

He was sitting tensely on the edge of his chair, leaning forward across the table, his voice flat and deliberately unemotional. But, as the general had raised the ghosts of his visit, Churchill saw the color drain from his face.

"So I don't need any more lessons about war being more than just military objectives. Now I understand your passion. There's no man alive who wants so much to dance on that bastard's grave, and if it meant leading a column to Berlin myself and digging the hole with my bare hands, I'd do it!"

"But I'll warrant you haven't come here to offer me second-in-command of this hypothetical column."

The American shook his head. "Nothing would give me greater pleasure. I can tell you with all my heart that I haven't cared for the . . . misunderstandings which have come between us recently. We shared so much in the months we were planning the campaigns in North Africa and Europe together. I had come to regard you as a close friend."

"You were right to do so, General." There was a determined set to Churchill's jaw as he contemplated what he might say next. He was still battling inside with his pride. "This seems to be a moment for honesty. Well, let us not dance in shadows. We have had no 'misunderstandings,' as you put it — we have understood each other all too well. We have shared differences of opinion which were profound, and we both fought our cases hard. You have won, and I accept your victory with considerable regret. I fear that when Marshal Stalin gets hold of half of Europe, as he now certainly shall, it will be the prelude to a forest of concentration camps that will spring up through a long Siberian winter, and the peoples of Eastern Europe will have exchanged one terror for another. But the die is cast. In politics, as in life, we must move on."

Having conceded defeat as gracefully as he could, Churchill stopped to take a cigar from the flap pocket of the one-piece siren suit he had himself designed and worn almost every day throughout the war. He had worn it today largely out of nostalgia; the war was all but over, it would soon be time to dispatch such wartime trivia to the back of the closet.

Eisenhower leaned across to light the Old Man's cigar. "There's more."

"Thought there might be," Churchill muttered, still full of hurt. "Didn't have to come here to tell me yet again that I wasn't going to get Berlin." He was staring moodily into the flame that rose and fell as the tightly packed tobacco leaves began to smolder, his broad and upturned nose seeming to point at the General like an artillery piece made ready to fire.

Eisenhower's tone was as soft as his words were chilling. "When I said I'd lead a column to Berlin to dance on his grave, I meant it. But he's not going to be there."

The flame stopped dancing.

"The Germans have gathered all their leading atomic scientists in the Black Forest, just south of Stuttgart," Eisenhower continued. "They're also transporting a small pile of uranium and other supplies to facilities around Berchtesgaden."

"Dear Lord, is it really happening . . . ?"

"And worse than we ever thought. The Alpine redoubt a reality. Endless war. And Hitler with an atomic bomb."

Churchill sat silent as the word sank in.

"No one knows for sure how close they are to putting together a bomb, but sure as hell it doesn't look as if Hitler's ready to give up yet."

"Now I see why you came yourself." Churchill slumped back in his chair, cigar forgotten. "General, I must confess that when I contemplate what my scientists tell me about the power of the atomic bomb, I am filled with awe. I begin to believe the world is changing so fast and for such terrible ends that I no longer wish to play a part. Or perhaps I am no longer capable . . ." His head went back and he looked to the heavens. "Roosevelt gone. Hitler and Mussolini soon to follow. The French Republic swept away. Poland, the country for whom we went to war in the first place, practically ceased to exist . . . There is a tide of history and it seems to have turned against me." His words faded as he slumped back in his chair looking aged and vulnerable, like a discarded rag doll, a crumpled old man in a child's siren suit.

"Wouldn't be the first time, would it?" the general countered in a loud, belligerent voice. "I've lost count in recent weeks of how many times I've cursed and fretted, called you stubborn, cantankerous, cussed — and plenty of other things besides. You got in the way, held things up, went behind my back." His diction slowed to emphasize his words. *"But* . . . never once have I lost sight of the fact that if it hadn't been for you, and your infernal stubbornness and your mule-headed refusal to accept defeat, then this war would have been lost long before we Americans even got here. You talk about a tide of history. Well, there are some occasions when one man seems to stand his ground and just refuses to accept getting washed away. That's how we arrogant Americans won the New World. And that's how you, Mr. Churchill, have saved the Old World." He leaned over to grab the other man's hand, trying to rekindle the friendship and trust. "But for you, the whole of Europe would by now be one vast concentration camp. Nobody's ever going to forget that."

For a while Churchill continued to stare at the heavens, hiding the turmoil. When eventually his head came down his cheeks were moist. "Thank you, General." He nodded his gratitude, yet the eyes stared fierce and uncompromising, the bottom lip jutting forward. "But I was right about Berlin. You'll see."

"It would have been empty . . . deserted." Eisenhower threw his hands up in exasperation. "Hitler's not going to be there!"

"We should not have let him escape. Dealt with him, sir, like a mad dog! No mercy. No Fuehrer. No redoubt. No endless resistance. No bomb. And we would have had Berlin!"

The military man shook his head. "Kill him? Ridiculous."

"Why? We slaughter his armies freely enough."

"It would have been . . ." Eisenhower searched for the argument.

"Immoral?" There was no mistaking Churchill's impatience. He slurped his tea dismissively.

"Impractical. We never know precisely where Hitler is. Nothing we have could get through that much concrete. There's no way of getting at him, not even with a whole army of parachutists."

"Not an army. One man. On the inside."

"Be serious!" Eisenhower exclaimed in astonishment. He had tried, dammit he had tried, to bring the Old Man back on side, but the stubborn bastard wasn't prepared to give an inch. His hand slapped down, the coffee spilled, staining his trousers, but he did not notice. "Where in mother's name could you have got one man? On the inside . . . ?"

On the other side of the North Sea, on a spit of sand which before the war had been a favorite loitering place of North Germans seeking sun and relaxation, a figure, scarcely discernible in the pale moonlight, was washed up on the shore. For several minutes it made no movement except for the languorous waving of the legs in the receding tide. Then it coughed and threw up before starting to cough again. Slowly and with obvious pain the figure began to claw its way up the sandy beach to the dry dunes and to safety.

Peter Hencke was home.

PART THREE

CHAPTER 9

"War sets the stamp of nobility upon the peoples." He couldn't remember who had said it, the words were but a vague echo in his mind from one of the interminable pre-war wireless broadcasts. Nobility . . . He wondered how close the author could ever have got to the stench of battle. Never as close as this.

The journey from Hamburg to Berlin would normally have lasted only three hours, but already it had taken eight, and they had still another sixty miles to go. In many places the autobahn was impossibly cratered or blocked by ruined vehicles, and the stretches still open were being bombed and strafed regularly by British Mosquitoes. One moment they were forced to climb cautiously around potholes and piles of vehicular wreckage, the next maneuvering past the bloated, gas-filled carcasses of dead horses, frequently being left with no option but to leave the autobahn altogether for the side roads that ran through the towns scattered along the banks of the Elbe. It was there the journey became even more hazardous and disjointed as they encountered a flood tide of humanity streaming toward them. The whole of Germany seemed to be on the move, shuffling west, away from the advancing Russians, carrying with them what they could. In two hours Hencke reckoned they must have passed almost 100,000 refugees, old women pushing barrows laden with linen and decrepit husbands; lines of young girls, many barefoot, shuffling behind as they pushed prams or dragged carts; mothers struggling to carry wounded children who stared out of dirty bandages with enormous, frightened eyes. There were farm girls driving cows or pigs, or trying to round up stray chickens, women in fur coats covered with dirt, women in their best suits, women in rags and women in peasant costume still marked by the signs of toil on the land. But there were no men, at least none capable of walking, and there were precious few boys above the age of ten. They walked and stumbled, heads down, carrying whatever they had salvaged of their lives on their backs, resigned to the idea that whatever lay ahead could be no worse than what they had left behind.

These were the survivors, what was left of Germany, trudging away from terror toward a future that none could comprehend. And this was but one road, in one corner of the country, a small piece of a kaleidoscope of misery which was being repeated throughout the land, as the German people were scattered like chaff.

The tide of shattered humanity was so thick that choking gray-brown dust rose in great clouds as far as the eye could see, and no amount of bellowing, leaning on the horn, or threats could part it. The shouts of the driver were met with red, exhausted eyes that did not understand, while in those few that did began to smoulder the spark of hostility as they saw the black Mercedes, clearly an official limousine complete with curtains and cocktail cabinet, trying to batter its way back to Berlin. Hencke sank deep into the red leather of the seats and his companion couldn't fail to notice the blaze of anger that spread across his face.

"I can understand how you must be feeling, you of all people. When you see sewer-Deutsch like that, it makes you wonder why we bothered," the other man sneered. "In my book deserters like these should all be shot. Still, maybe they soon will be. The British front line is less than ten miles from here. That's why Reichsminister Goebbels sent his personal car for you. We couldn't afford to take the risk by plane."

Captain Otto Misch sat erect and resplendent in his SS uniform with its FBK insignia, staring straight ahead and trying to avoid the hostile glances cast at him from the straggling crowd of refugees. He toyed nervously with the Iron Cross pinned at his neck. It wasn't that he was afraid of the human flotsam outside his window, he simply didn't understand them and the lack of understanding made him uneasy. This wasn't the valiant resistance against the enemy that had been planned in Berlin and which he had been led to expect. As he twisted at the medal he noticed Hencke staring at his mangled hand.

"Moscow. I left the fingers in Moscow." He waved his hand with a casual pride. "I'm going back to reclaim them one day."

"Not in this damned car you're not," the driver muttered as he swung the wheel sharply to avoid another crater, but his violent efforts succeeded only in running the car into a charred beam thrown across the road by recent bombing, and their progress came to a jarring halt moments before they would have run into yet another group of refugees.

"*Scheisse*, it would be quicker by bulldozer!" the captain swore.

"And a damn sight safer," the sullen driver responded. "The front wheel's gone. I'll have to change it. I'll need help."

"Then get it!" Misch snapped irritably as an artillery shell landed less than a hundred yards away, sending up a malevolent plume of cement and brick dust. So close to the front not even Goebbels' bullet-proof limousine was safe.

It was dusk and they were on the outskirts of a small town, semiderelict and ghostlike, over which a pall of brown smoke drifted as British artillery sporadically pounded what was left. Through the dust thrown up from the ruins of houses and by the tramp of a thousand feet, they could make out a group of people gathered around a campfire at the center of a crossroads; in front of them lay a tram which had been thrown on its side and filled with rubble. It was a primitive barricade, behind which the defenders would be expected to fight tanks, armed with little more than rifles and the one-shot *Panzerfaust* being churned out from back street workshops and bicycle sheds — from anywhere with a bench and a primitive set of tools. The driver set off toward the barricade in search of assistance, leaving his two passengers listening to the radio, tuned to pick up warnings of air raids in their sector. He was soon back, shaking his head.

"They say they're too busy to help — got problems of their own," he reported glumly.

"Did you tell them that this was Reichsminister Goebbels' personal car?" Misch, instantly annoyed, slapped his gloves into his half-hand.

"Sure. They said if that was so it was the first official car they'd seen all week which wasn't headed full speed for the British lines."

Misch ground his teeth in fury.

"I told them they were wasting their time with the barricade," the driver continued laconically. "That it would take the British only twelve and a half minutes to get past it."

"Twelve and a half minutes?" queried Misch, taken aback by the exactitude of the estimate.

"Sure. Ten minutes splitting their sides with laughter, two minutes to bring up an artillery piece and thirty seconds to blow the whole fucking thing into the river." Insolence was written all over the driver's face. Hencke noted that although he was in uniform the driver hadn't saluted Misch once. This was not the German army he remembered. But this was scarcely the Germany he remembered, either.

Consumed by rage, the captain slammed the door of the car and stalked off in the direction of the barricade. Hencke followed and found still more to astonish him in the new Germany. In the rapidly failing light the campfire threw lurid patterns onto the buildings surrounding the crossroads, all of which had been reduced by battle to empty hulks standing sightless and open-mouthed where once had been windows and doorways, homes. Dust and smoke drifted like witches' breath through the gaping apertures, as the thunder of exploding artillery shells rolled all around. By the fire in the center of this primeval setting stood an elderly man and a dozen boys. Scattered around them lay a motley collection of rifles of varying vintages, some from the First World War with fixed bayonets, and by the curbside lay a canvas bag which appeared to be filled with grenades. The man was perhaps in his sixties, the empty right-hand sleeve of his jacket pinned to his side. None of the boys was older than fifteen, all were filthy and covered with grime, a few were in the uniform of the Hitler Youth and one who had a split lip and a bruised temple was sobbing pitifully. Into their midst strode Misch and instantly there was silence. The old man looked up at the tall captain; his face filled with anxiety as he saw the unmistakable markings of the SS uniform.

"Heil Hitler!" Misch barked, snapping to a straight-armed salute which demanded a response. Immediately he flushed with self-ridicule as he noticed the empty sleeve, and his awkwardness did nothing to improve his temper. "What the hell is going on here? I ask for assistance to repair my car. How dare you refuse!"

"I'm . . . sorry, Captain. I am the local schoolmaster, these are my boys," the man stammered. "We were having a little difficulty . . ."

Immediately the tearful youngster resumed his crying.

"What difficulty?"

"Nothing, nothing at all, really. Perhaps we can help you fix your car now." But the schoolmaster's tone was a little too nervous, his words too rushed to hide his anxiety.

"What difficulty, you bastard? I want to know!"

A conspiratorial silence fell over the group, punctuated only by the youthful sobbing and the spitting of the fire. The old man, overwhelmed, cast his eyes down to the ground. Misch hit him hard, a single blow across the cheek.

"Tell me!"

Blood trickled down the old man's cheek where Misch's heavy ring had caught him and fear flooded into his eyes, but still he said nothing. Several of the boys were looking in the direction of the sobbing youth.

"As members of the *Hitlerjugend* you are all under military discipline. I order you to tell me what is going on here. You!" Misch pointed to one of the boys who already bore two medals on the breast of his uniform. "Come here!"

The boy, who appeared no more than eleven years of age, ran forward.

"Tell me! No, don't look round at the others." Misch shook him savagely by the shoulders. "Tell me!"

"It was Hausser, sir," he responded in a shrill treble. "He . . . ran away. So me and Pauli had to go and drag him back."

"Ran away. Where?"

"To his mother, sir. They were preparing to hang out a white sheet . . ."

Quiet fell across the gathering once again, but it was of a different, more menacing kind. Gone was the silence of conspiracy, replaced by oppressive guilt. All eyes were on the youth, tears still trickling down his cheek and mingling with the traces of blood smeared across the adolescent down on his upper lip. Misch strode toward him.

"Get up, soldier."

The boy made no move.

"Get up, I said." Misch kicked him hard on his bare thigh just below his shorts.

"There's no need for that," the schoolmaster pleaded, rushing across to grab Misch's arm. "Leave him alone. For God's sake, what's the point? Can't you see? It's all over. *Verloren.* Lost. Lost."

Misch threw him off and the old man fell heavily to the pavement. "Nothing is lost while there are decent Germans still willing to fight!" he screamed. His face was blue with anger, his knee trembling; he was losing control of himself. "It is only cowards and deserting pigs like this one who are losing us the war."

"Let them all go back home, they're only children." The schoolteacher stretched out his arm in supplication.

"They are soldiers defending the Reich. And this one is a deserter." Misch looked around the group of boys, saw the look in their eyes which grew more haunting and fragile with every falling shell. He had seen it before, in front of Moscow, in the eyes of conscripts just before they turned and ran away through the snow and slush. It was why they had lost Moscow. It was why he had lost his hand. And it was why they were losing the war. As the suffocating dust thrown up from a nearby explosion drifted across the scene, he knew that one more near-miss and they would be gone, blown away like autumn leaves even before they had sight of the advancing enemy. For Misch, and for the forces that had taken him, the hungry son of an unemployed printer, and turned him into a feared and bemedaled warrior for whom people stepped out of the way and over whom women drooled, it was almost over. It was all crumbling away in front of him. A savage tremor ran through his body. He was about to be thrown back on the rubbish heap, or worse. Because of cowardice like this!

"If any of you soldiers are thinking of deserting your posts, remember. There is only one punishment for vermin who choose to run away and leave their defenseless mothers and sisters to get raped!"

"This boy has already lost his father and three elder brothers in the war. For God's sake, how much more do you expect him to give?"

"Shut up, teacher!"

Misch's voice had an edge of hysteria; his mutilated hand felt as if it were on fire. His revolver was already raised, pointing at the boy, who stared straight at him, face flooded with incomprehension as he looked into the twitching eyes of this stranger. He still did not understand, even when the bullet struck him an inch above the right eye. For a moment his body twitched and froze, his eyes still staring straight at Misch, until belatedly and slowly his whole form seemed to crumple. He fell back, bouncing once off the bricks beneath him, and lay broken among the rubble.

No one moved, no one screamed. No one knew who might be next.

"Hang him from that lamp post," Misch ordered. "As an example to anyone who cannot remember his duty."

"As a monument to the Third Reich," whispered the schoolmaster, still on the pavement where he had been thrown.

"You want to join him?" Misch turned the pistol on the old man, and his hand was shaking violently.

"I no longer care to live. What is there to live for? You have murdered our future."

Misch turned to the boys. "Hang him! And put a placard around his neck that says 'Deserter.' And if you can't spell 'Deserter' I'll shoot the teacher."

No one doubted his word. As one boy stirred from his petrification, the others followed. Not until they had carried out the orders to the full did Misch replace the pistol in his holster. He was nervous and uneasy, his pale cheeks unnaturally flushed, shocked by the belated realization of what he had done. "Back to your posts," he commanded. The schoolmaster nodded, and they returned silently to the building of the barricade, trying to keep their backs toward the lamp post.

Misch turned away and for the first time seemed to notice Hencke, who had stood silently behind him throughout. "You'll understand, of course. After all you've been through." Misch smiled nervously. "The Fatherland means everything to me."

"I think I need a piss," Hencke responded, and clawed his way over a pile of bricks to the shell of a gutted building. He disappeared for a few moments behind a wall before reappearing. "Hey, Misch. Come and see what I've found."

He beckoned him over and Misch clambered after him until they were both hidden behind the wall.

"What's up? What have you discovered?"

Hencke turned to face Misch until they were no more than inches apart. "I just wanted you to know what I thought of that little episode outside, Misch."

The quizzical look was still on Misch's face when the bayonet that Hencke had filched from one of the boys' rifles caught him between the ribs. Then there was surprise, the pain hadn't yet hit him. Only when Hencke twisted the blade upward, snapping two ribs and penetrating the heart, did Misch's eyes bulge as the agony forced him on to the tips of his toes. He grabbed Hencke's shoulders with what was left of his rapidly ebbing strength, until they were eyeball to eyeball. Hencke could feel the fear and panic in Misch's hot breath as he began to choke on the blood rising in his gorge.

"But I thought you'd come back to help save us . . ."

"No, you murdering bastard. I've come from Mr. Churchill. To kill Hitler."

He gave another twist of the bayonet blade and Misch fell back dead at his feet.

CHAPTER 10

Hencke arrived at his destination well after midnight. The Royal Air Force had finished with their nightly bombing attack on the German capital, and there was a lull in the early hours as the survivors waited for the return of the American bombers by day. It was a routine with an awesome familiarity for Berliners. Somehow the city still functioned; hundreds of thousands went about their duties, baking, selling, stamping ration cards, clearing the streets, keeping the water and electricity flowing, distributing newspapers, even delivering mail — anything was better than sitting back to wait for the arrival of the Russians. Although there was a blackout, the driver was able to see his way without difficulty; a choking cloud of soot and phosphorous smoke hung low across the city, and the light from innumerable fires reflected back into the desolate streets, giving even darkest night a sickening edge of brightness. It was the fresh piles of rubble and unfilled craters scattered across the roadways that made the passage so difficult; wide boulevards had been turned into obstacle courses. Several times they had to turn back and divert away from streets that were completely blocked or had turned into great tunnels of fire. More than once Hencke had helped the driver shift obstructions; they wrapped wet handkerchiefs around their faces to protect themselves from the hot, suffocating ash and fumes. At one point their way was obstructed by a body. The driver got out, grabbed the body under the shoulders and dumped it to one side.

"Was he dead?"

"Who knows? If we stopped for every body, we'd never get there."

Since Hencke had returned alone to the car, the driver had dropped any vestige of military discipline and respect. He had a job to do and he'd do it, but he didn't have to pretend to enjoy it. When Hencke explained that Misch "hadn't made it" back from the growing chaos on the other side of the barricade, the driver didn't bother to ask why. It was too frequent an occurrence to arouse even his slightest interest; his only regret was that Hencke hadn't suggested they turn round and head westward with all the others.

They passed beside the Brandenburg Gate in the very heart of Berlin. It stood largely intact and shining in the glare of nearby fires, an awesome reminder of sights that seemed buried deep in a time when it had been illuminated by the torches of victory parades and the Fuehrer had taken the salute of adoring millions. But the military bands and the tramp of marching feet had gone; there was only the explosion of time-delay bombs and the shudder of collapsing buildings to interrupt the complaints of his driver and the low growl of the Mercedes engine.

They drove directly into the underground garage off Hermann Goering Strasse. Even by night, and with many of its windows blown out or boarded up, the looming edifice of the Reich Chancellery was clearly recognizable. Teams were at work dealing with the rubble from the most recent aerial onslaught, but it was no longer being taken away and hidden, merely pushed aside to allow access. Inside the building the upper storys had been vacated, parts of the roof and most of the windows having gone, but on lower floors and in the cellar there were still hundreds of people scurrying about their business. Indeed, as Hencke emerged from the garage into the heart of Berlin's main government complex, he entered a different world. While outside the great capital city lay in ruins, inside there remained at least a semblance of discipline and control. Even the driver had started saluting senior officers again. Telephones still jangled, commands were barked, soldiers scampered to obey. Yet as Hencke was led by an orderly through a maze of underground cellars and tunnels, he couldn't help but notice how fragile seemed this veneer of order. There was no hiding the weariness in the limbs, the ashen signs of exhaustion in the faces of men who had survived too long on too little sleep, the soiled uniforms which bore the dust and filth of excursions into the outside world and which no one bothered any longer to clean or replace. In many places the refuse of meals and drinking sessions lay uncleared, and Hencke passed two generals who were obviously drunk. Strangely, their uniforms bore the least signs of battle grime, the only stains seeming to have come from spilt wine and soup.

Soon they were out of the cellar and up to the ground floor, where spartan utility gave way to the splendor of marble floors, rich carpets and still finer tapestries, all of which were spotted with the marks of fallen plasterwork. The lights burned brightly for the windows were heavily boarded and, as the orderly led the way down corridors and through rooms that echoed to their footsteps, Hencke was conscious of the soiled splendor of a once magnificent showpiece. Drawing rooms had been transformed into sleeping quarters bursting with metal cots; where great receptions had once been held were piled man-made mountains of provisions and wooden crates; a burnished Steinway in the music room had been pushed aside to make way for an array of maps surrounding a briefing table, and everywhere there was a sense of desperate struggle to avoid the short descent into chaos. But still the heart of government was beating, even if the effort involved was proving colossal.

The orderly, a lieutenant, stopped outside a towering pair of carved doors and instructed him to wait. He knocked sharply, and from deep within there came a muffled order to enter. He disappeared for a second and exchanged a few brief words before reappearing. "He's ready for you," was all he said before ushering Hencke through the doors.

The room behind the doors had once been a small reception room — small, that is, only by comparison with the great halls through which they had passed. It was a good thirty meters long, and decorated with gilded mirrors, oil paintings of traditional hunting scenes, and a vast crystal chandelier that cast a delicate light across the inlaid oaken floor. Whatever furniture had once adorned the room had gone. In the middle now stood a large baize-covered table surrounded by chairs, sufficient for a briefing meeting of thirty, with a huge map of Berlin and its approaches pinned up at one end of the room. At the other end, beside a fireplace whose ornate mantel was covered with fine pieces of blue and white porcelain, was a vast pillared desk with a marble top all but hidden beneath neat piles of paper. And beside the desk stood the unmistakable, reedlike figure of Josef Goebbels.

"Hencke! Is it really you inside those rags? What a spectacle you make! But you are most welcome!" Goebbels paced stiffly across the room, his right foot pointing awkwardly inward, extending his hand in greeting. A smile of amusement played on his lips as he studied his unkempt prize. While the undersized Reichsminister was dressed immaculately in a conservative double-breasted suit with a pearl-white shirt, his dark hair brushed back and glossy with brilliantine, Hencke made a miserable sight. The change of clothes provided by the local police after his rescue on the beach had never fitted properly; now they were stained with mud and dust from shifting obstructions and rubble. His boots and trousers had become soaked from the flooding of broken water pipes, a dark brown stain of dried blood clung to his left sleeve, and around his neck still hung the grimy handkerchief he had used to protect his mouth from the burning air.

"Ha! I see you come well gift-wrapped," Goebbels chuckled, clapping his hands in delight. He was clearly exultant. "I am not a superstitious man, Hencke, but to have you delivered back to us, on such an auspicious day, is more than even my skepticism can take." He saw the bewildered look on Hencke's face and led him toward two comfortable chairs that stood on either side of a low occasional table. "Sit down, my dear Hencke. We have much to talk about." He poured coffee from a silver pot and began.

"Do you know what day it is?"

"Herr Reichsminister, I scarcely know what year it is. I have been in a prison camp, on the run, in fishing smacks on the Irish Sea, and in a submarine at the bottom of the North Sea . . ."

Goebbels stretched over to grasp his hand and still him. "The twentieth of April, my dear Hencke. The Fuehrer's birthday. I have organized a very special celebration for him. And a very special prize. Hencke, *you* are that prize!"

"I . . . am to be presented to the Fuehrer?"

Goebbels' saturnine face was unusually animated. "Yes. Oh, yes. The arrival of perhaps the bravest man in Germany represents the return of hope and good fortune. My God, it will be better medicine than anything those quacks have poured into him in months." The long creases about his face became suddenly harder and his voice lost its celebratory edge, becoming quiet, almost conspiratorial. He leaned close to Hencke as if afraid his words might be overheard, the blood vessels at his temples swelling as he strained forward. "You must realize, Hencke, the Fuehrer may not be the man you remember. The assassination attempt at Rastenburg last year . . . it caused him grave damage. He was so close to the bomb it was a miracle he survived, his ear drums shattered, his hearing damaged, his sense of balance gone . . ." Goebbels was talking slowly, choosing his words with care. "The worries he has borne over so many years on our behalf have taken their inevitable toll. He has given so much of his own strength to our cause, it is vital for us in turn to replenish it with our full support and encouragement. He is tired, unwell. He needs reassurance. While he has the will to carry on, so does Germany. Later today all of the party's leaders are arriving from their posts around the country to honor and strengthen him, to reinforce his desire to carry on in his great task. And that is why your arrival is so timely and so important. You are the embodiment of the German spirit to continue the fight; he will regard your presence as an omen of good fortune, a harbinger of victories yet to come."

"I fear I will disappoint the Fuehrer . . ."

"Hencke, you are Odysseus escaped from the clutches of the Cyclops and returned to Ithaca. This is no time for modesty. You have achieved more than any other captured German since this war began . . . But tell me, we know so little of you — no more than your name." He was on the edge of his chair — like a cat waiting to pounce, thought Hencke. "Tell me more about yourself."

So they sat while Hencke talked, of his childhood in the Sudetenland, the German-speaking part of Czechoslovakia, which had been almost the first of the Third Reich's territorial claims in Europe, stripped from the Czechs in 1938. Of his modest life as a schoolteacher, of his even more modest entry into the Wehrmacht as an ordinary infantryman, of his capture outside Bastogne on Christmas Day last as the Ardennes offensive turned to ignominious rout, of his incarceration and of his run for freedom. And as he spoke his mind was in turmoil. He'd only just arrived and already he was taking coffee with Goebbels — they were going to *push* him at Hitler! — could it all be so easy? Of course not. He needed time to think and his confusion and obvious exhaustion were causing his words to stumble. He took refuge in a yawn, mumbling an apology before Goebbels interrupted him.

"I have tired you enough. There is much for us to discuss still, but you must get some rest before our celebration this afternoon — it would not do for you to fall asleep on the Fuehrer! And we must do something about your gift-wrapping . . . Hencke, I am appointing you to the Leibstandarte Adolf Hitler, the most elite division in the Waffen SS. Its name is synonymous, as now is yours, with valor and dedication to the Fuehrer. I congratulate you! So, rest. There are a few hours before the Americans return to snatch our sleep from us and wake the dead. We can continue this later . . ."

Hencke's head swam with fatigue and the overwhelming atmosphere. He hadn't seen Goebbels give any signal, but when he looked up the orderly was waiting to escort him away. He rose stiffly with Goebbels' hand on his elbow for support. "Sleep well, brave Hencke," the Reichsminister said, assisting him toward the door. At the threshold he paused, taking Hencke's hand.

"I have never been able to fight in the front lines, but you seem to have shown enough heroism for both of us. You're a very brave man, Hencke. Indeed, coming from the Sudetenland it could be said that you were part of this war even before it began."

Hencke nodded. Goebbels didn't know how right he was.

"Tell me, where in the Sudetenland were you born?"

Hencke froze. The hand that held his, that had supported him across the room, had now become a restraint, a manacle holding him back: their conversation had become interrogation, and he would need all his wits about him. But his tired body no longer wanted to fight the fatigue, and he felt paralyzed by the touch of the hand and the brush of the seemingly innocent words. Goebbels' dark eyes and lean, saturnine face had the hypnotic power of a swaying cobra. For a moment it appeared as if Hencke could say nothing. He knew why Goebbels had asked.

"Eger," he said softly. "February the second, 1910. I was born just outside Eger."

Goebbels nodded. "They will be very proud of you. Well, good night, Hencke. And don't worry about a thing. We'll take care of you."

And Hencke was gone. With a thoughtful look Goebbels walked back to his desk. He spent some time pondering over a slow-burning cigarette before he lifted the phone.

"Bormann? Hencke's arrived. In Berlin. In the Reich Chancellery. Look, you're the man with the records. I want you to find out a little more about him. Schoolteacher. Born second February 1910 outside Eger in the Sudetenland . . . No, seems fine, but he's too valuable for us to take chances. I've arranged for someone to keep an eye on him, just in case. At times like these you can never be too sure . . ."

Replacing the receiver he checked his watch. He opened a large drawer in his desk and switched on the small radio that was inside, fiddling with the tuning dial before settling back to listen to the news service of the BBC. Nowadays it was the only way he could find out precisely what was going on. And Goebbels always insisted on knowing what was going on.

* * *

The orderly, who had not spoken a word on the journey through the Reich Chancellery to Goebbels' study, seemed to have relaxed. Once the Reichsminister appeared satisfied with his guest, the tension had seeped out of the lieutenant, to be replaced by a stubbornness and even pugnacity. Hencke thought he could smell alcohol on his breath.

"How well do you know Berlin?" he inquired of Hencke.

"Not at all. I'm from the Sudetenland."

"Rumor says you've come to save the city. That's nice of you, very generous," the lieutenant continued, oozing sarcasm. He clearly had little time for heroes, particularly new ones. "So let me show you a little of what you've come to save." Without waiting for any sort of response, he led the way along a back corridor and down a staircase. They were headed once more for the cellar. Soon they had left behind the lofty ceilings and soiled splendor of the upper floors, and were down once more in the low, bare, monochrome world of hollow expressions and deep-sunk eyes rimmed red with fatigue. They proceeded along the corridor that ran through the cellar complex, to a point where it became cluttered with bundles of blankets and rags. Inside the rags were soldiers, all badly wounded, some of whom already appeared to have given up the struggle and to be dead. There was a sweet, disgusting smell in the air and flies buzzed around freely. Up ahead Hencke could see doors, and the lieutenant was headed for them, but barring his way was a broken, toppled figure, once a full man, now unable even to continue sitting propped against the wall. The body was hunched, the eyes bruised and tightly closed, the only sign of life being a low moan of despair coming from between swollen lips. Judging by the gaudy brass buttons that still clung to what was left of his uniform, the body appeared once to have been a young recruit from a naval training college. It was clear he would never return there. The lieutenant picked

LAST MAN TO DIE

him up and gently leaned him back against the wall.

"Come on, old chap. Can't hold up progress," he whispered in the lad's ear. He lit a cigarette to place between the puffy lips, but the lad seemed to have neither the strength nor the spirit to respond and the cigarette fell to the floor. The lieutenant crushed it angrily with his boot before looking back at Hencke. "Looks as if you're too late to save that one. Never mind, plenty more inside."

They went through the door, and the scene in front of them banished any last vestige of tiredness from Hencke's mind. Beneath a solitary lamp stood an officer and two women. The officer wore a barely recognizable uniform covered with blood, some old and caked, much of it fresh. The two women, scarcely less bloodied, were obviously nurses. On a high table between them lay a body with its stomach open and entrails pouring out on either side of the incision. The doctor was having trouble, since the body was twitching, and he was uttering curses about the lack of morphine. His eyes were as red and smeared as his uniform, his face gray from lack of sleep. One of the nurses was crying silently, not tears of weakness or fear but tears of compassion; the body before them seemed to belong to a youth no older than sixteen. Set back from the table, on a hard bench where he lay supported by a large stuffed cushion, was an old man. Even at a glance he was clearly not long for this world, yet between racking bouts of coughing he was giving instruction and advice to the surgeon, who sought counsel frequently. Perhaps the man wielding the scalpel was not a qualified doctor at all. In one corner of the improvised surgery lay four other forms on stretchers, waiting their turn.

No one took the slightest notice of Hencke and the lieutenant. Not even when one of the nurses slopped something into a bucket and brought it over to the large bin close to where they were standing did she look at them. Hencke saw that the slops were yards of entrail, and the bin contained amputated arms and legs, some still with their boots on, in addition to much gore. He desperately wanted to vomit, but looking at the nurses made him feel foolish. He swallowed the bile and clenched his jaws until he thought his teeth would crack.

The lieutenant seemed unaffected; he had seen it many times before. "Come with me," he said, and dragged Hencke toward a door on the other side of the room, which required them to push past the table. Still no one looked up. Hencke suspected they would still be there, bent over the table, even when the Russians came.

As he and Hencke walked through the door the lieutenant switched on the flashlight buckled to his belt, for whatever was on the other side was in semidarkness. It was a large room, packed with beds jammed side by side which could be reached only by narrow passageways at their feet. There were well over three hundred beds, all full, many with two patients sharing each narrow palliasse. In spite of the hum of a ventilation fan the stench was appalling, a rancid mixture of death, decay, gangrene, sickness and broken bowels. By torchlight a handful of nurses were floating about the room, ministering, comforting, cleaning. One was carefully unwrapping the bandages from a corpse, laying those which appeared the least soiled on a table for later use. The door of a medicine cabinet on the wall stood ajar, the shelves inside bare.

"I'm sure they'll be happy to hear you've brought them hope," the lieutenant said. "Still, a truckful of aspirin might have been more practical."

Their journey was not yet over. Hencke was led along the side of the room, past patients who groaned with pain, some of whom reached out and implored them for a cigarette, many who seemed to lack the strength either to complain or to implore. Without knowing where he was going, Hencke hurried on. At the far end of the room was another door like the one through which they had entered; Hencke approached it with a feeling of considerable relief. The lieutenant stood back to allow him through first, proffering the flashlight.

Hencke's first impression was that this was another hospital ward, for he could see rows of cots lined up in the gloom. But as soon as he took a breath he could tell this was not so; the stench was gone, or was at least different. He flashed the torch around and could see bodies on the beds.

"Turn off that fucking light, you fool," a voice growled in the dark. Hencke shone the torch in the direction of the sound. In the beam of light he could see an overweight pink body stretched out on a bed. It was one of the drunken generals he had seen earlier that evening. Astride him, her breasts bobbing up and down as she tried to get some rhythm going, was a young woman. He shone the torch away and played it quickly over the rest of the room. It needed no more than a second for him to realize what he had intruded upon. The room seemed to have been intended as a small extension to the main hospital ward, but the beds were strewn around in haphazard fashion. On many of the beds lay men entwined with women, sometimes with two women, either actively involved in sex or taking a break with a bottle or cigarette. To one side several beds had been pushed together, and on top of this platform Hencke saw the confused and contorted shapes of group sex. The men appeared to be mostly elderly, the women all young. "Angels of the night," whispered the lieutenant, "who work just as hard as the girls next door. They call this the Recovery Room." From somewhere in the gloom, accompanied by raucous laughter and much crudity, a young female voice began to groan and then rise, unintentionally mimicking the anguish of a wounded soldier. Hencke felt sick again.

"Join in if you want. You don't have to make reservations,"

the lieutenant muttered. The angry snatch of Hencke's head gave him his answer. "OK, if you've seen enough, follow me," and they passed through a side back door into bright light. They were in a rest area, with comfortable chairs and sofas arranged round coffee tables. It was yet another world, and officers sat exchanging conversation and bonhomie with each other and a variety of women while orderlies passed among them dispensing drinks. Hencke shook his head to clear his thoughts, trying to ensure that what he had just witnessed was not simply the product of an exhausted mind beset by twisted dreams. But the stench of the hospital still swirled in his nostrils and he knew there was no mistake.

"I need a drink," the lieutenant said, and without asking went across to a table that served as a bar and ordered two. He and Hencke tossed them straight down.

"Who are these women?" Hencke inquired.

"A mixture. Mistresses. Secretaries. Civilian personnel. Even housewives. Some are just spectators, here for a gawk and a good time, but many of them have run to the Reich Chancellery terrified of Ivan, fleeing from what they imagine is going to happen when he gets his hands on them. It seems that most of them, after a drink or two, prefer German hands, and plenty of them."

The door behind them opened and the general, now fully clothed but with his uniform jacket unbuttoned, came through. He was pink with the exertions of his latest victory and raised a triumphal paw in greeting at a fellow officer who was drinking with three women. He strolled over to join them; there was no sign of the girl he had left behind.

"Down the corridor there's a dental surgery," the lieutenant continued. "You know, big black leather dentist's chair which can be adjusted to different positions. The latest trick is to strap a woman in it and tilt it to whatever angle you fancy. Two men often have a go at the same time. Then you stop for a drink, strap her in the chair some other way, tilt it to a new angle and start all over again. It's a particular favorite with the generals."

"Rape?" Hencke was incredulous. He had thought himself no longer capable of surprise.

"Don't be a fool. The girls are queuing up for it. Look around, do you see anyone complaining? It's like collective hysteria. There's nowhere else for them to go. They've probably lost their husbands or lovers in the war, they're alone and frightened. They come here and throw themselves at the nearest man with a pistol on his belt, desperately seeking protection and a way out. But after a couple of days and nights down here in the cellars they seem to catch the contagion. They call it *Kellerkrebs* — cellar cancer. As long as they can't see the war or hear it too well behind twenty feet of concrete, they manage to persuade themselves that it no longer matters, that Ivan's buggered off and they're safe. They drown everything in drink and fuck away all their cares. Live for today, for tomorrow we die . . . Who knows? When you think of what is going to happen, maybe they're right."

He turned to order another drink and as he did so, three prettily dressed women wandered into the room, and the hubbub of conversation momentarily became subdued. They were in their late twenties or early thirties and appeared to be looking for a friend, for another woman detached herself from a group of senior officers and hurried to greet them. After exchanging a few moments of girlish laughter they all left together, and the conversation in the room resumed unabated.

"Who were they, Lieutenant?"

"Them? Doesn't pay to notice them, Hencke. Particularly not in this part of the Chancellery. Forget you ever saw them."

"It seems there is a lot this evening I am supposed to forget."

"No, Hencke. Don't forget the rest. I want you to remember all that sewage we've just waded through, because that's the Berlin you've come back to save. And if you're half the savior Goebbels supposes you to be, it makes you the most dangerous man there is in this insane city."

CHAPTER 11

Hencke awoke to the sound of bombing overhead. It was shortly before noon; the American air force had returned for their daily visit. Down in the cellar of the Reich Chancellery where Hencke had been billeted in one of the crowded sleeping quarters, the noise was like the rumble of distant artillery fire, the thick alluvial sand on which Berlin was built cushioning and deadening the effects of all but the most direct of hits. Yet after months of saturation bombing, almost everything had been directly hit, several times. The lamps overhead swung as if agitated by an imperceptible subterranean wind, fine plaster and cement dust settled on every surface, and nobody seemed willing to talk as they listened for the one that had their name on its nose cone.

Underground the routine of bombing seemed the only way

of distinguishing between night and day. People ate when they felt hungry, drank when they wished to forget, slept when they were too exhausted to stay awake any longer or, if they had the energy and desire, went in search of a signalwoman. Many, particularly those with no front-line duties, had found reason to be there a very long time. The longer they accepted the shelter of the cellar and the less contact they had with the outside world, the more unreal it became. And Hencke was told that the Fuehrer had been in the cellar almost constantly since mid-January.

Before Hencke had managed to scratch the sleep from his eyes the lieutenant was at the foot of his bed. "Knew you wouldn't sleep through this lot, not yet. Takes a couple of days before you no longer give a damn . . ." He held some clothes and boots. "Try these. The boots are waterproof. Might come in handy, just in case you get caught short while you're busy saving Berlin." As he mocked he threw the items on the end of the bed. They were the black dress uniform of the Waffen SS, complete with silver piping, distinctive collar markings, armband of the Leibstandarte Adolf Hitler division, and captain's shoulder flashes. Hencke looked at the officer's pips incredulously, rubbing them with his thumb to make sure they were real.

"Why, didn't they tell you, *Captain?*" the lieutenant goaded. "Way things are going you'll be a general by the end of the week. Or dead. Sir."

Hencke decided not to argue the point — he wasn't here to argue, and he was too confused as to what was going on. The lieutenant enlightened him.

"Lunch — or, in your case, breakfast. Then you'll be taken to the birthday knees-up. Your big moment."

"Where is the Fuehrer?" He hoped it seemed a perfectly natural question, but Hencke held his breath, waiting for the response. He couldn't afford to arouse suspicion.

"Where he always is. In the Bunker, of course."

"The Bunker? It's separate from the cellar?"

"The whole of this part of Berlin's been tunneled out into several cellars and shelters. Under the Chancellery, Propaganda Ministry, Air Ministry. There's a little world of underground empires down here, all crisscrossed and interconnected; half the time you expect the Minotaur to pop his head round the corner. But there's only one *Bunker*. No, I lie. Two. A *Vorbunker* where most of his personal staff bury themselves, and then down to the *Fuehrerbunker* proper. Twenty feet below sewer level, the underworld of Berlin. They say even the rats come out with a headache. Although the fact that the air conditioning doesn't work properly is supposed to be a state secret. Hey, they might even shoot me for telling you." His face brightened for the first time that day.

"And the birthday celebration is there?"

"Good God, no. Too damned small. Get Goering and two fat housewives down there, and the rest would suffocate. No, the Fuehrer's going to honor us by coming up to face the daylight for once, and look Berlin in the eye for the first time in months."

So maybe that would be it. His one chance of success. He wouldn't get more than one chance, and perhaps not even that. He washed and changed into his uniform, *the* uniform. He felt like an ancient knight donning armor invested with evil powers. The fit was immaculate, yet the collar felt unbearably tight around the throat as if it were trying to grip and strangle him. As he fastened the last button on the tunic his chest heaved and he had trouble breathing — somehow the uniform seemed to be trying to take him over, to make him one of *them*. Only when he checked the leather holster and found the Walther 7.65, cleaned and with a fully loaded clip, could he begin to fight back against his anxieties and convince himself that he, not the uniform, was in control. Like everyone else he was sweating in the accumulating heat of the cellar, yet every few minutes a cold river of apprehension would flood down his backbone. *They were going to take him to Hitler.* Just like that. Could it really be that easy? Or had he already been sucked into this underworld of madness and illusion, where nothing was as it seemed? He waited for over three hours, trying to control the writhing knot in his stomach, wondering if he would be forced to take the lieutenant's advice and use his boots.

He quickly discovered that nothing was going to be as easy as it might have seemed. When the lieutenant returned they walked several hundred yards without once leaving the Reich Chancellery. It was vast and very crowded, bustling like a railway station. The remnants of an entire city and several Wehrmacht armies had been poured into its cellar and lower floors, until the building had filled and overflowed. Growing piles of suitcases and kitbags were tucked away in corners and there was the constant clatter of people arriving; those departing did so less obviously. Armed soldiers were everywhere, and he thought it could be only moments before one of them spotted the unmistakable blush of treachery which he felt certain marked his face. But they all seemed too busy with their own affairs to pay attention to him.

It changed when they ran into the checkpoint. They had arrived in the antechamber of the so-called Court of Honor, and armed guards were everywhere, relieving guests not only of coats and bags but anything that might conceivably resemble or contain a weapon. No one was exempt, not even high-ranking staff officers. All had to give up side arms and briefcases, the women their handbags. The Walther on which Hencke had focused so many ill-formed hopes in the last few hours was taken, and a record entered in a huge ledger that had once been used to keep the accounts of the Chancellery kitchen. Even ceremonial dress daggers were confiscated. No chances were being taken; nothing, it seemed, could get past.

Yet even that was not enough. Four more FBK guards were waiting as they proceeded from the antechamber, two to watch with machine pistols poised, while the other pair saluted each guest before submitting them to a careful body search. Women were dealt with in a separate corner by two female adjutants who looked as if they could take on a whole parachute platoon and still be through by breakfast. Passes and identity cards were inspected and checked against a master list; at Hencke's turn the lieutenant produced a sheet of paper, flourishing it at the guard and nodding toward Hencke. The guard seemed impressed.

"Here you are." The lieutenant handed the paper to Hencke. "Your pass. Signed by Goebbels himself. For Chrissake, don't lose it or they won't let you out this side of World War Three."

Only then were they permitted to pass into the magnificent Court of Honor, the *Ehrenhof*, the traditional place of celebration. Never had it looked more incongruous. The chamber glittered with its finery of medals, bejeweled batons, party insignia and gaily bedecked womenfolk, though the pride of Nazi society milled around like cattle at pasture, penned into one section of the room behind a cordon of guards, while those still waiting to join the festivities formed an obedient, shuffling line leading through a final security check. The absence of people from much of the hall gave the proceedings an eerie, echoing quality. Only when he looked up beyond the lofty marble columns did Hencke understand why. Although the polished stone floor had been swept of debris since the last bombing run, full across the gilded ceiling ran two cracks wide enough to take a man's arm to the shoulder. The ornate chandelier of a thousand pieces of crystal was lit, but lurching at a sickening angle from broken supports. No one could be sure when it would come smashing down, only that it must, and probably before the coming night's air raid was over.

His pass was inspected once more, his face examined, but still no one detected any mark of guilt. At last he was among the guests and, as he looked round, his knotted stomach gave another savage wrench. Almost beside him, sweat pouring down his face, was the huge, bursting figure of Goering in full Reichsmarschall's regalia, beaming broadly, sipping his drink and taking regular, nervous looks at his watch. He seemed like a man who had an urgent appointment somewhere else, his agitated eyes suggesting that he didn't mind it being anywhere else, so long as it was outside Berlin. Nearby stood the diminutive figure of Himmler, oddly shaped forehead, thick glasses, no chin, no trace of humor in his face, also looking distracted, unable to concentrate on the conversation of his companions, his eyes moving restlessly around the room. There was Bormann, and Speer, Ribbentrop, Axmann . . . The whole damnable hierarchy of the Nazi party seemed to have gathered, yet Hencke could sense something amiss. There were bursts of jocularity and laughter, but the appreciation of a neighbor's attempt to raise spirits was perfunctory. A laugh, an edgy smile, and the faces returned to grimness. A five-piece military band struggled to provide entertainment, but their scratchy performance suggested they had been hastily gathered and never played together before. There were also cameras and a film crew moving round the gathering to capture the scene for the instruction and admiration of future generations in the Thousand-Year Reich. All the formalities and substance of an historic celebration had been brought together, yet the spirit was missing. There was little attempt to circulate, few of the leaders showing even the slightest interest in talking to their senior colleagues, preferring to bury themselves in small talk and joking with more junior personnel or the women. It was difficult to escape the atmosphere of unease and mistrust. Only Goebbels, dressed in the freshly pressed brown jacket of his party uniform, seemed intent on circulating, shaking hands, talking, encouraging, listening, nodding his head in approval or wagging his finger to emphasize a point. He appeared to be the only common factor, the only remaining link among the remnants of what had once been the most formidable political organization Europe had ever seen.

"Ah, Hencke. You're here. Come forward, don't be shy." Goebbels had spied him, hovering uncertainly, and the Reichsminister raised his hands above his head and clapped for attention.

Hencke stepped forward, feeling like the pig being paraded in front of the revelers at *Schuetzenfest* before they fell on the creature and tore it apart. Their eyes devoured him, stripping him, probing, questioning, wondering what sort of man was this. The sea of bodies parted and he was drawn onward, his legs leaden with trepidation, his bladder as tight as the new boots, certain that at any moment some accuser would step forward to denounce him, as he followed the diminutive figure of Goebbels toward the far side of the gathering. The band's leader, nervous of his responsibilities and with no one to guide him, struck up the Horst Wessel song.

Zum letzen Mal wird nun Appell geblasen! . . .

The signal sounds for one last charge!
We stand ready for the struggle.
Soon Hitler's flag will fly above all,
The days of slavery will be shortlived!

The words seemed apt, but the Nazi carol was a marching song, intended for raised voices and the crashing of boot leather, and its strains played at slow tempo on clarinet and violin seemed ludicrously out of place.

Then he was there. In front of him. Face to face with Adolf Hitler.

The band trailed off in relief as Goebbels started to speak. "My Fuehrer," he began. His voice was gratingly loud, although he was standing close beside his leader. "I have the pleasure to introduce the man who has scorched the feathers of Churchill's tail, who took on the English war machine and won. A proud German who knows his duty both to you and to the Fatherland, a symbol of Germany's indefatigable desire to continue resistance until final victory." It was cheap theater, everyone with their appointed role.

"I present to you Captain Peter Hencke!"

Slowly a hand extended toward him, and Hencke reached out to grasp it, raising his eyes to those of the German leader. As their hands touched and eyes met, Hencke felt paralysis grip his wits as confusion flooded through his senses. He remembered the Hitler of the newsreels and the great victory parades, the strut, the confidence and arrogance, the raised chin, the flicking hand gestures with which he brushed aside opponents and orchestrated the world. The man of legend who had devoured nations and terrified the world. But that was someone else. The man in front of him was a physical wreck. Every inch told of a body and a spirit in decay. The once smoothly slicked hair was unkempt, the crystal blue eyes that had charmed so many German women were watery and bloodshot; the cheeks were unnaturally puffed, the complexion sallow from lack of daylight, the chin badly shaved, the mustache graying and limp. There was a slight dribble from one corner of his mouth. The body was hunched, the shoulders slumped like those of a man many years older than one celebrating his fifty-sixth birthday. The once immaculate plain gray jacket he habitually wore was crumpled and marked by food stains and slops; his left leg was entwined around a chair as if to provide support and balance. And the hand that clasped Hencke's was like ice, flabby, with no strength; trembling.

"*Mein Fuehrer,*" Hencke whispered, lowering his head.

"Speak up, Hencke!" Goebbels commanded. "No need to let your voice get lost in the hubbub."

But Hencke noticed that the entire assembly had gone quiet, and Hitler was leaning forward, stiffly, as if better to catch what was said, while still attempting to keep his leg wrapped firmly around the chair support.

"I am overwhelmed to be here, my Fuehrer!" Hencke raised his voice, and Goebbels nodded in approval. "I bring you greetings from all your forces across the seas." He wondered whether he had said the right thing, since practically all of Hitler's forces across the seas were stuck deep inside Allied prison camps, but Hitler responded with a nod of pleasure. Or was it merely an uncontrollable wobble of the head?

"I . . . am delighted, Hencke. Thank you." The voice was weak, croaking. "You are a very brave man." He turned his head to signal, and an aide was immediately at his side proffering something. Carefully Hitler took it in his right hand and reached toward Hencke. "The Iron Cross, First Class. Wear it with pride." The patter of applause began to rise, but Hitler was having problems pinning the medal on Hencke's breast. His left hand came up to assist, but the coordination between the two hands seemed remote. The medal was in danger of being dropped to the floor, and the diffident aide stretched forward to help while the applause died away in embarrassment.

Hitler cleared his throat, and when he spoke again his voice had regained some of its powerful timbre. "My friends," he said, addressing the entire company, "you have done me great honor, coming from many parts of the Reich. But there are armies to command and battles to be fought." Goering raised a quizzical eyebrow; the Fuehrer seemed not to notice. "Continue with the celebration with my thanks. But I must return to my duties. So farewell to you all, until the next time."

There came the clicking of heels and a series of salutes from around the room as Hitler prepared to leave, and the band struck up the national anthem, but no one sang. He had commanded people to risk their lives crossing from all parts of the Reich to be at this birthday celebration, yet no sooner had he appeared than he was preparing to leave. Goebbels was at his elbow once more, whispering in his ear, guiding him toward one corner in which a small group of dirty street urchins had been standing, looking miserable and bewildered. They wore a kaleidoscopic array of stained uniform jackets and military caps, all of which hung on them loosely. They reminded Hencke of the group he had found at the barricade; none of them was older than fourteen. An orderly pushed them hastily into line as the Fuehrer approached, accompanied by the retinue of cameras. Goebbels' little play was not yet finished.

"My Fuehrer, these brave soldiers are all orphans of the savage war inflicted on us by our enemies. They have lost everything, but still they are proud National Socialists. They have come from many different parts of the Reich to celebrate your birthday, and to volunteer to defend to the very end this great capital city of Berlin!"

One of the boys began to pucker his brow and shake his head, either in disbelief or disapproval, but quickly decided it was not worth the effort and went back to looking sullen. Hitler shuffled along the line, accompanied by the cameras, taking each boy by the hand, not saying a word. One of the younger boys in the middle of the line had golden hair and a less weary expression than the rest. Hitler patted his cheek affectionately and turned to the next, but Goebbels intercepted him to whisper yet again in his ear. Again without a word, Hitler returned to pat the child's cheek, this time right under the eye of the hastily repositioned cameras, before moving silently on. Then it was all over, and Hitler was walking past on his way out. As he did so he grasped Hencke's arm, leaning on it heavily. "You must have tea with me, in a little while. An orderly will show you down." With that he departed, dragging his left leg behind him.

No sooner had the hunched back of Hitler disappeared than the conversation started once again, much of it the formalities of good-bye as many made a scarcely disguised dash for the exit. The exodus brought Himmler and Goering together for the first time.

"Must rush. Armies to command and battles to fight," Himmler explained, his reedy voice dripping in sarcasm as he mimicked the Fuehrer's words.

"See you in hell, Heinrich," Goering snapped, ignoring the proffered gloved hand.

Within seconds both were gone, and within minutes at least half of the remaining guests had followed. The boys still stood in line; no one had told them they could move. Hencke wondered how many of them understood what this grim little ceremony had been about, or why they had been brought from what was left of their homes to this place. And how many of them would be alive in a week? Perhaps they would all be decorating lamp posts, like candles on a birthday cake.

"Bormann, I'm glad I caught you before you . . . disappeared for the evening."

Martin Bormann, Hitler's personal secretary and deputy leader of the Party, looked less than pleased at the interruption. He was leaning close to one of the female secretaries and chatting in a tendentiously informal fashion as they prepared to leave the Ehrenhof. He was notorious for his double life. Within the bunker he was the soul of efficiency, the most loyal and devoted of all Hitler's entourage, and a master at controlling the floods of paperwork and information that still cascaded toward the Fuehrer for his personal attention. As such, even those who disliked him intensely — and they constituted a large majority — were forced to admit his worth in the smooth running of affairs, particularly when the city was falling apart. But once out of the Bunker he was a braggart, a drunk and a womanizer, who spent long evenings lost in various corners of the vast Reich Chancellery cellar. By the way his hand was pawing the arm of the secretary, he had plans for this evening too, although as Goebbels advanced on him he was obliged to release her and with obvious reluctance wave her into a corner out of earshot.

"Any news of Hencke?" Goebbels enquired.

"Christ, you only asked me at four o'clock this morning. D'you think everyone in the records offices is an insomniac like you? What's the almighty hurry?"

"I want a double-check on Hencke. I'm not going to announce his arrival to the whole world until I know everything there is to know about him. I don't want to know if he scratches his ass, I want to know which hand he uses."

"Why so picky? Hasn't just stopped you offering him to *Der Chef* like a tasty piece of birthday cake. Bit late to start having doubts, isn't it?"

"Some risks have to be taken to keep up the Fuehrer's morale. But that's no excuse to relax and forget what we're here to do."

"Anyway, you're out of luck. All the records departments are having the shit blasted out of them by the bombing. The Wehrmacht offices received a direct hit last week, all their paperwork's in chaos. It'll take days to find anything in that mess."

Goebbels sighed peevishly. "Then check the civilian records — birth, school, university. He's a teacher, for heaven's sake, there's got to be some information on him. Get the Buergermeister of Eger out of his bug-ridden bed and looking for what we need. It's called using your imagination, Bormann."

"OK, OK," he muttered, looking ruefully in the direction of the secretary. She would have to wait for a little while. "You really are the most suspicious bastard I know. Can't you just trust in your good luck?"

"I don't trust to luck, Bormann, any more than I trust people. They have an unpleasant habit of letting you down. You make your own luck in this world, and your own mistakes. So I'm not going to launch him as the savior of the German nation only to discover that he's some stinking Jew-lover or drowned his baby sister in her bath. I want him checked out. Now!"

"The Fuehrer is ready for you, Captain."

Hencke started as an orderly plucked him by the sleeve. "Where are we going?"

"Why, to the Bunker."

Hencke tried to compose himself as he was guided once more into the cellar and onward through a bewildering maze of tunnels and underground corridors, but he found the task difficult. A lethargy had settled over his wits and limbs as Goebbels had performed the introduction, the tension swamping his faculties. He needed fresh air and a moment to think, but he was to get the chance of neither. As they proceeded downward, into the bowels of Berlin, everywhere there seemed to be checkpoints, guards armed with machine pistols and hand grenades, studying the papers and identity of all who wished to pass. They walked through a dank, bare concrete tunnel more than a hundred meters long that dripped with water and reminded Hencke of a rabbit's warren in autumn, while waiting at the end was another set of guards wanting to know who and why, double-checking everything. Every time his papers were scrutinized, his face examined, he felt another layer of determination and fortitude being stripped away, leaving him like a rabbit trapped in a beam of light. Except rabbits have somewhere to run; for Hencke, in the tunnels, there was no way out. Every step farther underground seemed like another step into his own grave.

Finally the orderly moved aside to allow him past a heavy steel door, and he was inside the Vorbunker, the staff quarters. He entered a narrow corridor which also served as the dining room and rest area and, as he did so, he almost choked. The atmosphere was fetid from the body heat of people packed into the tight space. Twenty or so men and women, not all in uniform, seemed to be making strenuous efforts to recover from the general misery of the previous hour in the Ehrenhof by holding their own private celebration. Hitler was strictly teetotal, and there had been no champagne served at the formal reception; down here the staff were making up for lost time. The clink of glasses and the music of a waltz being scratched out from a gramophone somewhere nearby mingled with a loud voice as one of the men related a story of the early days in Munich. The room had meagerly decorated walls and bare overhead lighting, which blanched the faces of all color. It resembled any of the low-life nightclubs or dive bars Hencke had visited as a young man, particularly the unlicensed ones. But the memory served only to remind him how far he was from home, deep underground, surrounded by people with ghoulish, unnatural faces, like goblins in a gruesome fairy tale, except with armed guards on every corner. Suddenly he was overwhelmed with the realization that it was all impossible. It was madness, had always been madness, an aberration. He knew now that he could not possibly succeed. Did it really matter any more? Perhaps he was already beginning to catch the *Kellerkrebs*.

With leaden spirit he continued behind the orderly. They were still descending, down a spiral metal staircase with yet more bulkheads and FBK guards at both ends, and they entered upon a short corridor. He didn't need to be told, he knew this was it.

The Fuehrerbunker. Several open doors ran off the corridor and through them Hencke could see how small and claustrophobic were most of the rooms, with low ceilings you could touch. Then another short corridor, another guard and yet more doors running off into tiny rooms. Shelves along the corridor were spilling over with a disorderly collection of papers, manuals, candles, bottles, uniform caps and other paraphernalia — but nothing that might be used as a weapon — and a twisted assortment of cables and hoses ran along the bare concrete floor, a sign of impromptu repair work to electricity and water supplies. From nearby, Hencke could hear the whine of a generator and could smell latrines. This was the Emperor's palace.

It was quiet down here, the atmosphere colder than the crowded Vorbunker, with no comfort of conversation or music to break the silence. It reminded him of a medieval castle near Asch where he had once taken a party of schoolchildren. They had descended into the catacombs, dank and oppressive, with a smell that brought a funny taste to the back of the throat and left even the bolder boys anxious to leave. The Fuehrerbunker gave him the same sensation, parching his mouth, putting him on edge, filling his thoughts with dark memories. Suddenly Goebbels, always the stage manager, was there in front of him.

"Remember, Hencke. Don't tire him. And above all don't irritate or contradict him. Not if you don't want that Iron Cross shoved up your ass. Your job is to encourage, that's all. Go in. He's ready for you."

Hencke found himself in an office, scarcely ten feet square, decorated in simple fashion with blue Frisian tiles and a bare oak desk upon which stood two well-burnt candles, as might be found on a chapel altar. Above the desk, dominating the room, hung a large oil portrait of Frederick the Great. A voice beckoned from the far door.

"Is that you, Hencke? Come in, come in!"

He entered another room no larger than the office, furnished as a sitting room with carpet, coffee table, blue and white velvet sofa and chair. On the table stood a small, feminine Dresden vase filled with fresh tulips, and in the chair, beckoning, sat Hitler. He seemed more at ease sitting down than he had been standing, and his smile of welcome was genuine. He was scratching the ear of an Alsatian puppy which sat contentedly in his lap. As Hencke advanced he saw an orderly hovering in the corner kitted out in military uniform. Even in his inner sanctum, Hitler was not alone. And the nearest thing resembling a weapon was a sugar spoon.

"Sit. Have some tea. A most refreshing drink. Probably the best reason for conquering the British Empire there is." Hitler grimaced in self-mockery. "They tell me you are a man of few words, Hencke. Good for you. Suggests a man of action. Take Goebbels, now he's a man of many words. But action? If I had to rely on shrivel-legged little runts like him to beat back the Russians I might as well shoot myself straight away. I only need one Goebbels but, oh, what would I give for a thousand Henckes!"

Hencke was taken aback at the greeting and sat silently on the sofa.

"You know, Hencke, you and I have so much in common," Hitler continued, lowering his head unsteadily to meet a piece of cake held in an equally unsteady hand. "We are both men of valor, holders of the Iron Cross," he said, wiping smudges of cream from his mouth with the back of his hand. He pointed proudly to the medal, the only decoration on his tunic apart from his tiny gold party button, which had been awarded for bravery under fire as a courier, a mere corporal in the First War, before he was gassed and invalided out. That had been in the distant past, more than a generation ago, in another world.

He was muttering away through mouthfuls of cake. "And

me as an Austrian and you from the Sudetenland, we understand the need to build a Greater German Reich, to bring all Germans together — not like those feeble minds and faint hearts who nowadays flood out from every sewer to question why we ever needed to send soldiers across the blasted Rhine! They're like a plague . . ." His pale face colored rapidly with indignation. "All about me there are men who think they know better, who disobey my orders, who betray the Reich. The generals are the worst. I, almost singlehanded, gave them the continent of Europe." His voice rose, bits of cream cake spraying across the table. "Everything but England, that puny island governed by the son of a pox-ridden aristocrat. I gave it to the generals, Hencke, and what did they do? Prick-pullers every one. They've thrown it all away!" His voice had gained a remarkable strength for someone so frail. There was still passion in those glassy eyes, a flickering glow like a candle trying desperately to revive itself on the last traces of wick. The willpower and determination were still there, struggling to find some remnants of physical energy on which to cling. The puppy discreetly jumped down from his now-exposed position and waddled out the door. "Not one of them knows what it is like to have been under fire, to have an enemy trying to shoot the balls off you, that feeling of exhilaration when you realize the bastard's missed. They've never risked their lives in battle, like you and me. They have betrayed us both, those aristocrats from their military academies. Why else were you left to rot in a prison camp? Why — else — am — I — here?" His hand beat down on the table, but the effort and animation were rapidly tiring him. His lips could no longer keep pace with his anger, and saliva dribbled down his chin, which he did not bother to wipe. He settled back once again in his chair, the flame subsiding.

"And the German people . . . I wanted so much for them, expected so much of them. They have failed me. The Reich has turned into a great field of white flags for the Russians and Americans to harvest; and you won't find a single German who can ever remember supporting the Party, let alone coming to one of my rallies to cheer until they were hoarse. Do you remember, Hencke? Berlin, Nuremberg, Munich — rallies of more than a million wonder-filled people. Where have they all gone?"

His mood had become depressed, and a look of anxiety crossed his face. His mustache and nose, swollen and pulpy in old age, twitched in agitation, and he began biting one of his fingernails until it was red and ripped to the quick. "Tell me, what was it like waiting to die, in that submarine? On the bottom of the ocean?"

Hencke couldn't see the purpose of the question; he didn't know how to react. He decided to be honest, answering slowly.

"Terrifying."

Hitler nodded, as if he understood. "Different from facing death in the field, in the open air? Tell me, is there anything noble about . . . waiting to die? Stuck in an underwater tin can?"

Or stuck in an underground box, thought Hencke. So that's what is getting at him. Facing the Russians in his bunker won't be the same as facing the French in the trenches; he's worried he may not be up to it. "No, nothing noble."

Hitler sighed, the breath rattling in his lungs. "Hencke, look at me. As you see, I am not a well man. I am not physically strong. There are those who see this and believe that the war is over. They wish me to make an end of it, here in Berlin. Particularly some of the generals. The war is lost, they say, but we can still save Germany if we end it properly, nobly." His hand came up to tap his forehead and his bleary eyes stared directly at Hencke. "But I have not lost my mind yet, Hencke. What damned purpose is served by dying like rats in a cellar, tell me that? Where's the nobility of a Russian bullet in your guts — or worse! Having your body dragged through the streets of Moscow behind some hairy-assed commissar?" He leaned forward, his brow wrinkled with concern. "And then there are the women to consider; it's not just me. They have served me so loyally, more faithfully than any man. They have stood by me when the men were trampling on babies in their rush for a seat on the plane to Switzerland. Would it be *noble* of me to leave them to their fates here, under the bellies of subhuman Russians who don't give a damn whether it's a dead woman or a dead sheep and will screw the lot? That's how my noble Prussian generals would repay their loyalty." The flame in his eyes had found more fuel. "They underestimate me, those cretins. I may not be able to fight at the front any more, but I'm not yet finished. No, not by a long way! Those cowards in the High Command forget that Julius Caesar was an epileptic, but it didn't stop him conquering half the world. I don't forget! I don't forget that no enemy ever defeated Caesar, his stinking generals stabbed him in the back!"

He reached over to grasp Hencke's hand but his fingers were so unsteady he had to use his other hand to quell the shaking. He was already breathless and wheezing painfully. "Hencke, I have a plan. The war will not end. We shall stay in Berlin a few days longer and give the Russians a bloody nose. Then we shall fly to the mountains! We can fight for months from there, up where the air is sweet and the sun will shine upon us. We shall leave this shit hole of Berlin for the Americans and Russians to fight over. Jewish capitalists marching from one side and Jewish Bolsheviks from the other. Imagine! The mightiest blood-letting history has ever seen. They can lob artillery shells at each other over the fucking Reichstag, for all I care. We are *die von dem Berg*, people of the mountain. We don't need vast panzer divisions, and to hell with all those miserable, whining, double-crossing generals. Just a few thousand of us, carefully chosen. People like you, Hencke. We can stay up in Berchtesgaden until the Americans get bored and limp back home, after they've stuck their bayonets up the bums of half of Russia. We shall have new weapons, deadly new nerve gases, Tabun, Sarin, atomic weapons perhaps. Then — will — be — our — time — again!"

He collapsed back in his chair, exhausted, unable to continue.

Hencke, too, was incapable of speech. Deep inside, in the parts where men cry and rant about the injustices of life, he cursed whatever forces had brought him to this underground bedlam. They had brought him into the lair to inflict his mind with further madness, shown him an evil beyond comprehension, filled him with such horror that he knew he would burn in hell if he failed to wipe out this evil. And yet he had been left powerless, stripped of means or ideas to end it all. He could see no shadow of a chance.

"It can work, can't it, Hencke?" Hitler asked, interrupting his thoughts.

The endless Alpine war? Hencke had to admit to himself that, like so much madness, it just might. He nodded.

"I knew it. You are my lucky mascot, Hencke, sent to let me know that with valor like yours we can still achieve anything we want." He shook his guest's hands limply and he had started to mumble with exhaustion. "This is a happy day . . . very special one for us both . . . miserable bastards, to hell with the doctors and their suicide pills. They can shove them up their wives' . . ."

Suddenly Hitler halted his litany of abuse; Hencke looked up to see that they had been joined by another figure, a woman, pretty, lithe, smiling, early thirties. It was one of the group of friends he had seen laughing in the cellar of the Reich Chancellery. Hencke expected outrage at this unannounced interruption but, instead, Hitler gathered his energies and rose unsteadily to his feet, straightening his jacket, kissing the woman tenderly on the hand. Gone was his rambling coarseness of a moment before.

"Hencke, allow me to introduce you to Fräulein Braun, a

dear and trusted friend of mine." Having effected the introduction, he sank down heavily in his chair.

"I came in to make sure you weren't tiring yourself," she said to him. "It seems I came not a moment too soon." There was a scolding tone in her voice, and her blonde, shoulder-length hair fell about her diamond-shaped face as she leaned over Hitler. She turned to Hencke. "Captain, forgive me, but I think it's time for the Fuehrer to rest. He has so much still to do . . ."

"No, one last thing," objected Hitler. "Hencke, I have something for you." From beside his chair he produced a red leather case which he thrust at his guest. "Something special."

Inside, Hencke found a solid silver photo frame. Inlaid into the metalwork was a small gold swastika. It carried a photograph of Hitler and there was writing, a dedication in a practically illegible scrawl that he struggled to decipher.

Hitler hurried to cover the embarrassment of his growing inability to control a pen. "It says: 'To Peter Hencke, A brave and devoted follower. From your Fuehrer, Adolf Hitler.' I don't give those to everyone, you know."

"I find it difficult to know what to say."

"Well, that's it. Time for a rest. Perhaps see you later, Hencke." With that he pulled himself awkwardly out of his chair. Having straightened himself, Hitler bowed courteously to the woman and shuffled off into a neighboring room. The interview was at an end. Hencke never had a chance.

The office was dark, the only illumination coming from a candle on the desk. The power had failed again. Bormann was in foul mood. He loathed Goebbels, for the intellectual gifts which Bormann could never match, for the significant role he had played in the early days of the Movement, for the access to Hitler which this gave him, and for his role as *Der Chef*'s oldest — and nowadays seemingly only — trusted counselor. Over the years

Bormann, as the archetypal bureaucrat, had outmaneuvered and outlasted most of the others, but he had never learned how to handle the Reichsminister for Propaganda. Goebbels always seemed one step ahead. And Bormann seethed when he remembered how Goebbels had spoken to him, in the presence of the young secretary, too. No one else would get away with that . . . He was in no mood to tolerate the stalling he was getting on the telephone from the Buergermeister.

"Look, I don't want a debate on logistics, I don't want to hear how busy you are and I don't give a damn if your pet dachshund keeps crapping on your best carpet because of the shelling. This is not an inquiry. Nor is it a request, you little jerk. This is a *Fuehrerbefehl,* an order direct from the man himself, and if it's not obeyed I shall come down personally to the Ministry and string you up on a meat hook with my own hands. So, if you want to live to see tomorrow night, I suggest you drop whatever else you are doing and get me some answers. Can I make it any clearer than that? . . . That's right. H-E-N-C-K-E. Peter. Check his birth certificate, his university records, his teaching diploma, his collar size, his taste in music, everything . . . I don't know if he's married, cretin. It's your job to find out! By midday tomorrow. Understand?"

He was just about to throw another barrage of abuse down the receiver when the connection went dead. Bormann stared at the mouthpiece, unable to decide whether the phone had been put down on him or the land line had once again been cut. He was still looking at it when the secretary, kneeling directly at his feet, ran the tips of her fingers across her heavily rouged lips.

"Shall I continue now, you big bear?"

"Captain Hencke, I know your plan. I think you have come here to cause the most extreme havoc."

Hencke froze; his brow creased in bewilderment as he saw

the young woman's green eyes staring directly at him.

"Do you realize that four of my best friends are at this very moment threatening to murder each other, in order to decide which of them is going to be the first to be seen with you in Berlin?" Her face lit up in mischief and a peal of laughter echoed around the small bunker sitting room. As she laughed she swung her narrow hips, causing her silk dress to rustle.

"Fräulein Braun, I'm not sure I understand . . ."

"Come on, Captain. You surely don't think it's only the likes of Goebbels who take an interest in you."

"I fear I would be a miserable disappointment for one lady, but for four?" He shook his head in self-condemnation.

"Don't fool yourself, Captain. You might have evaded the clutches of Churchill and the entire British Army, but I can assure you that you will not escape so lightly from my girlfriends. They have instructed me that if you refuse I am to get the Fuehrer to sign a personal order!" She laughed gaily once more, and Hencke was still wondering who this extraordinary woman was who had walked in on Hitler and then propositioned him on behalf of her friends when her laughter suddenly died. Her face puckered and her hand came to her forehead.

"Oh, this bunker! The atmosphere is so oppressive, my head is ringing. It feels as if the entire roof has fallen in on me . . ." She was in genuine distress.

"Perhaps some fresh air," Hencke suggested. "I would offer to escort you, but I'm lost beyond the end of the corridor."

She studied him carefully for a moment. "Would you mind, Captain? I'd be grateful. Let me show you the way."

Left with little choice, he followed her out into the corridor and past the guard, but not the way he had arrived. She guided him in the opposite direction, past a foul-smelling latrine and through yet another guarded steel door, but this time no one stopped to check him, the guard simply saluting him — or was it her? — and stepping back. Then on to a concrete stairway, which rose four flights, until he could feel the soothing brush of fresh air on his face. They emerged into a garden from underneath the cover of a huge concrete blockhouse, twenty feet high, with an unfinished pillbox tower looming beside it. A broken cement mixer leaned drunkenly against its bare walls. In the fading light he could see the garden was mostly planted to grass, with a few trees, but the lawn was badly churned from the impact of bombs and shells and most of the leaves had been stripped from the trees. Even the high walls of the Reich Chancellery surrounding the garden had been unable to provide much protection. A greenhouse nearby stood sagging and badly shattered; Hencke could smell the fragrance of jasmine wafting through the broken panes, made all the sweeter by the acrid smell of smoke that hung across the city.

They started walking along a narrow gravel path. She breathed deeply of the evening air, and the creases on her forehead vanished as quickly as they had come.

"Where are we?" Hencke inquired.

"The Bunker garden. We've just come out of the emergency exit. You're not supposed to use it, of course, except with the Fuehrer. Or me. You must be careful, Captain. Here less than a day, and already taking tea with the Fuehrer and walking in his private garden. There are those who will grow jealous." Her mood was light and easy, but he had the impression that her words should not be dismissed as idle chatter.

"Who?"

"You're very direct, Captain."

"I've only just arrived, remember. And I doubt whether I've got time to learn all the subtleties."

"Ah! Too direct, I fear, for this city. It's not the habit here. People prefer to talk in code or riddles, and you need an interpreter or an astrologist to find out what they really mean. Why, only an hour ago I heard that tub of lard Goering profess undying faith in the Fuehrer, yet already he is on his plane flying as far south as possible. With such faith, whole Reichs could be toppled, eh?"

Hencke's brow puckered as he heard the bluntness of her comments aimed at one of the most powerful men in the land. Who was this woman of the bunker? "I'm confused. Forgive me . . . Who are you?"

"Me?" She smiled, lowered her eyes, blushed a little? "Of course, you've never been in Berlin, and Goebbels makes absolutely sure that nothing ever appears in the newspapers." She shrugged. "But you'll know as soon as you ask any corporal in the Chancellery, and you seem to prefer directness . . . I am Eva Braun."

His expression told her that the name meant nothing to him.

"I am the Fuehrer's companion. His mistress."

"Then it would seem that you, too, should beware in this city of jealousies, Fräulein Braun, for you certainly have far better access to the Fuehrer than me."

She clapped her hands with delight, her green eyes sparkled, and her voice fluttered with laughter. She moved gracefully, athletically; her body was slim, almost boyish, her teeth white and her lips naturally red, and she had a dimple in the middle of her chin. Although she could never be called a beauty there was an untainted naturalness about her that belied her age and her fashionable clothes. She seemed and sounded much younger than her thirty-odd years. "You are not like the others, Captain. I feel I can be honest with you. They all play games and intrigue against each other. I hope you won't be long enough in Berlin to catch their disease."

"You don't seem to like Berlin."

"I hate it. I'm a Bavarian, from the mountains."

"You must be looking forward to returning there."

"It . . . would be wonderful." Her words were wistful, as if she were describing a dream rather than the reality of a few days' time.

"I thought it was decided. Yet you sound uncertain, Fräulein Braun."

"We have made so many plans, over these past years . . ." She trailed off, her gaiety gone.

Darkness had fallen and a chill was catching the air. There were goosebumps on her bare arms, but she seemed not to notice. She was wrapped in thought and her words came cautiously.

"I've had fifteen wonderful years with him, Hencke. Every year has been like a lifetime, and I have been so happy. I'm not afraid to die, if I have to. If that's the price." She was twisting a ring on her little finger, the only jewelry she wore, and it had obviously come from him. "I know everything has to come to an end. Some time. I'm not complaining, really . . ." She was biting her lip hard, losing her carefree composure.

"You feel that much for him?"

"He's . . . been so kind to me. So considerate. I was only seventeen, an assistant in a photographer's shop when we met. He's older, of course, much older, and I'm such an emptyhead, where he's so wise. Like a father. He trusts me because I don't play games like the others. I don't discuss politics or push new military strategies. And I never argue with him — I daren't. We just relax together. He says that if he closes his eyes and reaches out he needs to know that someone will be there, not with a knife in their hand but with virtue and steadiness in their heart. And all the rest are liars, every one of them. Goebbels tries to manipulate him for his little propaganda games, Goering promises to defend the skies above Berlin with planes he hasn't got. And as for that disgusting toad Bormann . . . He hates me, because I'm the one woman he knows he can never have. He tells fearful lies, even pretends that he's a nonsmoker and vegetarian like the Fuehrer. Vegetarian! One night one of the girls found a salami hanging behind his pillow. And she says that's the least of his revolting habits. But even with an oaf like him I have to share the Fuehrer.'' She sighed with resignation. ''I have to share the Fuehrer with the whole of Germany at times. I shouldn't mind. I've been at his right hand all these years. That should be enough for any girl, shouldn't it?''

Hencke was the schoolmaster once more, listening to a girl pour out her heart and her confusion, and in spite of her protestations of loyalty he knew there was something missing. ''But it hasn't been enough. Has it?''

''All these years, at his right hand, but never properly by his side. Sharing him with so many. Worrying that the difference in our ages was so great he must take me for a silly chattering girl. Wondering what love was like, for all the rest . . .''

Hencke tried to imagine the decrepit old man he had seen that afternoon lying beside this young, vibrant woman. But he couldn't. No matter how hard he tried. He realized it couldn't be, or couldn't have been, not for a very long time. So that was the problem. A young woman. Facing death. Alone. She deserved it, of course, for the folly of a loyalty so blind. She could be condemned for a love that was twisted, unnatural, obscene many would call it. But even as he shared in the distaste he knew that he, of all people, could not join in the condemnation. Not condemn her for her love, for love could never be a crime. That he understood all too well. They sat down in a gazebo that had somehow remained untouched by the assault on the city, and he reached in the dark to touch her hand, as he would have comforted one of his pupils. He did it instinctively, without thinking, and she did not draw back. He could feel the warm splash of tears on his skin. But no sound, no complaint. Damn it, she was fighting hard.

"You are such a good listener and I am nothing but a silly blabbermouth, but I have no one else to talk to." She squeezed his hand in gratitude and tried a brave laugh, to pretend she wasn't hurting, but couldn't sustain it. "Tell me. Is facing death . . . difficult?"

In the semilight she was looking at him with the earnestness of a young woman, spoiled all her adult life and who had never grown up, never had to, but who had the honesty to realize it. Now she was having to catch up for those wasted years, to mature, to deal with pain, to face death, all in a hurry. Even in this place he couldn't help but have sympathy.

"Facing death difficult? I've found facing life much harder. Death is just another challenge, and not the most difficult. There is no pain in death, the pain is all in the waiting. You can spend every day of a whole lifetime fearing something that will come only once and, when it does, be gone in a moment. Why waste our lives fearing something over which we have no choice? You have only one really important choice, and that's nothing to do with dying, it's all about living. How long we have is of little consequence, what we do with it is everything. That's what makes facing death difficult, the regrets. The things you've done or, even worse, the important things you've left undone."

"Will you die with regrets?"

He paused. "I hope not."

The darkness had closed around them like a confessional. She had stopped crying; they were still holding hands.

"Have you ever helped anyone to die?"

He ran his tongue across his lips to moisten a mouth which had suddenly run dry as he considered how best to answer, or if he should answer at all. He began hesitantly. "Once, many years ago, a friend asked me to help him die. He felt alone, victimized. His colleagues and family had rejected him. He was in despair. He felt he had nothing left to cling to."

"What did you do?"

"I gave him something to live for." Hencke's voice was no more than a whisper, as if every word had to be carved from his soul.

"And is he . . . ?"

"No, he's dead now. The war . . . But I think he died without regrets."

"Then he was a very fortunate man to have such a friend as you, Peter."

"Maybe."

They sat in the gazebo for some while, in silence, joined in spirit and by the touch of their hands. Eventually they were brought back from their private thoughts by the sound of heavy boots making their way up the bunker stairs toward the emergency exit.

"We have to go. My friends are waiting for me — for you, really; they'll be disappointed! — and I mustn't keep them waiting. I'm going to take a short cut through the gardens, but you must go back through the checkpoints in the Bunker and sign out. But Peter . . ." There was pleading in her voice. "Promise you'll help me, too."

"Help you? How?"

"Help me to live, to die if need be, with no regrets. Tomorrow. This time. Meet me. Help me."

"Where?"

"The reception area in the Chancellery. It's always crowded. Don't come up and talk to me. Just follow me. Please?"

He had no chance to consider or reply before she pushed him in the direction of the Bunker entrance, while she ran off, disappearing into the night, leaving him bewildered. What did she want? How could he agree to help her? He felt the uniform grabbing at his throat once more, and beads of perspiration gathered on his brow. Christ, Hencke, remember what you're here for!

As the sound of boots on concrete steps drew closer, he discovered he was still holding the case containing the photograph. He turned it round on all sides, rubbing his thumb over the soft leather, knowing what honor the gift implied, remembering the inscription. "A brave and devoted follower . . . From your Fuehrer . . ." He weighed it carefully in his hand, testing its weight before casting around to make sure no one was watching. Then he threw it down the jaws of the broken cement mixer.

CHAPTER 12

"Hencke, Peter. Born when he said he was — second of February, 1910. Born *where* he said he was, just outside Eger in the Sudetenland. Only son, father a local shopkeeper, killed at the battlefront during the 1916 offensive at Verdun. Left Eger to study at university in Karlsbad, never returned. No surviving relatives left in the area." Bormann's bullet-shaped head looked up from the slim folder that held the notes of his conversation with the flustered Burgermeister of Eger. "He checks out, your Hencke. He's all right."

Goebbels sat, staring into the fireplace, the corners of his mouth dragged down almost to the bottom of his jaw as he concentrated, giving him an air of unremitting gloom. It was a while before he responded.

"What else?"

"Else? Nothing else. I said, he left Eger. We're now checking with the people in Karlsbad and Prague. But what's your problem? The creep checks out."

"You're talking about nearly twenty damned years ago! Nothing since then. You call that 'checking out'?" The tone was accusatory, the look that Goebbels threw at Bormann far worse.

"For God's sake, what's bothering you? Haven't we got bigger things to worry about? Three hundred thousand men just surrendered in the Ruhr, Russian tanks already driving along the autobahn around Berlin, the Fuehrer a stumbling wreck, the last opportunity we've got of getting out of this hole rapidly going up in smoke . . . and you keep fussing about one lousy man. A man *you* brought here in the first place. What the hell do you think you're doing!"

Bormann's fingers were trembling, a flush creeping up his thickset neck and across his bony features. He was angry, exasperated, frustrated, but Goebbels could see it was more than that. The man was scared. A shaking leaf. It was as simple as that.

"Don't you see? It's precisely because we want to get out of this hole that Hencke is so important. If we just scuttle off to the Alps, the whole of Germany will think we're running to save our wretched skins. White flags will sprout like weeds all the way across the Reich, and the war will be over within days. Dammit, as soon as we start heading for the aircraft they'll be ripped apart by those being left behind. We'll look like deserters. But with Hencke, with the example of a man who's risked everything to fight at the Fuehrer's side, we might still make it appear like an inspired move to a new fortress, a brilliant plan to outwit the Russians. An example that might keep resistance burning throughout Germany."

"You don't sound too bloody sure . . ."

"Of course I'm not sure, you idiot! What do you think I am, a witch doctor? But I know one thing for damn certain. If we stay here we're all going to have our balls dangling on the end of Russian bayonets before the end of the week. So make your choice. Hencke? Or singing castrati for the Communists!"

Bormann made no reply. His head sagged and he looked mournfully toward the floor, while Goebbels took several panting breaths to regain his composure.

"So, my dear Bormann, check out in Karlsbad, check out in Prague, get them sifting through the records of the Wehrmacht, inquire anywhere you might find out something about Hencke. Check, check, check. We need this bastard firmly under our thumb, because next to the Fuehrer, he may be the most important man in the Third Reich . . ."

The reception area of the Chancellery was crowded still, but something had changed since the previous day. There were fewer armed guards standing around than Hencke remembered from his last visit. The piles of packed suitcases seemed to have grown higher, more people were off in corners whispering anxiously among themselves. They appeared to be discussing more than where to spend the evening. The vast foyer retained the bustle and atmosphere of a railway station, but one in which the last train was about to leave, with not enough room for all the passengers. A new form of greeting had become common around the Chancellery — "How's your family? Where are they?" Anybody with sense was trying to get their families moved west, away from the advancing Russians, and those with influence were trying to join them. A major with responsibility for issuing transportation permits had been busy the previous day, dealing with a long line of applicants, shouting down the phone to discover when the next train, road convoy, or airplane was leaving; today the queue had gone and he sat listlessly by a silent telephone, head in hands. Nobody was bothering with permits anymore, the transportation system was shot to hell and it was every man for himself.

He saw her descending the huge marble staircase. She didn't look up. She was wearing a bright floral print dress with long sleeves, and carried nothing but her handbag. She wore no make-up. Her shoes clipped purposefully across the marble floor as she headed toward a side door off the reception area, her well-cut dress brushing across her legs. Once again he noticed the athletic grace with which her hips swung and her body moved. He also noticed many men casting similar furtive looks as she passed by, but, unusual for this place, their appreciation remained silent. Nobody mentioned it, or offered any of the usual ribald remarks.

She passed close by Hencke but gave no sign of recognition. He allowed a respectable distance to develop before following her out through the side door, striding after her. She led him quickly away from the central reception area, with its crowds, into increasingly remote areas of the Chancellery where many fewer people scurried around. For several minutes he followed along anonymous corridors, up and down flights of stairs, through reception rooms, until he had become completely disorientated. It was as if she were trying to lose him — had she already changed her mind? He hurried around yet another corner to find himself in a bare corridor echoing in its emptiness. She had gone, disappeared. He'd lost her and lost himself into the bargain. He had no idea where he was or what she wanted of him. Why the secrecy? What was he doing here? Where the hell had she gone? He was stumbling mystified along the corridor, growing more bewildered with each step, when a hand reached out and dragged him into a doorway. It was Eva. Putting a finger to her lips, she pulled him into a small, windowless secretarial office with two desks and typewriters, and papers strewn across the floor. The room had been vacated in a hurry. She showed no interest in their surroundings, and was leaning against the door, ear to its paneling, listening. He moved across to join her but once more she raised a finger to her lips, demanding silence. A few moments later came the sound of booted footsteps approaching from the way they had come, hesitating, scraping in uncertainty, then quickening and moving sharply onward. Before they disappeared completely the footsteps broke into a run, bringing a wry smile of satisfaction to Eva's face.

"I thought as much. They've put a man to keep an eye on you," she whispered.

"Following me? Why?"

"I told you many would be jealous."

"They suspect me? Of what?"

She smiled reassuringly as she saw the look of alarm twitching around his eyes. "*Everybody* is suspect in this city. It was only a few months ago that generals in the High Command tried to kill the Fuehrer. And you they suspect because you're different, you're new, dropped in out of the blue. They don't yet know what your vices or ambitions are. Everybody in Berlin has vices and ambitions, and they're all recorded somewhere in somebody's files. But not yours, not yet. Perhaps you should make it easy for them, present them with a written list," she chuckled impishly.

He showed no sign of appreciating the humor. "Who are 'they'?"

"Practically everybody. No . . ." She paused while she considered her response, her ear to the door once more, checking for further sounds of pursuit. "Come to think of it, probably Goebbels or Bormann. The rest of them seem to have lost interest in what goes on here. Yes, probably one or the other of that rotten pair."

The lids closed slowly over his eyes and his lean face sagged as he contemplated the horror of his position. Under constant watch, with seemingly no chance of finding the opportunity he sought. Now locked in some mysterious conspiracy with Hitler's mistress. His eyes flashed open. "What am I doing here?" he demanded.

"Come with me," was all the explanation she volunteered. She grabbed his hand and, after listening once more for sounds outside, proceeded to lead him through the labyrinth that made up the service areas and passageways of the Chancellery. Several times she stopped to ensure they were not being followed. But they were deep inside the disused section of the Chancellery, evacuated because of bomb damage, and there was no one about. They started to climb, up flights of stairs littered with debris, fallen chunks of plaster, and the occasional brick or abandoned file. In one section the wrought iron balustrade had fallen away, and paintings sagged at drunken angles from the wall; elsewhere the lights had failed, but she seemed surefooted and to know precisely where she was headed, leading him onward with the aid of a small flashlight she had taken from her handbag. They were several storys above the inhabited section of the Chancellery before they came to a set of tall doors. She tried the handle; the door refused to budge. Once more she tried, before appealing to Hencke. He put his shoulder to it and it gave way with a shudder — not locked, just jammed — covering him with a shower of plaster dust.

He was still brushing the dust from his uniform when she pulled him inside. Even in the darkness he could see they were in a magnificent library, perhaps forty meters long, with towering mahogany bookcases on all sides. Some of the bookcases were empty, their contents strewn on the floor, or thrown into packing cases that stood abandoned in the center of the room. Every one of the tall French windows was smashed, some hanging crazily off broken hinges; yet elsewhere the room seemed almost untouched. A sumptuous tapestry adorned the far wall, and fine oil paintings still hung in their places between the bookcases. Beautifully carved chairs, desks and expensively covered chaise longues were scattered around, and a tray of coffee waited on one of the tables. Hencke picked up the pot, but it was stone cold, and there was a deep ring of dust around its base. It hadn't been touched for several weeks.

"What on earth are we doing here?" he demanded once more.

"I wanted to show you the view," she said, leading him to one of the windows. Outside there was a small balcony that afforded a panorama of the city. A huge sweep of Berlin was scattered before them in the early night, from the Brandenburg Gate and the wooded Tiergarten lying behind, to the ruined Reichstag that had burned in 1933, and onward to the ministries, embassies and hotels that crowded along Unter den Linden. Many of them were burning now. Through the low-hanging clouds of smoke and dust that swept across the city, they saw the silhouettes of great cathedrals, hospitals, monuments, boulevards and railway stations, thrown into stark relief by the fires that glowed all around. Away into the distance the whole city was lit by flame. In some places conflagrations burned out of control and consumed whole blocks, where the firefighters had given up in despair; in others there rose the flicker of fiery geysers where a gas main had been breached and was burning, despite the order issued days before to cut off the last of the supplies. Elsewhere, on street corners and in courtyards, they could see the flickering campfires of the Hitler Youth, lit not so much for physical warmth as to comfort the spirit while they manned roadblocks and waited for the assault. Where buildings still stood they burned, where they lay in ruins they smoldered, and this once-great city of Berlin was cast in the light of its own pitiful destruction.

Yet it was the sounds, the noises of a city dying around them, that made the deepest impact. There was no sound of warfare; the artillery bombardment had stopped for the moment and, although they couldn't know it, the Anglo-American aerial bombardment had stopped too, for good. The Russians were now so close that the pilots of the British Lancasters couldn't know at night whether they were bombing ally or enemy. But there were other sounds; in place of the noise of battle came that of the capital tearing itself apart. The screams of a battered city yielding to final assault; the pathetic cries for help of the injured and maimed still trapped in the rubble; the drawn-out death rattle of masonry as buildings gave up the struggle and collapsed; the crackle of flame; shattering glass; frantic shouts of alarm as a horse-drawn ambulance tried in vain to force its way through the chaos; the tears of children wandering the streets in search of parents who would never come home. The howling of dogs driven frenzied with terror. Yet, as in the madness of a nightmare, though assailed by the cries of misery, they could still hear raucous shouts, laughter even, as many of those who were left anesthetized themselves in drunkenness, lust, revenge. While naïve civilians cowered in their cellars, still praying for salvation, soldiers who had given up all hope wandered the streets looking for distraction. Occasionally a shot would ring out, whether as a sign of success or failure in that search there was no way of telling, but news of what was going on in the cellar of the Chancellery had spread like disease, and with it had been wiped out any last vestige of military discipline and self-control.

"I wanted you to see this, Peter. When I see what is happening to Berlin, I know it's all nearly over. Down in the Bunker the retreat to the Alps might make sense, but not up here. The whole world seems to have gone insane, and I don't think anyone can save it." They stared across the burning city, standing side by side, until he found her hand in his.

"Peter?" The voice was tremulous, anxious, full of uncertainty. Gone was the self-confident authority of the chase through the Chancellery, the uncertain schoolgirl had returned. She clutched his hand still more tightly as his eyes turned upon her, but he said nothing. Already he knew what she wanted. He had turned to face her, still said nothing, but now she held both his hands. Tentatively, hesitating as if at any moment she might change her mind or be rebuffed, she raised herself unsteadily onto the tips of her toes, leaning against him for balance, her body pressing into his as she craned her slim neck. When their lips met it seemed scarcely a kiss, more a light brushing, a dance of butterflies, testing her own resolve as much as his. But she was committed now and searching more eagerly for him, her fingers working their way up his back to force his head down, her lips taut, inexperienced, the kiss for all its earnestness that of a woman many years younger. In many ways she was still a child, an innocent in this city of slaughter. "No regrets," she whispered. "Help me die. With no regrets."

Like an attentive pupil she had listened, and thought she understood. She led him back into the great library, to the far end where a chaise longue stood beneath a wall-length tapestry. It was a classical scene of bacchanalian excess, in stark contrast to the intellectual aspirations of the rest of the room, as naked women were carried off into the dark oak forest by half-men, half-horse, for purposes that the skillful weft and warp took no steps to hide. And, in the half light thrown through the windows, scarcely before he had time to notice, Eva too was naked.

"Your uniform," she whispered, "your uniform." Her fingers were eager, everywhere. The belt and its holster clattered to the wooden floor, the buttons of his tunic sprang open one by one as her hands found their way inside his shirt. Her kisses, still tight and over-conscious, began to cover his neck. In a moment she was all breath, heat, energy, wetness. She was inside his trousers now, examining, exciting, pulling him on top of her as she lay across the chaise longue.

"Please, Peter . . . ," she breathed. "You're the only one I can ask. All the others are liars and swine; I don't want to end up as an item in one of their wretched files. Help me."

He held back. He was on her, but not in her or, she could sense, with her. She grabbed his head.

"Please, Peter. I can't just sit back and wait to die! That's all there is left, no matter what anyone says." There was a catch in her voice. "I'm scared, for God's sake. At least for a while, can't we forget what's waiting out there?" She shook her body, urging him on.

He knew he had to. There was no choice; to reject Hitler's mistress, to make an enemy of her, was certain disaster. She was crying now, tears of passion, of frustration, of growing anger at his indifference, tears of a lonely and frightened girl, who had never hurt anyone, whose only crime had been to fall in love with the wrong man and who was waiting to die as bravely as she could. He understood, sympathized, even cared. So he started, trying not to think, to feel, losing himself in the enormity of it all.

It was not to be. As they lay entwined, thoughts only on each other, their private world was shattered by the explosion of a thousand brilliant flashes from beyond the windows. Lightning seared through the night sky, followed by a devastating and unending blast of noise. They froze. Death was rattling at the window frames and their moment was gone.

The sexual tension drained from her as the fear forced its way in. "The Russians. Those are Russian rockets and artillery. The final bombardment has begun," she said quietly.

From around them came the pandemonium of falling shells as they erupted to pile new rubble on top of old, to seek out those corners of the city that had somehow survived, and reduce them to ashes. They were back in the real world, the world of insanity and destruction which, for a short time, they had left.

"It will all be over soon, Peter." Her voice was plain, matter-of-fact.

"I'm sorry."

"Don't be." Tears were falling again but there was no sobbing, no self-pity, only release from the tension.

"If only we'd had a little more time."

Very slowly, tenderly, she pushed him away, until he lay beside her, face to face, while she stroked the hair gently back from his damp forehead. "We've had enough time, Peter. Enough to show me that at least I can die my own person, not simply . . ." She hesitated, considering the word carefully. "An appendage. Not just an extension to his life. This, us, here — it wasn't so much doing it as the act of deciding to do it. To break away a little, to make up my own mind for once, be sure I could be myself. So it's done. I can return to him. My own woman. My own choice." She was trying to smile through the tears. "I've lived so much for him over all these years, I needed to know that I could face up to dying for him, too. Now I do know. Thanks to you."

She had learned more than he had realized. She kissed him again, gratefully and with passion, not taut like the schoolgirl, but openly, and lay back on the chaise longue as more shells burst about them.

Hencke rolled away and onto the floor. "Eva, take this." He was down on his knees, scrabbling in the semidarkness for his belt and holster. The Walther was in his hand. "Put this in your handbag. Just in case. It will get chaotic, very dangerous, neither I nor anyone else may be there when you need us most, to protect you."

"To help me die, you mean."

"Take it, just in case."

She stretched up to brush his cheek, grateful for the concern, then she took the gun and placed it in her handbag.

He watched her dress in the flickering light of the bombardment, smoothing the rumpled cotton as best she could. He shivered as he felt a cold river of fear run over him, not from the shells raining down but from what he knew had been the touch of Fate. It had not been planned, he couldn't possibly have foreseen this. He had gained a friend on the inside. And possibly, just possibly, through Eva Braun and her handbag, he had broken the iron ring of security around the Bunker.

A few minutes before midday Hencke received the command to report to Goebbels in the Bunker. As he strode through the Chancellery it was clear that the established routine of the building had suddenly changed. No longer was it built around the twice-a-day pattern of Allied bombing; the bombers had left for good, and in their place had come the incessant and insistent pounding of Russian artillery and fire-belching "Stalin organs." The message of the barrage was unmistakable; there was no longer a time to sleep and a time to work in the Chancellery; only a time to die.

In the Vorbunker there seemed to be other ideas. Where before he had seen little but unrelieved grimness in the faces of its inhabitants, in its place had come a new tension, an excitement, a glow of hope in their eyes. Everywhere there were signs of preparation for departure. Packing cases were being nailed shut, suitcases locked, papers being sorted and discarded, crates being carried out. Instead of the maudlin atmosphere of the birthday celebrations there was purpose, energy, urgency, the noise of rushing feet echoing from the concrete walls.

"The Fuehrer has given the order," Goebbels explained, eyes bright. "The breakout begins!"

He paused in issuing instructions for the safe transportation of various cases, and turned to study Hencke. Less than an hour ago he had received the report of the officer detailed to follow Hencke, and who had lost him in the maze of the abandoned Chancellery. Why had Hencke gone there? Out of curiosity? Souvenir hunting? Yet the report had said he seemed to know precisely where he was headed, not tarrying to look. And there appeared no doubt that he had deliberately lost his tail. What had he been doing during those lost hours of the night? Yet what harm could he possibly do in the empty section of the Chancellery? Hencke was a puzzle, and Goebbels neither liked nor trusted puzzles. Particularly now.

Two of Goebbels' children were playing at his feet, a little girl with a doll and a boy with straight blond hair who was bouncing a ball. It ran loose toward Hencke, and he stooped to retrieve it.

"To think they will be playing in fresh Alpine air in two days' time." Goebbels smiled as he took possession of the ball, looking directly at Hencke. He arched an eyebrow. "And the Fuehrer has instructed that you will join us."

Hencke remained expressionless as he tried to figure out the import of what Goebbels was saying. The little girl started crying, and the Reichsminister stooped to gather her in his arms; only when he had finished comforting her did he return his attention to Hencke. He took from his pocket a dog-eared gas station map of Berlin and its suburbs, smoothing out the creases on the table.

"The Russians are rapidly encircling the city. Their advance troops are already in Koepenick and Spandau; in a few days there will be no way out. So we start. There's an emergency airstrip in Kladow — here. We use small planes to ferry us out to the Rechlin airbase" — he stabbed again with his forefinger — "where they've assembled an entire fleet of Condors and Junkers 390s, enough to fly us to China if we wanted, more than enough to get several hundred of us to Berchtesgaden in a few hours. With luck they may be able to make two, even three trips. For everyone else it's the autobahn routes to the south and west, for as long as they stay open." His carefully manicured finger ran across the map, indicating the way. "So we leave tonight! Hencke, the fight back begins!"

"Why are you telling me all this, Herr Reichsminister?"

Good question, thought Goebbels. Was it because Bormann had received fresh information from Karlsbad, confirming that Hencke had studied at the university there, had no record of political agitation or other trouble, had kept his nose clean, and graduated into a respectable teaching post in the small town of Asch? His story was checking out; still Goebbels was not content. Something about the whole situation gave him the feeling of needles being stuck into the nape of his neck. And there was still no trace of Hencke in the records since 1938, since the annexation of the Sudetenland. Perhaps, as Bormann had suggested, it was because all the record-keeping systems had changed, and the new records were kept separately. He was still checking, he was sure they would come through with the full story. But Goebbels remembered there had been trouble in Asch and other towns that had been "liberated" by the Sudeten Freikorps, who had left a trail of blood and broken bones in their wake. It made him uneasy.

Was it because he wanted to see how Hencke reacted to the news, to see if there were any clues in his response? If so, the Reichsminister was disappointed. Hencke's eyes remained unmoved and impenetrable. Or perhaps it was because Goebbels, his faculties sensitized by his twisted frame and a lifetime of physical inferiority, knew that his own fate and the fates of all of them were inextricably linked with Hencke? Salvation or annihilation. Somehow Hencke would decide.

"I tell you, Hencke, because you will soon hear about it anyway. I shall broadcast news of the breakout to the world as we leave tonight. In six hours. It will be too late then for the Allies to react and stop us. The whole of Germany will know that the fight is not yet over, that resistance must still continue. A new chapter in our history, Hencke, one which you have helped to write. Because I shall also announce that you are with us, by the Fuehrer's side, showing the world that Germany still has the will to resist. And I want you to say a few words of encouragement, too. What do you think of that, eh?"

"It goes far beyond my wildest dreams, Herr Reichsminister."

"You are of great importance to us, Hencke. Next to the Fuehrer you may be the most important symbol in the Reich."

Hencke swallowed hard, scarcely able to believe what he heard.

"Oh, yes. That is why I have to give you new instructions. These are dangerous times, crucial times for our survival. We can afford to take no unnecessary risks. So I am giving you an armed guard, Hencke, to ensure as best we can that nothing befalls you. They will be with you day and night. Doesn't that make you feel better?"

Hencke felt a sharp edge of pain as the final window of opportunity slammed shut across his fingers.

Goebbels nodded to someone behind Hencke and immediately there was a crashing of boot leather as a guard snapped smartly to attention. "Sergeant Greim here will look after you. He's one of our finest commandos, utterly trustworthy. You'll like him, I'm sure."

"I don't know how to express my thanks, Herr Reichsminister." As Hencke looked into Goebbels' dark eyes there was a flicker of contact and understanding between them. Goebbels knew. Not for certain, and not the details, and not enough to order any immediate action against him, but he knew. It was written all over his crooked smile. Hencke was trapped, and any time after the evening broadcast he would become dispensable. Goebbels could indulge his instincts and drop him down the nearest crevasse. He might not even make it to the Alps. That's what Greim was there for.

"You will excuse me, Hencke." Goebbels gave a condescending nod. "I have a radio broadcast to write. I shall see you in six hours."

Regrets. He had regrets, plenty of them. To have come so far and to have got so close made the regrets that flooded in on him all the more difficult to bear. He knew he couldn't make a good death of it, not now. He didn't have to die, of course. He could slip the guard and lose himself in the ruins of Berlin, taking his chance with the rest. But as difficult as he found the prospect of dying with his regrets, it was nothing to the prospect of having to live with them. The memories of the school and its burning books and broken bodies came back. He had sworn revenge, it was the only way he had been able to live with those nightmares. Yet he had failed, and he knew the pain of the memories would suffocate and destroy whatever life was left to him. There was no way out.

Almost blindly he wandered back into the Chancellery, pursued by the dogged Greim. They didn't talk — what was the point? The signs of growing chaos and collapse were everywhere, yet he could take no comfort from them. In a makeshift command post, a general was conducting a furious argument with an engineer about the flooding of the subway tunnels. The Russians will use them to infiltrate right to the heart of Berlin, screamed the general. They are the only shelter for hundreds of thousands of Berliners, who will drown if the tunnels are flooded, argued the stubborn engineer, and would not obey. The exasperated general stormed off in search of another engineer. The veneer of military discipline that had hung over the Chancellery in previous days was finally blowing away. The apple had been cut open, only to reveal a writhing mass of maggots.

He felt an overwhelming need to have something other than solid concrete above his head. Walking slowly down the steep steps leading from the Chancellery entrance, he saw makeshift barricades being erected out of tree trunks, wrecked vehicles, sandbags, anything that was heavy yet could still be moved. Waffen SS troops were being stationed at every point around the Chancellery, as if a direct attack were expected at any moment. The troops were speaking not German but a mixture of foreign tongues — French, Norwegian, Latvian, even Russian. These were the foreign volunteers, skimmed from the occupied countries, renowned for their ferocity and total indifference to casualties. They had little to lose, since dying in battle offered a far better fate than any they could expect if returned as prisoners to their native countries. Hencke wondered if anyone else saw the irony, the heart of the most racially pure Reich in history being defended by foreign mercenaries.

Choking clouds of smoke and dust swirled through the streets around the Chancellery. In spite of continuous shelling and high risk of death, there were lines of women with buckets drawing water from standpipes. The city's water supplies had been shattered, there was little left to drink and nothing with which to fight the flames or wash away the sewage. The stench was appalling. On another side of the street was stacked a pile of weapons, rifles of many makes and descriptions, boxes of grenades and ammunition, pistols and *Panzerfausts*, at which both men and women picked, equipping themselves with weapons and trying to find ammunition that matched. Several old men, armed with Italian rifles and a handful of bullets each, were being marched off in the direction of the U-Bahn tunnels, while a detachment of Hitler Youth on bicycles collected antitank weapons before riding east. At every point along the broad boulevards was destruction. Shattered tanks, trucks, buses, artillery wagons, scattered like children's toys. A field gun lay twisted, with its barrel resting on the ground in symbolic surrender. From the back of a nearby ambulance — with its driver dead at the wheel — came the screams for help of the wounded. There were bodies everywhere, young, old, women and children too. No attempt was being made any longer to collect or cover them. Many of those that lay in the roadway had been hideously crushed under truck wheels or tank tracks.

By the side of the Brandenburg Gate there lay the smoldering wreckage of a light airplane with its single wing pointing accusingly toward the sky, the victim of a desperate attempt to put down on the emergency airstrip by the Gate. The wreckage had been pushed aside by a tank, to allow other planes to take their chance on the rubble-strewn runway. In the wooded Tiergarten beyond the Gate the trees stood stripped of all leaf and many branches. Hencke had to remind himself that it was spring, that they should all have been in blossom and bud. Trunks of uprooted trees were being hauled away by teams of men and horses to act as barricades, while from the branches of many of those still standing swung the bodies of Germans, some in uniform and some not, hanged for desertion and cowardice by the flying squads of SS and SA troops who were combing the city in an attempt to stem the growing flood of capitulation. All around there were craters and shell holes, the fresh earth thrown up in the form of gaping mouths, like graves waiting to receive their dead.

This was the reality of Berlin, the reality which those in that madhouse of the Bunker wished to maintain and extend through endless war. Except Eva. She had seen through it, recognized the self-deception, the futility of it all. If only her infatuation and loyalty hadn't blinded her to what was necessary to end the madness. But there was no hope of that, she was devoted to Hitler. There was no more chance of her acting to thwart him than a shadow might trip its owner. Poor Eva.

In the midst of the battered Tiergarten, he came to an abrupt halt. A thought gripped him, all but choking his heart. Impractical, impossible, but a flicker of hope. And what had he got to lose, except his regrets? He started to run, back toward the Reich Chancellery.

"What? What's that you're saying? Speak up, I can't hear a damn thing. What about Peter Hencke?"

Bormann was bawling down the telephone, trying to make head or tail of the sputter pouring from the earpiece. The phone lines from Karlsbad had all but collapsed, and it was the third attempt they had made to get through to him. The Czech city was surrounded by American forces, who were pounding the place into hell on earth. It might be only hours before Hausser's Army Group decided to ignore the *Fuehrerbefehl* to fight to the death, and started surrendering. It didn't help that Soviet troops were also scarcely twenty miles away, willing and eager to finish off the job if the Americans couldn't.

"Speak up, speak up!" Bormann screamed, but it was no good. The phone was dead. He rapped the receiver a couple of times; there was no response. He snorted contemptuously as he replaced the instrument in its cradle. If it was that important, they would phone back again. He resumed his packing.

All was confusion inside the reception area of the Chancellery. Hencke had to force his way past milling crowds of soldiers, rather more of whom seemed to be armed with suitcases and knapsacks than with rifles. Little pretense remained that effective control or defense of the city was still possible. At one desk, abandoned by its duty clerk, an officer gabbled down a phone making arrangements for his departure. He was obviously talking to his mistress, instructing her to pack immediately. Another phone stood unused on the desk, and Hencke grabbed it anxiously, rattling the cradle for attention. He demanded to be put through to the Bunker switchboard, and was mildly surprised when the connection was immediately made. He was still more relieved when, as he requested, they connected him to Eva's suite. Either his name meant something to the switchboard operators or, more likely, they no longer gave a damn.

When she answered the phone he could hear the noise of children laughing in the background. He surmised she was playing with Goebbels' children, and that there were probably other women in the room. She was coy, but there was evident warmth in her voice.

"Captain, you are well, I trust?"

"You've heard? About the breakout?"

"Yes, of course. I shall be leaving with the Fuehrer tonight." There was little enthusiasm in her words. "It's my duty," she added. She clearly felt the need to explain.

"I have been instructed to leave also."

"I know. I suggested to the Fuehrer it might be a good idea . . ."

"I don't want to go."

"What? Why on earth not?" she exclaimed.

"I came back to Germany to fight for what I believe in. I think I can do that best by remaining here in Berlin."

"But you are the Fuehrer's mascot, his symbol . . ."

"How much better a symbol will I be if I stay behind to help lead the resistance, to fight to the last? That's the sort of symbol that will keep the white flags from flying!"

"Peter, do you really want to die that much?" In her surprise and confusion she had dropped the discreet formality.

"No. I don't want to die. But this way I can die without regrets. Remember?"

"How could I forget?"

Their words were guarded, wary of eavesdroppers. Greim was drawing closer to him, clearly curious.

"I have a favor to ask."

"Anything."

"I want the Fuehrer to release me from his order, and allow me to remain in Berlin. And I want the opportunity to bid farewell to him personally. It would mean everything to me."

"He doesn't see many people on their own anymore. He says they only ask to see him alone if they have terrible news, or want to tell him the war is lost . . ."

"Help me! There is so little time left. I would ask Goebbels, but he is too busy for such matters, and I know of no one else to ask. Could you, this afternoon, take me to see him? It would mean everything." Greim was edging nearer, in a moment he would be beside Hencke and able to hear every word.

"It's very difficult . . ."

"Please, Eva. Remember. It's an honor I'm willing to die for."

The voice on the other end of the phone trembled with emotion. "You are a very exceptional man, Captain Hencke. I'm so very glad I met you."

Hencke was becoming desperate. He turned his back on Greim, as if trying to shield the receiver from the noise of the officer who was shouting on the next phone. "The Fuehrer, Eva. Can you arrange it?"

There was a long silence. Greim, making no pretense as to his intentions, came round and sat on the desk beside him, cocking his ear to catch every word.

"Tea. In my room in the Bunker. Four o'clock sharp. Don't be late." With that the phone went dead.

Hencke threw an evil look at Greim, but the sergeant's attention seemed to have been distracted. At the next phone the officer had abruptly ceased shouting and was staring with incredulity at

LAST MAN TO DIE

the receiver. A moment before he had been talking to his mistress in the suburb of Wannsee, scarcely ten miles from the Reich Chancellery. Now all he could hear coming out of the phone was a guttural male voice gabbling in what sounded very much like Russian.

Greim followed Hencke like an unpleasant smell as they walked down the tunnels and toward the Bunker. The checkpoints were all in place; whatever other chaos was going on, the FBK still seemed certain of its duty. Hencke was anxious that the security checks might delay him, make him late, but at last he entered through the final steel door and was in the corridor of the Vorbunker. She was there, too, smiling. He offered a formal nod of respect and she took his arm, leading him toward the stairs that led down to the Fuehrerbunker.

As they started to descend the wrought iron staircase there came the clatter of Greim descending after them. Eva turned to him.

"Sergeant, where on earth do you think you're going?"

Greim looked uncomfortable. "I have instructions, Fräulein. From Reichsminister Goebbels himself. I am to accompany the captain everywhere and ensure his safety."

She laughed gaily. "I assure you that he will be perfectly safe taking tea in the Fuehrerbunker with me. Or do you suspect me of wishing to attack him?" Her tone was light but mocking.

Greim began to stammer with embarrassment. "No, Fräulein, but my orders . . ."

Her gaiety had gone, in its place only taut impatience. "Sergeant, your orders do not require you to be either ridiculous or impertinent. I promise you the captain will come to no harm."

Greim writhed, a picture of misery. "But I shall have to report to the Reichsminister . . ."

"And if you continue your insolence I shall be reporting to the Fuehrer!"

She was staring angrily at him, defying him to continue down the stairs. Greim felt himself caught between the hot breath of a firing squad and the frozen gales of Siberia. He had to choose between Goebbels and Eva Braun, and knew whatever he decided he couldn't win. He looked once more into her indignant eyes. Shit! She was here and Goebbels wasn't. It was bound to be all right if he stood guard at the top of the stairs. As the slut said, what the hell could happen down in the Fuehrerbunker?

Greim turned on his heel and disappeared.

Bormann threw himself down the corridor as if the hounds of hell were at his heels, his face beetroot red and spittle-covered from the exertion and his growing sense of panic. The telephone call had got through just as he was completing his packing in the Chancellery. The line from Karlsbad was as terrible as ever, and held out for less than three minutes, but three minutes had been enough, and — string up the entire milk-sucking Signal Corps from piano wires! — when he in turn tried Goebbels in his Bunker office but a few hundred yards away, he found the land line chewed to pieces by a Russian shell and out of action. So he'd been forced to run. He was very unfit. The sweat poured down his face, and he thought he was going to bring up a bellyful of salami and sauerkraut. Since the telephone call, there had been a terrible pounding in his temples, and for a moment he wondered whether he was having a heart attack; it seemed a considerably brighter prospect than anything Goebbels was likely to do to him when he heard. He forced his tired legs onward.

The sight of a wild-eyed Deputy Fuehrer charging down the tunnels toward the checkpoints unnerved some of the FBK guards — perhaps the Russians were already here . . . or Bormann had cracked, he was always the one most likely to . . .

perhaps they should shoot him. But such was the bull-like charge that he was past them before they had a chance to think. He hauled himself through the bulkhead door that led to the Vorbunker, took a huge lungful of air, and bellowed.

"G-o-e-b-b-e-l-s?"

A bewildered adjutant paused from his packing, the sight of such animalistic fury rendering him utterly incapable of response.

"Where's Goebbels, you bastard?" Bormann screamed. He lunged toward the adjutant who had begun to tremble. He was about to lay his huge paws on the wretch, when the soldier waved toward one of the doors leading off the corridor.

"But . . . but he's recording his radio broadcast. He mustn't be disturbed."

With a wild sweep of his hand Bormann threw him aside and crashed through the door.

Eva Braun's suite led directly off the Fuehrer's sitting room, and was furnished in similarly frugal style. Only a coat of pale yellow paint on the walls differentiated it from the other dingy cubby holes of the Fuehrerbunker. Hencke sat in an armchair while she busied herself on the small sofa pouring tea, moving to one side the vase of fresh flowers on the table. It was a scene almost identical to that of the Fuehrer's own tea party for him. Except there was no orderly. And the nearest guard was in the corridor, out of sight and out of earshot.

"Thank you for your help, Eva."

"It wasn't easy. I haven't had a chance to explain things to the Fuehrer; I've simply invited him to tea, our last time in the Bunker. He'll be along any minute. I hope he won't be angry with me . . ."

From within his black officer's tunic Hencke took a one-armed toy bear. It looked sad and exhausted, as if it had had enough. He placed it on the table beside the tea cups.

"My lucky charm. It's been with me all the way . . ."

"Peter, how sweet. You with a teddy bear! You really are the strangest man."

She picked up the battered toy to examine it, glowing with pleasure like a girl sharing presents with her schoolfriends, trying to stroke fresh life back into its tattered fabric. For a moment she scarcely noticed that Hencke had risen from his seat and was by the small bureau near the door, where she had left her handbag. When she looked up again she saw he was opening the bag and reaching inside.

"Peter . . . ?" The smile had gone as she saw him take out the Walther. "Peter, what is it . . . ?"

It took him less than two full strides to cross the room. He was leaning over her. He didn't want to, from deep down within him he absolutely didn't want to, this was no aunt-image; but he knew she would leave him with no choice. Her mouth was open, and she was about to scream, when his hands went round her neck and he began to squeeze, choking off the cry of warning. Her right hand came up, clenched in a fist, striking him fiercely in the testicles and he winced with pain, but kept squeezing. She tried to kick, but her feet were obstructed by the sofa. Her face was rapidly changing color. After another futile attack on his groin, her hands were up trying to tear his fingers away from her neck. The harder she fought, the tighter he squeezed. Her body was shaking, seeming as light in his hands as a pillow, and her strength was ebbing fast. Her tongue was out, her jaw was slack, her lips pursed in a silent scream of fury, and her large green eyes stared up at him accusing, beseeching, uncomprehending. While they stared, he dared not let go.

It seemed forever before he realized she was dead, that the eyes, still full of accusation, retained no life.

His own eyes brimmed with tears. "No regrets, Eva. No

LAST MAN TO DIE

regrets," he whispered. With great tenderness he leaned down and kissed her on the forehead.

It was as he stood up that he heard someone enter the room behind him. He turned round to find himself looking straight down the barrel of a gun.

"Bormann, you oaf. Can't you see I'm recording a broadcast?"

"Fuck the recording. It's Hencke we've got to worry about."

"Oh my God. What is it?"

"It's not Hencke, it's not him!"

"Make sense, man!"

"I've just had Karlsbad on the phone. They've found out more about Hencke. The reason we haven't been able to find any recent records for him" — Bormann swayed, breathless, with fatigue — "is that he's dead. He died seven years ago."

"How? Where?"

"Hencke was a schoolteacher all right, at the time we seized the Sudetenland, but some idiot Freikorper threw a grenade through a window during the troubles. It exploded in the middle of his classroom, killing Hencke and half a class of schoolchildren."

"This cannot be serious," whispered Goebbels.

"There's more. Seems he never married and was living with another man, a Czech. Probably a pillow-biter, some of the locals reckon."

"Then if Hencke is dead, who the hell is this one . . . ?"

As one they sprang for the door.

Hencke stared into the glassy expression of Adolf Hitler. The gun in the Fuehrer's hand trembled as he gazed open-mouthed from Hencke to the body of Eva Braun and back again. His wits

280

seemed dull, his reactions slow, his attention unable to focus, to settle on either, moving backward and forth as if by searching hard enough he would discover his eyes had deceived him. He shook his head, to clear his senses, to refute all that he saw. Eventually, agonizingly, as he stood looking at his lover's lifeless body, as the truth pierced through to his befuddled brain, his watery eyes began to dissolve.

Hencke watched transfixed as the tears began pouring down Adolf Hitler's cheeks.

"Where's Hencke?" Goebbels and Bormann shouted in unison as they burst into the corridor.

This time the adjutant was completely incapable of speech and it was not until Greim, disturbed by the commotion, put his head around the bulkhead door from his position at the top of the stairs that they got their reply.

"Hencke? He's . . . down with Fräulein Braun," Greim whimpered. "They went to have tea . . ." He trailed off in terror as he saw the look on Goebbels' face.

"You shit-eating scum!" Goebbels pushed past him. "You're dead!"

The Reichsminister was hobbling, dragging his braced leg behind him, yet Bormann, in panic as to what they might find, gladly let the other lead the way. As they stumbled in their haste down the corridor, Goebbels trod on the head of a china doll with which his young daughter had been playing. It shattered into useless, unrecognizable fragments.

They clattered down the metal stairs, Goebbels forced to take them one at a time and slowing Bormann and the FBK guards who had joined the pursuit. They rushed into the lower corridor of the Fuehrerbunker, Goebbels shouting ahead to the guard stationed outside the entrance to Hitler's rooms.

"Where's the Fuehrer?"

The guard pointed through the door, and Goebbels lunged frantically past. Inside the Fuehrer's sitting room they hesitated, unsure which door to try. A single shot rang out. It came from behind the door leading to Eva Braun's suite.

Goebbels already knew what he would find as he burst into the room. Hencke was standing over the body of Eva Braun, a gun by his side. Directly in front of them, slumped on the floor, his face pointing to the ceiling, lay the body of Adolf Hitler. There was a gun in his hand and a bullet wound in his temple. He lay as dead and as useless as the shattered doll.

There are moments when time stands still. It did so now for Goebbels, as he took in the scene before him. The Fuehrer, a single bullet wound in the temple. Eva Braun, open-eyed, distorted lips, the agonies of death etched across her face. A small porcelain vase of flowers tipped over on the table, the water dripping mournfully on to the floor. A scene to be remembered for all time. Suddenly a pistol was thrust over his shoulder and Bormann was firing. The first bullet struck Hencke full in the chest and spun him round; but like a man possessed Bormann continued to fire repeatedly into Hencke's body until it was slumped against the wall, covered with angry, raging wounds, and Bormann had run out of ammunition. Yet still he pulled at the trigger and the hammer clicked against empty chambers, until Goebbels forcibly restrained him.

In the icy silence that followed, nobody moved. Then one of Hencke's eyes twitched open, a flicker of flame shone from somewhere within, and through lips twisted with pain and effort he whispered: *"Nelipuje."* A thin, triumphal smile brushed briefly across his face, and he fell back dead.

"What did he say, what did he say?" Bormann was quivering with shock.

"It was Czech," Goebbels responded quietly. "It means 'No regrets.'"

There was another long period of silence before they were distracted by the gathering of curious guards beyond the outer door.

"Keep them out. They have no business here." Goebbels was calm. He seemed very much in command, almost serene. At last he turned to face Bormann. "It's over. The end."

Bormann shook his head, unwilling to accept. "But surely we can fight on. There's still the Alps."

"Without the Fuehrer? Impossible. Tomorrow we are dead."

"No, no. We can still escape from Berlin." There was fear in Bormann's florid face.

"Hopeless!" Goebbels snapped. He pointed at the corpse of Hitler. "The head and the heart of Germany are here in this room. The war is over, Bormann. All we have left is the idea."

"What the hell are you talking about?"

"The cause, it must live on. And for that we need martyrs and a noble myth, not some shabby little scene played out in an underground sewer, the Fuehrer dead beside the body of his mistress and some sniveling Czech laughing in our faces. Is that what you want future generations to remember, for God's sake?" Goebbels had grown animated as he struggled for one final time to rearrange the pieces of history.

"But what can we do?"

"I tell you what you do. You find a notary and get him to marry these two." He waved at the corpses of Hitler and Eva Braun.

"But they're dead . . ."

"Do you want the world to know that Hitler died with a whore? You get the notary, and once he's married them, get rid of him. We can't have anyone going round telling tales."

Bormann blanched.

"Then you dispose of the bodies. Burn them. We can't have

them falling into the clutches of the Russians." He stood amid the carnage, struggling to summon up the energy and adrenaline for his task. Suddenly it became all too much, and somewhere inside him a switch was thrown. Shoulders sagged, the long face wilted, and he closed his eyes for a moment, seeking composure. When he spoke again, his voice had taken on an uncharacteristic mellowness. "You do that. And I will announce to the world that the Fuehrer has committed suicide, his new wife by his side, fighting to the last to defend the Reich capital of Berlin. An heroic death which will inspire great histories to be written. Only you and I will know, Bormann."

"What of him, the Czech?"

"Place him in a side room for the moment, out of the way of prying eyes." Goebbels paused to consider the man in whom he had placed so much faith and who had betrayed him with such devastating effect. He shrugged, the energy for hate gone. "Then give him a proper burial. He died a soldier's death after all, whoever he was."

"The last man to die, maybe?"

Goebbels sniffed in contempt as the other man's fear filled his nostrils. But what did it matter any more . . . "You get out of Berlin, Bormann. If you can."

"You, too?"

Goebbels kicked a one-armed toy bear lying on the floor. "No, I don't think I'll bother . . ."

AUTHOR'S NOTE

"Hencke" was not the last man to die.

After arranging for the disposal of Hitler's body, Goebbels and his wife Magda prepared their six young children for bed in the family's quarters within the Bunker. Frau Goebbels dressed them all in clean nightgowns and brushed their hair, before feeding them chocolates laced with poison. The six tiny bodies were then wrapped in white shrouds.

Afterward the parents went up to the Bunker garden, where Hitler's and Eva's bodies had been burned in a shallow trench. Standing by the cremation site, Magda bit into a capsule of cyanide. As she fell to the ground, Goebbels put a bullet in the back of her head. He then bit into his own capsule, shooting himself in the right temple as he did so. They both wanted to make sure... An SS aide poured gasoline over the bodies from a jerry can, and set fire to them. The semicharred corpses were discovered by the Russians two days later.

Bormann attempted to break out of Berlin the night after Hitler and Goebbels died. He got less than a mile from the Reich Chancellery before he disappeared. His skull, identified through dental records, was dug up by developers preparing the site for an exhibition park nearly thirty years later.

The notary who had performed the wedding ceremony, Walter Wagner, was shot dead the same evening.

Sir William Cazolet, Bart., KCMG, CB, CVO, lived to old age, showered with public esteem and honors for the sagacity which he had brought to prime ministers and monarchs alike. But he, too, was near death when I met him.

I had written to him after reading a volume of the wartime diaries he had published in retirement. In it, he had referred briefly to a mass escape of Germans from a Yorkshire transit camp. And to one who nearly got away. Peter Hencke. The same name I had found two years earlier on an old photograph while rummaging through a junk shop in the rundown district of Niederschoenhausen, in what used to be East Berlin before a thousand tiny hammers had chipped away the Wall. In the drawer of an oak desk lay a battered photo frame covered with the grime of many years, containing an anonymous sepia photograph of an aging woman. Beneath the grime I had found solid silver with an intricate gold filigree, also a jagged hole from which a piece of the ornamentation, perhaps a swastika, had been ripped. Beneath the photograph of the old woman I had found the original for which the frame had been intended, of the Fuehrer, magisterially staring left to right into a future he imagined to be filled with endless victories. There was a signature in the characteristic spidery scrawl. And a dedication. To Peter Hencke.

The name had meant nothing to me — how could it? — and

with some distaste I had left the photograph and its dedication amid the dust and decay of Niederschoenhausen. Until I had read Cazolet's diaries. And remembered.

So I had written, and had been summoned. I had no idea how ill he was. The nurse was astonished he had accepted a request from a complete stranger; perhaps it was because there was no family, she suggested. He lay propped among the pillows, wasting, waiting, the parchment-thin skin stretched taut across his skull, veins gray at the temple, a sad drooling from the corner of his mouth evidence of the chaos which was eating him away inside. In the sea of white cotton, chalk skin, bones, antiseptic walls, only the eyes sparkled, blue, dimmed but not yet extinguished by the glaze of death creeping across them. I told him of the photo I had found and left behind in Berlin. And he had talked. From afternoon into early evening, with an energy and desperation I could never have imagined his frail body to possess. Of Churchill's prayer that he might forestall any possibility of an Alpine redoubt, of the Old Man's desolation when his dreams had crumbled and he had lost Berlin, of the guilt which had thereafter plagued him for the rest of his life and which Cazolet in some measure had shared. And of Hencke, "the insurance policy" as Churchill had called it.

"Could it be?" Cazolet had whispered, exhausted by his tale. "Did he after all make it? Find out. Please, find out!" He did not need to ask; I was already captivated by his tale and fired by his earnestness. I promised to try.

"Hurry," he urged. His time was short.

But the junk shop in Niederschoenhausen was gone and the rest of the street with it, swept away in the redevelopment of unification. Of the owner there was no trace, nor any of the photograph. I drowned for days in the microfilm of the archives recently flooded with new material from what had been the East, but there was no sign of our man, no proof he had ever existed.

Nine days later I found it, in the Allied War Cemetery, amid the thousands of white-stone tributes to the American, British, Australian, Canadian, New Zealand, Indian, South African and even five Polish servicemen who had died in and above the war-wrenched capital. A single cross, carefully scrubbed like all the rest:

"An Unknown Czech Soldier. Died April 1945."

The Old Man's crazy, impossible dream had worked. Their man had got to Berlin, after all, and if he had got this far it seemed probable he had gone all the way.

That same evening I arrived back at the gentle hospice overlooking the Sussex downs, but Cazolet had already slipped into a coma. Mercifully there was no pain. He lay amid his pillows, eyes closed, lips stretched back against his gums as he clutched for air in ever shorter, shallow gasps. The nurse shook her head as I held his fingers of bone, gnarled like a bird's claw, already cold. I leaned across until my lips were close to his ear.

"He got there. Made it. All the way to Berlin!"

Could I have imagined it, the smile, that final triumphant gesture, in the moments before he died?